Street Karma

a novel
by

Pain

𝕾treet
𝕶arma

WHERE
HIP HOP
LITERATURE
BEGINS...

© 2019 Jeffery Appolon.
ISBN 978-1-935883-91-3

Novel by Pain
Edited by Anthony Whyte
Cover model: Jerimyah Appolon

Augustus Publishing paperback November 2019
www.augustuspublishing.com

I dedicate this project to DA'RYL
—A pure fan, and true friend.
Your motivation has kept me in the game.
In your words, Let's go!
And of course Mother… Love is Love.
To the world: Strap your seatbelts.
LETS GO!

KARMA

is based on the theory that every deed done
Irrespective of right or wrong will be recorded
And bound to come back full circle...
A good deed is multiplied thousandths of times
But a wrong deed not only comes back
It comes back worse than the original wrong done...

What goes around comes around
like a hula-hoop
Karma is a bitch...
Well just make sure that bitch
is beautiful...
The Carter IV, She Will

−Lil Wayne

"Your destination is on your right…"

As soon as the Garmin GPS sounded, Low got out of his ride, and slowly strolled by the basement's parking garage entrance of a massive, twelve-story, luxury building. It had been fifteen years, but Low still retained the pass code that would grant him access inside the compound. How could I ever forget my son's birth date? Low wondered, entering the code then getting back inside his car. Slowly pulling into the driveway, he proceeded to the back of the building. He stopped at a short metal fence, and placed the Buggatti's gear in neutral. Low stepped out the car with his shotgun locked and loaded.

Through the night sky of Boca Raton, a thick, black cloud gave way to a torrential downpour. Raising his night-vision binoculars to eye level, Low located the Palm's luxury condominium buildings. Scaling the floors, Low scanned the top floor, and zoomed in. There she was sitting in the dinning room. Time had been good to Michelle. Her face was still as beautiful as the day Low first met her in high school. Aiming the binoculars to the right, Low saw a young teenager sitting on the living room's sofa. Remote in hand, the youngster chomped on pizza while scrolling the television channels.

While Low focused on Michelle, he saw Rob suddenly coming from the kitchen area, carrying a pitcher of red juice. Watching Rob and Michelle in the dining room, Low felt his rage overwhelming him. Rob placed the pitcher of juice on the dining room table, and took a knee in front of Michelle. Reaching between her legs, he gently massaged her stomach. Low zoomed in so close he almost lost his grip on his binoculars.

The sound of booming thunder exploded, and lightning illuminated the entire sky turning it from gloomy to bright gray. Massive thunderstorms or the heavy rain would not deter him. Low dreamed about this moment for what had seemed like an eternity.

Cocking the Mossberg pump, he glared with deadly intentions. Then Low turned and broke into a deadly charge. There was murder in his eyes as he jumped into his car. The boss was gone. He had been left for dead—to rot. His status, and family was stripped from him. Now this was his time to take it all back. His revenge on hand, Low grit his teeth and closed in.

PART 1

GRAND
THEFT AUTO

INTRODUCTION

In 2009, American Troops were finally being pulled out of Iraq. This brought an end to a long, bloody, and seemingly pointless war. The wait for George W. Bush to finally finish his lame-duck term was over. Then in what seemed like a miraculous turn of events, the first black President in United States History, Mr. Barack Obama became the 44th President. Even though there was cease-fire in the Middle East, a war continued to be waged throughout the inner cities of the U.S. The war on drugs had been on going for the past twenty years, and claimed countless young lives in the process. Despite all efforts, the drug war remained as bloody and cutthroat as ever.

From the West Coast of California to the East Coast of New York down to the various seaports of the south, billions of dollars a year remained at stake. Millions of hustlers and pushers put their lives on the line trying to move every drug possible. Young men with broke pockets made desperate efforts to turnout substantial profits. Products that were available for distribution included marijuana, methadone, ecstasy, and prescription pills, like Oxycontin and Percocet. Then there was the mother of all drugs and by far the most popular, cocaine. This was the drug game in 2009. Millions of hustlers out there were playing in a tax free, multi-billion dollar industry. Welcome to the American Dream.

Now enter the mind of an ultimate hustler, a young Black male. Milow 'Low' Pierre not only played the drug game, but he succeeded—making it in the fast life. By the night his thirty-sixth birthday rolled around, Low had been a hustler in the drug game for the last twenty years. The streets were all he knew, all he figured he needed to know in bid for survival. Low experienced the ups as well as the downs of the game. Fortunately for him, the downs were few, and very far between, leaving many to call Low a lucky-ass motherfucker. He was unlike the majority of hustlers in the game, who ultimately end up failures due to death or jail. The game dealt Low tons of success, and turned him into a legend around his town of Decatur, and Atlanta.

His rep steered him to being one of the best of a very few who played the game, and remained alive to enjoy the fruits. Along with his hustling credentials, Low was notoriously known on the streets to be a coldhearted killer. If you dare cross him, everyone knew that Low wouldn't hesitate to bring an end to your life.

Those two qualities made a deadly combination that had to be respected. There were those who doubted, but Low always managed to make believers out of them in the end—dead, but believers nonetheless.

A close friend nicknamed Low, 'the untouchable', and even though he lived his life as an untouchable, he was far from naive. Low knew that a twenty-one year stretch in the game was unheard of, and was only possible due to very good fortune. A very strong believer in Karma, Low knew very well that as much as Karma was a bitch, Karma from the streets was five times worse. In his mind, it was always just a matter of time.

Street
Karma

Low was certain he had his coming. After twenty-one years of blood, and bad deeds in the game, the thought of Karma never really bothered him much. He had made up his mind for the day he would have to face his past. Never in a million years did he ever imagine that Karma would return like it did.

CHAPTER

1

THE BEGINNING OF THE END

"Oh yes, baby! Oh yeah…Oh!...Yes! That feels soo good! Take it! It's yours, baby! Yes! Yes baby! Oh yes, yes! I feel you all over, baby."

Damn, you a straight up freaky bitch. Low was thinking while the satisfied smile on his face was all he was wearing as he pumped his dick in and out of her tight, brown hole. He was busy making all her sexual fantasies come to fruition. So the fingers of Low's right hand steadily fingered her throbbing pussy. He thrust three digits in and out of her, leaving her twat wet. Low removed his fingers from her moist tunnel, and put them inside her mouth. He felt like he was big pimping, smugly smiling while enjoying the pleasure of her tongue licking, and sucking her juices dripping from his hand.

She felt his dick tearing down the thin flesh of door to her forbidden hole, and shouted, "Smack my ass!"

Obliging her freakish demand, Low gave her caramel complexioned butt a firm smack on the left cheek. Smiling at the rippling effect that made her ass jiggle like Jell-O, he watched as she arched her back. Suddenly a tsunami of moans erupted.

"Hmm… Oh…ah yes baby. Yes!"

The mixture of pain, and anal pleasure reached a crescendo, sending her into a whirlpool of sheer bliss. Reaching back, she grabbed Low's balls into her soft palm, and playfully juggled them between her fingers.

"Ah…" Low hissed.

The massage, and her tight asshole gloving his pulsing penis only intensified the euphoria Low was experiencing. The two Ecstasy pills she had convinced him to pop earlier reached their peak. His blissful rush now exponentially heightened, Low found himself feeling almost too good. Closing his eyes, and tilting his head back, he couldn't stop moaning his pleasure aloud.

"Uh yeah… Ah yeah, girl!"

"I'm 'bout to cum!"

When Low heard her screaming, he viciously plunged his pipe deeper into her ass while continuing to finger fucking her gushy pussy. She closed her eyes while intensely rubbing her clit. Hollering in pleasurable pain, her gorgeous body shuddered as an intense orgasm began building inside her like a volcano. Only seconds away from a great eruption, she screamed, "Ooh… I'm… ooh baby, yeah!"

Squirming, her body shook violently while reaching her climax. The feeling of being stimulated three different ways caused a strong wave-like orgasm to stream from her warm crevice. There was no room for recovery because Low was still pumping his dick furiously inside her. The beast within him was unleashed, and her tight ass raised high welcomed it with lust. Low slowly eased his hand from her clit. Reaching back, he grabbed her ass, stuck his thumb slightly between her cheeks, and quickly plugged her hole. The sudden heightened stimulation that she felt caught her totally off guard. The feeling of having both his dick and balls pleasured simultaneously overwhelmed Low. An intense sensation flooded him, causing his knees to buckle.

"Cum for mami, baby!"

She seductively tightened her ass muscle, and Low felt an orgasmic rush take over him. His ecstasy induced high heightened the sensation, and made his entire body feel like one-big dick.

"A-h-h!" Low whimpered, blasting off inside her.

Then immediately collapsing on the hotel's super king-sized bed, Low was sweating, panting, and gasping for air. He was exhausted, and with eyes shut, he rolled onto his back while trying to catch his breath.

"Damn girl, you's something else," he gasped.

With a pleased smile, glancing at Low, she said, "Yeah, I am. But daddy, I ain't done."

Inching closer toward him, she began seductively kissing his neck, gliding her moist tongue down Low's chest, and slowly easing her way down his stomach. On reaching his manhood, she grabbed a hold of his slowly hardening meat.

"Hmm, I see you ain't done either," she salaciously smiled then began licking the tip of his dick like a chocolate Tootsie Pop.

Lifting his head, Low stared at her in surprise. His dick was solid as a rock. Fuck Superman, he thought wearing a smug smile. These fucking pills got me feeling like super-dick. Those double-stacked ecstasy pills with five point stars he popped earlier were only an hour and a half into the nine-hour ride. A night Low would never forget was in the beginning stages. It seemed to be going well. Low kicked back, and delighted in some serious sexual pleasure.

Closing his eyes, his mind was enchanted. Damn! This bitch must be a seasoned pro. Her head-game was terrific, and she was expertly giving his cock the deep-throat treatment. Occasionally gagging when the tip of his dick temporarily clogged her esophagus, she was putting him in a trance.

Grabbing a hold of her long silky black dreads, Low used his hand to navigate her rhythm, controlling her pace while fucking the shit out of her mouth. She reached for Low's nut-sack then gently rubbed, pulled, and massaged his balls. The added pleasurable sensation made Low's toes curl. Instinctively, she knew Low was on the verge of another explosion. Low's volcanic buildup reached its peak. His body went tense, and he erupted. Wrapping her full lips around the tip of his meat, she sucked him into her mouth like a Hoover vacuum. His semen gushed through his dick like milk from a cow, Low's entire body shook in convulsions, and he grimaced.

Lying comfortably on the bed with his head reclined on two plush silk pillows, he took a drag on a Newport, and slowly exhaled. Then he scrolled through his iPhone 8, and released a tiresome sigh. He was feeling drained, and exhausted from fucking for the past two and a half hours. But at the same time, he felt very much satisfied.

"You must work for Bell South, girl cuz you done sucked all the energy out of me," he laughed, pressing send on his phone when he located the number. Then he continued. "What was your name again?"

"Karma…"

Sighing seductively while winking at Low, the sexy woman glanced up. A sly smile was pasted on her lips. She wanted to be free, and have fun tonight. Wiggling her sexy hips, she returned to crushing the double-stacked Batman-stamped E-pill in a square shaped tin foil. The pill was almost powdery, and ready to mixed with about two grams of fresh crypie weed she brought with her on her flight from school. Ass fucking, and smoking weed-laced with ecstasy were two habits she picked up while attending the University of Miami. Her bachelor's degree in sports medicine, and communications was a past accomplishment, and she was ready to take the next step on the ladder of success.

An occasionally dabbler in coke, she mostly cultivated a taste for fine wines, partying, and pills. She also developed a deep interest for thug-ass niggas with big dicks, and loads of cash. Low met all her qualifications. She was hooked after her first boyfriend at the U turned her out, exposing her to the fast life, illicit drugs, and sex. Torri was a good girl gone rotten. Her first love, Troy Moore was the star quarterback of the Miami Hurricanes College Division 1 Football team. He was a lock to be in the first round of the upcoming NFL Draft.

All the women on campus wanted him figuring he would be a guaranteed meal ticket. Torri felt fortunate and was grateful to be the girl that he chose. He treated her like gold, buying her everything her heart desired. Throughout her four years at school, Troy made sure she wanted for nothing. In return she was loyal to only him, catering to his every need and desire. Even obligingly allowing him to engage in threesomes with her and her dorm-mate on the night of his twenty-first birthday.

That night, he also enjoyed a girl-on-girl freak show. The evening was topped off with her giving him anal sex for the first time. They were soul mates, at least she was sure of it. During their senior year, he proposed to her, and she was certain that the deal of becoming a rich athlete's wife was sealed.

Abruptly, he broke-off the engagement after being drafted first overall by the Dallas Cowboys in the NFL Draft, and signing a lucrative multi-million dollar contract. She was by his side, and expected to reap all the rewards of being his beautiful, and loyal fiancée. He moved to Dallas with his millions with a newfound sports agent and girlfriend. Devastated, she never shed a tear. Instead she used that heartbreaking experience as motivation.

The rest of her year at school was mostly spent at all the hot spots in Miami, chasing a good time and trying to find a millionaire baller to lock up and marry. This quickly became her obsession. Her search was definitely going to end with Low, if she had anything to say about it. She had hit the jackpot. She knew that Low's name was ringing bells even down in Dade County, Miami. The word on the street was that Low was large. People spoke of him like he was some kind of Tony Montana.

When Low first approached her at the bar of Atlanta Airport's Fliers' lounge and offered to replenish her half empty gin and tonic, her first thought was to tell him to go fuck himself. She gave his appearance - plain white T-shirt, khaki shorts, and cheap Reeboks the once-over with her gold-digging eyes. Then she quickly dismissed him as another petty-ass wanna-be hustler.

The fact that his cheap looking-ass even thought he was worthy of her time and conversation made her that much angrier. She just wanted to dismiss him as quickly as possible. Having just got into Atlanta from a long unpleasant flight from Miami International about an hour ago, she was experiencing a pulsing migraine, and was feeling beyond fatigued. The last thing she had time for was this lame-ass.

Her usual 'my shit doesn't stink' attitude almost crept out, and got the best of her. If it wasn't for the fact that she was on her third glass of gin and tonic, and was getting tipsy which slowed her reaction time in telling him off. Filled with attitude, her eyes began rolling.

Then she noticed the gleam coming from the glistening ruby stones on Low's Cartier wristwatch.

She recognized the piece immediately. Having taken, and completed a jeweler certification course in college, she knew jewelry. If her eyesight was correct, the timepiece Low wore on his wrist was worth anywhere from fifty to sixty thousand dollars, she quickly surmised. Instantly, the strained look on her face morphed into a big, warm smile.

"I have some time to kill," she smiled, inviting Low to sit at the bar with her. When he did, she sprung her plan on him. "I'll have that drink now," she added.

Wiling away the hours, the two chitchatted about this and that. Then she nonchalantly asked to see his watch. She inspected the five-carat VVS diamonds and rubies flooding the face of the Cartier, and realized that her initial appraisal of Low's watch was actually short by four hundred and fifty thousand dollars. The discovery that Low had a half a million dollars sitting on his wrist left her pussy wet and tingling.

It was a wrap. She was up in his presidential suite, and he was up in her ass so fast that she ditched her golden rule of never letting a man get the goodies on the first night. She decided to let Low fuck her brains out. She knew after she laid her pussy on him, he would be hooked, and be a fiend for more of her physical ploy. After tonight, her body would be off limits until she had his mind. Her plan was in motion, and there was no way she was going to let him slip her grasp.

When she was finished rolling the techno filled vanilla Dutch, she lit it, and inhaled deeply. Letting the smoke linger in her lungs, she exhaled the fumes, and began thinking. What would her older brother think if he knew how his supposed-to-be-virgin, saint sister that he sent away to college on his dime was really living? Even though he was aware of the devastation her breakup caused, he wouldn't be too pleased. The techno-blunt began making her buzzed. Quickly, all thoughts of her brother faded. She took another deep pull, and inhaled.

"Fuck it," she shrugged, exhaling.

The past would be kept secret, and set aside with her college years. Her brother didn't expect her home until tomorrow anyway. Plus, she knew she would have to leave the drugs alone around him. So tonight she decided to toast the town for one last go-around.

"Here baby, hit this blunt," she said, reaching out to Low, and putting the lit Dutch to his mouth while he spoke to Red on his cellphone.

"Okay then pimp. I see you got company over there huh, homey?" Red said, hearing her voice while she passed Low the Dutch. "Damn nigga, what room you in? I might have to come up there, and see what you working with cause that bitch sound fine as hell!"

"Yeah nigga. She sure is a bad one," Low smiled in agreement. Pausing, he took couple tokes then continued. "But I think I'm a have to keep this one to myself, my dude."

Glancing at her round apple shaped ass, Low watched her cuddle next to him. Then she began gently massaging his chest. The sight of her lovely caramel skinned nakedness mixed with her sensual touch made his dick jump. He kept puffing, and pretty soon he was getting horny as hell. Gently Low caressed her plump, soft ass. He slid two fingers between her cheeks entering her wetness, and began to slowly finger fuck her pussy from the back. The sensation of his fingers roaming inside her wet walls, teasing her G-spot, sent shockwaves through her petite frame.

"Ah… Ooh," she hissed with a guttural groan.

A series of desired-filled moan escaped her opened mouth as she gently sucked while licking Low's rising chest. Her breath came rapid letting him know he was getting her hot. Low knew he wanted to bust another nut before Red came to pick him up. He cut the small talk short on the phone with him.

"Yeah, so how long is it gonna take you to get here?"

"Ah nigga, you know you was always a cuffer," Red chuckled.

Red was aware of Low's habit of not sharing his women. He paused, listening intensely to the seductive moans coming from the other end of the phone. The sounds of lovemaking only served to make him think of the pussy he already lined up for later that night.

"I got something for tonight anyway," Red laughed.

"That's what's up. Do you?"

"I'm approaching College Park right now—I'm about thirty or so exits from downtown... I should be there in half an hour. I'll hit you up when I get out in front of the lobby, be ready my nigga."

"A'ight my nigga... One."

Low ended the call, tossed the iPhone on a night-stand, and stared at the beautiful body on the bed.

"Damn baby, your friend is coming to take you away from me already?" she asked, easing closer to him.

She teased with light, passionate kisses starting at his torso, and making her way up to his chin. Gliding her tongue toward his ear, she traced his earlobe with her moist tongue.

"If you leave you'll miss the surprise I have for you," she seductively whispered.

Grabbing Low's hand, she pulled his fingers out of her wet pussy, and stuck them in her warm mouth. Sucking, she licked her own juices off Low's digits. Then with a demure smile on her lips she said, "I know you don't want to miss what I have for you right?"

Her soft brown eyes were searing with vision of nasty sex. She continued licking and hungrily sucking on his fingers. Low took a deep drag off the Dutch and exhaled loudly, with a sly smile on his face. Her sexual banter was making his dick hard.

"Damn ma, I just gotta make this quick drop off and pick up my car. But I'll be right back in about an hour," he said, passing her the Dutch.

Taking a pull on the weed, she inhaled deeply while staring at Low. She exhaled then clipped the Dutch, placing it in the ashtray on top of the nightstand. She sighed deeply like something was wrong, and said, "By then I'll be sleeping like a baby." Smiling, she continued. "Well I guess I'll have to show you what I have for you right now," she said, shrugging.

"Carpe diem, baby-girl," Low smiled, watching her.

She quickly climbed on top of Low, and set herself into a sixty-nine position. Her round ass and moist pussy glistening from juices and sweat welcomed him. Grabbing a firm hold of his erect penis, she slowly stroked it.

"Now I know you're hungry, baby," she purred, teasing his stiff manhood with slow, wet licks of her tongue.

She saw the pleasure all over Low's face. Licking up and down the shaft, and tip of his magic stick, her tongue assault caused a slight drip. Wearing the most seductive smile, she said, "If you're gonna go then I can't leave you with an empty stomach. I suggest you start eating."

Then lowering her buttocks, she straddled his face with her wet pussy. Leaning forward, she feverously engulfed his dick in her warm moist mouth, and sucked his shaft. Low wasted no time in sticking his face into her goodies, devouring her. With both hands slightly spreading her ass cheeks apart. He began to gently suck on the edge of her pink pussy lips while occasionally flicking his tongue across her clit causing her to moan out ecstatically.

"Oh yes! Yes babe!"

She slowed the tempo of her strokes, and like the rhythm of an intimate love song she began to rock his world. Raising his anticipation to the highest crescendo, she stopped at the tip of his meat to circle the head with her tongue then swallowing him whole again. This calculated routine brought a feeling Low never before experienced. The techno-blunt heightened his ecstasy induced high so much that with every stroke she made with her mouth his entire body reciprocated.

It felt as if his whole body was being licked and sucked at once. Her oral antics left Low feeling so good, he obliged by returning the favor. She brought out the freak in him, and he let his tongue invade her gushy love box. Low traced the outer wet walls of her womanhood then eased his way to the bare area of skin separating vagina, and anus. With slow passionate licks, his tongue teased her.

"Oh no… No! Yes… yes!"

Ecstatic moans, and the shrill of screams burst like flares of delight across the room. Low snaked his tongue, sticking it deeper inside her tight asshole. With firm circular strokes he rimmed the tip of her anus. He spent a couple minutes tossing her salad. By the up tempo sway of her hips, and the intense grinding of her clit on his chin, Low realized that she was on the verge of an immense explosion.

"Oh baby, yeah! Yes!" She moaned in pleasure.

Low felt a humming vibration on his dick, sending waves through his entire body. In one quick motion, he eased his tongue out of her asshole, made it stiff, and plunged his tongue into her soaking, wet pussy. The tip of his tongue rubbed against her upper walls, springing her G-spot to life, and setting her entire body on fire. The ecstasy heightened the feeling so much so, she found herself unable to continue to please him anymore.

23

"Oh God! Yes! Yes!" She screamed.

Her fingers clutched the satin sheets as a heavenly orgasmic wave began building inside her. Her climatic elevation began vaulted to another level. The torturous nature of his tongue-action lifted her body up as if Lucifer possessed her. She rode the fuck out of Low's face. Nearing an apex, Low quickly plugged her anus with his middle finger, sticking it all the way inside her. Her eyes rolled to the back of her head.

"Ah-h!" She screamed when a vicious orgasm rocked her entire body.

Holding his head in place, she erupted. Her milky white juices overflowed in and around Low's mouth.

"O-o-h yes, daddy!"

Her body spasm, and shook in convulsions. When her body finally stopped shaking, she swiftly got off Low's face. Without missing a beat, she grabbed his rock hard cock. With a straddle hop, she quickly jumped on Low's dick in a reverse cowgirl.

"Hold on, baby," she purred devilishly while gyrating her hips.

Stretching her pussy walls, she allowed Low's massive cock engulfed her insides. Then she felt the tremors of an orgasm coming from the pit of her stomach. The sexy young woman seductively bounced up and down on his rigid pole like she was riding a mechanical bull. Raising his hips to greet her grind, Low plunged his massive tool inside her twat. Then he started thrusting in and out her wetness like his dick was a jackhammer. He fucked her so hard her screams were filled with the blissful mixture of pleasure and pain. She shook her head side to side, and her walls stretched. This sensation was followed by the instant delight of his cock rubbing her G-spot.

"Oh, yes! I'm cumming! I'm cumming, baby! Cum with me!"

Her body convulsed and she reached her peak, exploding on Low. His entire body stiffened, and semen flooded her tunnel.

"A-a-ah!" Low grunted, collapsing on top of the bed wearing nothing but a presidential smile.

RED

The blind stares of a million pairs of eyes looking hard,
But won't realize that they'll never see the P
—Tupac You Can't See Me

Red was straight zoning. Gunning his sports car south down Highway 85, bumping 2Pac, he raised the big bottle of Barbancourt Haitian Rum to his mouth. He took four thirst-filled gulps of the brown liquid like it was Spring Water. Wiping his mouth, he was careful not to scratch his lips with the one and a half carat diamond encrusted cufflinks on his black, silk Armani shirt. He carefully placed the bottle of rum between his legs, and raised the volume on the Bose sound system to the max. The four eighteen-inch Bose subwoofers blasted heavy, showing him what they were working with.

Speeding toward downtown Atlanta, the car's six hundred and eighteen horse powered AMG engine was effortlessly traveling at a hundred miles-an-hour. Red reclined comfortably behind the wheel, and the car's corn silk Italian leather fitted his body like a G4 jet pilot. Rapping along to the lyrics of 2Pac's, *You Can't See Me* blaring through the cars surround-sound speakers, he was in an exhilarated trance.

25

"See me in flesh
And test…
And get your chest blown
Straight out tha west, don't get blown
My adversaries cry like ho's
Open and shut like doors…
Is you a friend or foe?
Nigga you ain't know?"

Feeling on top of the world, Red took three massive gulps, and the rest of the liquor was finished. Red lowered his limo-tinted driver's side window, and tossed the empty two hundred dollar bottle liquor out. Quickly, Red reached behind him where three more bottles sat in the back seat. Grabbing one of the pint sized bottles, he opened the top, and took a heavy swig that went down smooth. Every part of his six feet eight inches, weighing around two hundred and thirty-five-pound frame was on fire. The hundred-proof-rum left him with a heated sensation, easing down his chest. Red blew air out his mouth as if he was exhaling smoke, causing his eyes to squint.

"That's some good shit right there," he smiled, muttering to himself.

1:44 a.m. His night was progressing exactly as planned. Red's smile reflected that of a hustler finally reaching the apex of his game. Fueled by the potent alcohol, Red was now officially stuck in a euphoric zone. Shifting his gaze toward the time on his canary diamond-studded, rose gold ice-link watch, he nodded his head.

Red's mentor, and confidant was Low. He was the reason Red finally accomplished his lifelong goal. Illegitimate or not, the fiery, ambitious teenager was now of millionaire status. For the division-1 college basketball prospect that dropped out of high school in his senior year this wasn't too bad. After abandoning his hoop dreams, and a full scholarship to any university in the country, Red made it in another game.

Ditching school for the grind of the street, Red chose to finance his sister, Torri's college education. He pursued the less guaranteed route, becoming a stellar street scholar. To gamble on such a critical decision would've been disastrous if he failed. So there was no room for any losses. Because of that Red didn't make a move unless his heart was completely with it.

Red was taking a great risk when he chose to hustle instead of going to college, but couldn't give up the chance of becoming a member of Zoe Pound. It was one of the most financially prosperous criminal organizations in the United States. He would be under the tutelage of the most notoriously feared drug lord of the nation's underworld—Low. This was a one in a million opportunity Red just couldn't pass up.

And I ain't stoppin'
'Til I'm well paid
Bails paid
Now nigga, look what hell made
Visions of cops and sirens
Niggas open fire
Bunch a Thug…

Gripping the steering wheel tightly, Red knew the last thing he needed was to have his spit-clean arrest record ruined by a reckless felony. He was in possession of an unlicensed handgun while driving under the influence. Red throttled the speeding car down to a respectable forty miles-per-hour. Then sucking his teeth, Red let out a long sigh. Activating the right turn signal, he guided the car to the exit lane, entering the Atlanta Hartsfield–Jackson International Airport.

Red hated being anywhere in the vicinity of down-town, ATL. He never partied or enjoyed nightclubs. Always about making that money, Red cast a hater's glance at 'the scene' and being seen. All of his clientele lived in and around the suburbs therefore being in the city was never a necessity. Only if he were heading out of state on one of his business trips would he drive to the airport.

Unfortunately for Red, his sister, Torri, was coming into the airport tomorrow, and he was scheduled to pick her up. The thought of that trip made him sigh heavily. Red was well aware of how freely the 'alphabet boys' – FBI, DEA, and ATF roamed this part of the city. Their headquarters were in the downtown area. Red held onto the common sense belief of not showing his face at the local strip clubs, celebrity restaurants, and social events.

Staying out of the spotlight was what a lot of hus-tlers failed to do, and became a portrait for the 'alphabet boys'. He was not only cautious, but was sharper than your average hustler. Red wanted to be in the game for the long haul, and avoided the 'scene' at all costs.

Taking the airport exit, heading toward the Royal Sonesta Hotel & Resort, Red shrugged off the dislike for being in the city. Torri would be returning home from four years of college at the University of Miami. Red hadn't seen his beloved sister since her last visit a year ago. He couldn't wait to see the huge smile she would be wearing when he presented the spanking new '09 db9 Volante Convertible, Aston Martin he bought for her graduation gift. Red went the extra mile with his gift. He had the luxury sports car shipped off to California, where it was gutted, and customized to his liking. Red even had 'Torri' stitched into all four of the car's head-rests in bold script.

He wanted to get himself, and Torri out the hood. Red accomplished this, but unfortunately he realized that Torri's heart was out of his hands. All he could do was help her move on from her broken relationship. Along with the new car, Red leased a two-bedroom luxury condo in Atlanta's exclusive Buckhead residential area for Torri. He also had fifty thousand dollars deposited into an American Express prepaid Credit card account. Torri was ready to start graduate school in the fall. Red planned on paying the full tuition—another surprise he wanted to reveal when she arrived.

Red guided his beluga black on black rims, two-door Mercedes Benz SLR McLaren to the front entrance lobby of the luxurious Royal Sonesta Resort Hotel, and Casino. He pulled to a stop in front of a valet. For a moment, Red wondered why Low booked a room at such a well-known hot spot. Then smiling, he quickly shook his head. Red knew that Low was a big-time trick, and a sucker for fine women.

The choice of hotel told Red that Low definitely had some five-star pussy up there with him, and he was trying to impress her. Two taps on the driver's side window broke Red's train of thought, and his smile disappeared into a frown. Turning the cars sound system off, he lowered the tinted window just enough for his eyes to be seen. Red glared at the young valet with a cold stare.

"Yo...?" he sneered.

"Uh... Yes, sir..."

A valet reluctantly approached when he saw the person sitting behind the wheel of the expensive vehicle. Smiling nervously, the valet said, "I was just kindly wondering if you had any luggage that needed to be taken up to your suite with you, sir?"

Sucking his teeth, Red said, "Nah, I'm just picking up someone."

Then he gave the valet an icy stare, and with a sweeping gesture of his hand, Red signaled for the valet to get away from his car. The valet flashed an uncomfortable smile.

"Very well, sir," he said, nodding, and rushing to another vehicle.

His driver's side window up, Red turned up the volume. Suddenly his iPhone vibrated. Shifting his gaze down toward the phones screen, Red saw the message.

Daddy I'm soaking wet. Where R U?

It was the fourth text in the past thirty minutes Lovely sent him. She was blowing up his phone, but Red couldn't blame her. He was supposed to be at her house an hour and a half ago. Red didn't bother to respond. Letting out a deep sigh, he reclined himself in the cars leather seats, resting his deep waves on the seat's headrest with a mischievous smile on his face, thinking. Lovely was one of Low's bad bitches.

Lovely's pussy was A-1. Behind Low's back, Lovely had given Red a taste of the goodies. Since then, Red could not get enough of Lovely. His young- ass was sprung. Grabbing his crotch, Red began massaging his erection through his Armani silk slacks. Wild thoughts of fucking Lovely had him going, and his smile grew wider at the thought of getting more of Lovely. He rubbed his palms together, thinking life was good. Eventually Red would have to tell Low that he was fucking Lovely. That could be done much later.

Even though it was damn special, her pussy was not good enough to jeopardize his future, and livelihood. He was aware that Low hated secrets, but figured that Low wouldn't give a fuck once he told him about Lovely. Women were an added luxury to a man of Low's status. A long time ago, Low made it clear to Red that only his wife, Michelle was off limits. Red wasn't going to allow Lovely to deter him from his destiny. This was a monumental turning point in his life. At this moment, Red's mind was on presenting Low with a million dollars in cash tomorrow. He needed the dough to complete the final stage of his initiation then he would be an official member of Zoe Pound.

Raising the money was the final test. It had taken four years to raise the amount. Red did this without the guidance or help of Low, and he didn't have the muscle of Zoe Pound. Low needed to see that Red was not only a hustler, but that he was sharp, and street smart. If Red were able to garner the resource to accumulate one million dollars without attracting the FBI, ATF, and DEA or getting set-up, or worse—getting robbed along the way, he would be worthy to carry on the torch of the Criminal Enterprise known as Zoe Pound.

2Pac's, *All Eyez On Me* album rolled on, *Check Out Time* flowed through the car's sound system. Nodding his head, Red's mind drifted further into the struggles he faced in the last four years. Setting the foundation, he was in the midst of making the necessary moves to get a million dollars tax-free. Success came down to making the right decisions. That philosophy never rang as true as it did when it came to the final connection that eventually got Red over the seven-figure milestone.

It was the most critical decision he had to make throughout the whole ordeal. Keys were going for twenty-seven-five up north in Massachusetts, and two determined hustlers out of Boston were in town, and looking to cop thirty of them at fifteen a piece. The thought of killing these out-of-towners, taking their money, and doing away with their bodies seemed like the easiest route at first. Red's long-term frame of mind kicked in. Quickly, Red realized that if these buyers were about money then not only would he surpass the million-dollar mark necessary, he would also have another out-of-state customer.

There was no necessity to flip coin on this deal. Red already had a solid circle of connections, and was making real good money locally. With close to seven hundred and fifty thousand dollars stashed away already, Red was not in a rush to get that last quarter million. Never the anxious one, Red knew it was better to be safe than sorry.

Knowing this deal could push him over the top, Red chose to roll with his gut feeling. He hit the buyers with the bricks they were requesting at a price tag of seventeen thousand dollars. The deal went down smoothly—that was three months ago. After hitting the Bostonians with their last ten keys earlier, and collecting one hundred and seventy thousand dollars, Red's net worth stood at nearly a million and a half.

Red put Low's million in a safe at his condo in Decatur. With the money he owed on the bargained price of two hundred thousand, Red was able to pay for a new Benz, and Torri's Volante. He headed straight to the Aston Martin dealership, and paid them off. Then he put fifty thousand on a pre-paid credit card for Torri. While shopping at an Armani outlet in DeKalb, Red bought a few dozen outfits.

He booked a V.I.P reservation at P Diddy's exclusive five-star restaurant, Justin's. It was there that he planned to entertain his sister in style on her first night back home. Four years ago, Red chose the street game over a shot at going to the NBA. Looking back at the decision, Red felt he made the right choice. Once he started working with Low's connections, twenty million dollars at the end of the year was a guarantee. Then he and Torri would reap untold rewards. It was a vow he had already staked his life on.

His vibrating iPhone broke Red out of his ruminations. Glancing at the screen, he saw another text from Lovely, sent with a video message. Scrolling, Red opened the video message. He could feel his eyes growing in size while looking at the screen. His mouth stayed open for the entire two-minute video of Lovely seductively rubbing her clit with a vibrator.

'*I'm on my third nut and counting Daddy! WHERE R U?*'

The message read, and Red felt an immediate response. "Ooh-wee!" He shouted, his dick already rock-hard.

Desperately pressing the reply button, Red was about to reply, but saw that Low was coming his way. He secured the phone on his waist, and shook his head, whistling in blissful anticipation of a booty-call. Sighing thankfully that Low only needed a ride to the stash-house, Red wanted to drop off his mentor, and haul ass to Lovely's condo.

"This nigga swear he fly," Red muttered under his breath when Low got closer.

Looking freshly dipped in Versace silk linens from head to toe, Low was his unflappable self. Flossing five-carat diamond cuff links on his ivory white and gold Versace button-up lit up with every step, Low's matching ivory white Versace silk slacks were tailor pressed perfect. Cuffed precisely over ivory ostrich skinned, round-tip slip-ons, his slacks were complemented by two large Versace sun pendants on the face of each shoe. Each pendant made of solid gold, with a three-carat diamond flooding the face of the sun—worth about fifty thousand each. Throw in his five-hundred-thousand-dollar, ruby studded Cartier watch, Low looked like a million bucks.

Making his way through the hotel's massive double doors, Low walked to the valet parking area. A car's horn caught his attention, and Low's face lit up when he locked eyes on Red's McLaren Roadster. Hustlers have a way of communicating without saying a word. The suicide doors swung open on the Benz. Red was telling Low that he was officially in the building. Then

Red, one gator foot at a time, stepped out the two-door coupe. Low's face straight beamed with a great smile. It was a joy similar to a father witnessing his son reaching a higher level of success.

"Okay then pimpin!" Low excitedly exclaimed.

Red glanced to his right, and began to lightly brush his shoulders off. Low threw his head back in laughter at the move.

"I see ya shining nigga!" Low joked, making his way over to Red.

"Yessir, I'm in my motherfucking bag!"

The two hustlers locked hands, embracing with a homeboy hug. Low stole a glance at Red's wrist.

"Damn, my nigga. You could've at least bought yourself a rollie," Low joked.

"You right," Red smiled.

"Fuck is this? What you need to know the time in Asia for? Nigga you ain't an international playa like me," Low chuckled.

"Nigga, you're laughing cause your old-ass ain't up on this new shit," Red retorted, gesturing towards his canary studded watch.

"That's what you think…"

"After tonight, even bitches in Japan gonna want a taste of this eggroll. Cause the boy knock down these bricks like King Kong in the flesh nigga!" Red laughed, giving the face of his iced-out watch two assuring taps.

"Say no more, playa…" Low said, jokingly lifting up his hand in an act of surrender before he continued. "But say bro, that's a mighty nice car you got there."

Low quickly gave Red's new ride the once-over. With a raised eyebrow, he glanced back at Red, and asked, "You got your license, my nigga?"

"Ah nigga don't trip," Red said in a serious tone. "You already know. I never leave home without my license," he declared, and raised his shirt exposing a.44 Smith & Wesson revolver.

"Good nigga, cause I forgot my shit upstairs," Low said.

"Look at you," Red said, shaking his head before continuing. "Fuck it. We ain't headed too far, right?"

Low's car was parked at the stash house. Low always stay strapped, carrying two.357 Magnums in armrest of his Bentley Continental Flying Spur.

"Oh for sure. You know my twins go nowhere else. Soon as you drop me off, I'll be good."

"Well a'ight then my nigga. I guess we good to go. Hop in so we can get the fuck up."

✦ ✦ ✦

The Mercedes' engine roared as Red maneuvered in and out of the highway's traffic lane. Low sat snugly in the passenger seat while Young Jeezy's, *Trap Or Die* boomed through the cars Bose sound system. Low adjusted the volume then reclined, resting his baldhead on the leather headrest. He lifted the crypie weed to his mouth, and lit it.

"Bro, I'm telling you..." Low began as he inhaled the thick weed smoke deeply into his lungs. Then he continued. "I think I just met the baddest bitch ever!" Low exhaled the laced fumes, and passed the weed to Red.

"Nigga, you trippin," Red snickered in amusement, took a long pull off the weed, and kept his eyes on the road.

"Man I ain't even bullshitting, bro," Low said.

"The bitch's bad as fuck, man. I swear she look like that broad... Ah... You know that broad we be seeing in all them King and XXL magazines?"

"Who...? You mean Angel...?"

"Yeah, yeah, that's the one," Low said, snapping his fingers.

"Yeah sure... Angel's bad. That bitch can't look that good," Red snickered, shaking his head then continued. "Angel's a straight up twenty-piece."

"You think it's a game, huh? I ain't even joking, bro. And the shit about it... You'd think a bitch that beautiful would be a straight up saint, right? Man, look-a here!"

Red was laughing as he switched lanes, and tried his best not to choke on the weed smoke. Red could tell from Low's enthusiasm that Low was about to become animated.

"Good thing I never let looks fool me, when it comes to these broads."

"Yeah, but I bet you was spitting that A-1 tech to her though," Red chuckled.

"Shit, nigga. I ain't even have to spit no game to that ho. Soon as the bitch seen them stones on the kid's wrist it was a wrap. She was instantly in the matrix!"

Red threw his head back in laughter, knowing well the effect his own jewels had on woman he first met. Then chuckling, he said, "Nah, you ain't have the bitch stuck on the stones like that bro."

"Man I told you I ain't had to spit no game. Soon as the bitch seen the rubies on the kids wrist the bitch turned into Roger Clemens, and straight fastballs me the pussy.

They both burst out laughing at Low's animation and his analogy.

"I swear, bro—word to the Pound. I tell this bitch my name...next thing I know, she's pulling out the visa, and started charging drink after drink to that shit. She even insisted on charging a room for the whole week."

Red glanced at Low, smiled, and said, "Man, I know you didn't have shorty maxing out her lil' credit card try-ing to impress you?"

"I was about to," Low said with a devilish smirk.

"Oh yeah…?"

"Yeah… But you know I had to let her see she was in the presence of a boss."

"Anyway bro… Soon as we get in the suite, the bitch pulls out a big prescription bottle full of these."

Red glanced down at Low's at opened hand. Skeptically eyeing the four two-toned, cloverleaf stamped pills for a brief second, Red immediately started laughing so hard he almost dropped the weed.

"Nigga, this bitch had you popping Viagra!" Red asked still laughing.

"Nah, fool. Nigga, this Ecstasy," Low said, passing Red one of the double-stacked Ecstasy pills. Then he continued. "All the young freak's popping these shits nowadays. I ain't even gonna front, that lil' broad just turned me out on to these pills. You ever tried one?"

"Nah, I never tried that shit," Red said while examining the green and white pills.

"Okay then—"

"But I heard they'll have your dick hard for like two hours straight," Red said with a smirk.

"Nigga what?" Low chimed in excitedly, grabbing his crotch. Then he continued. "These pills is the truth! Fucking have your meat hard like Rottweiler!" he laughed.

"Huh…?"

"Yeah nigga, been fucking for like two hours, and my dick's still hard as fuck right now! The shit just won't go down. Plus, the bitch was crushing these shits all in the weed, and shit. Man, I'm high as fuck, bro. I can't wait 'til you drop me off. I'm heading straight back to the telly to tear that pussy up some more."

Laughing, Red shook his head, and said, "Nigga, now I know why this weed taste funny. Shit, I got this bad one lined up tonight waiting to get blessed too."

"A'ight, I'm telling ya bro. Pop one of these babies, and then go see that broad. You'll see… Matter of fact, pop two," Low said, handing Red a second pill then he continued. "I'm 'bout to pop these two myself."

Red eyed the two ecstasy pills skeptically then he said, "Really…?

"Yes nigga."

"C'mon you know me. I ain't into all this extra shit like some of y'all old-heads. No disrespect. But I don't fuck with coke and—"

"I know you only fuck with weed, and liquor to get right, but you gotta take a chance on this shit right here."

The thought of fucking Lovely's brains out for hours on end without losing his erection made things seem quite enticing. Nodding his head, Red said, "A'ight, fuck it. I'm a fuck the dog shit outta this bitch."

He purposely left out Lovely's name. Instead, reaching around the backseat, Red retrieved a bottle of Haitian rum that he was drinking earlier. Placing it in his lap, he took a toke on the weed, lowered his driver's side window, and tossed out the roach. Then he swallowed both pills, lifted the bottle of rum to his mouth, and with one swig, washed them down.

"Damn nigga, I passed you my blunt, and your young-ass smoked that whole shit," Low said, realizing the weed was all gone.

"My bad, Low…"

Shaking his head, Low dropped the ecstasy pills into his own mouth, and got the rum in Red's hand. After swallowing he said, "Back in the day it was puff, puff, pass…"

They both laughed, and Low took another gulp of liquor, and his face wrinkled when the liquor burned his throat on its way down.

"Ah, nigga don't trip…" Red said.

"This liquor is potent—"

"Yeah, this stripper bitch I be fucking with her parents just got back from Haiti. Look at the backseat. I got twenty more cases of Barbancourt Haitian Rum at the crib. Nigga, that's enough juice to keep a nigga drunk till next summer."

"Be careful with this shit," Low said, taking another gulp.

Red took the bottle back, took another gulp, and asked, "How long it's gonna take these pills to kick in?"

"Don't worry. You'll feel it soon."

It was now 3 a.m. They were travelling for seventeen minutes, and Red could feel the ecstasy creeping on him. The car's sound system blasted Bone Thugs and Harmony. Highway I-85 was virtually empty. Red was doing a hundred and eighty miles per hour entering the city of Columbus where Low's stash-house was located.

The smooth ecstatic effect the pills gave Red, mixed with the flowing beats of the music left him in an excellent mind frame. His Kool-Aid smile was accented by occasional chuckles as he listened to Low's ranting about his sexcapade with the freak at the Hotel. Low was filled with animation while telling his story complete with details, leaving no room for imagination.

"Nigga, I stick my tongue in the bitch ass and toss her salad a lil' bit to get her loose, and ready. Once I replaced my tongue with this meat! Man look-a here! Whoever was hitting her off before me must've not been packing. Cause once I stuck this Anaconda in that tight ass, the bitch started screaming hysterically like she never took it in the ass before…"

Red threw his head back in laughter, but all he could think about was how he planned to punish Lovely later on.

"Man, you's a straight up freak, Low. Word up!" Red chuckled, shaking his head.

"Nigga, I'm soo old school," Low retorted.

Then he lifted the bottle of Haitian Rum to his mouth, and guzzled down about a half pint of liquor in one gulp. The Rum went down much smoother this time, but still caused Low to blow out air, and squint his eyes.

"Be easy with that hundred proof shit, my nigga," Red cautioned.

Licking his lips, and smiling, Red said, "Ain't no shame in ma-my... game."

The Rum left him feeling woozy, and the ecstasy had kicked in, heightening Low's drunkenness. In a span of five hours, he had popped four double-stacked pills, and was rolling something serious.

"A'ight, but take it easy anyway, old-school nigga," Red chirped.

"Shit, nigga y'all new jacks gotta start eating more pussy, and licking a lil' more ass. Might grow some hair on your chest, lil' nigga. Fucking with these young girls ain't gon' cut it," Low said, taking another gulp of the rum before continuing. "They don't even know how to clean themselves right yet. Might fuck around, and get a piece of turd on ya tongue. You need to find a woman about my age. You know thirty-six through forty, and let her throw dat grown woman pussy on ya. Ya might learn a thing, or two. Bet'cha won't be thinking I'm such a freak then."

Red smiled, thinking about diving into Lovely's pussy tonight, face first, made Red want to hear more of Low's tale.

"Nigga, you such a boss. You ain't have that ho' suck you off?"

"Lil' nigga, raise your hand when you address a boss!" Low jokingly sneered.

"A'ight..."

"Nigga, soon as I busted off, I took the dick out the bitch's ass, and stuck it in her mouth. And ooh-wee! That girl can suck some dick. She's a certified pro. Plus, a nigga was rolling on these pills. Shit, she sucked a nigga off soo decent... I started getting emotional. Damn near got teary eyed by the time she was done. On every-thang!"

"Fool, you crazy!" Red shouted, throwing back his head in laughter.

"I'm saying porn star quality..."

"Shit...if the head that good you might as well let ya lil' homie get in on the action," Red said with a wide grin.

"Shit, I fuck 'em. I don't love 'em," Low said with a shrug.

"I can't tell. Earlier I was try'na come up there to see what you working with. You acting like Captain-Save-A-Ho or some shit. Matter of fact, what's the bitch's name? Cause I done had me a few stallions 'round here. I might've done fucked the broad already, and you over here try'na cuff that," Red boastfully smiled.

"Ma-a-a-n, I'm so fucked up right now," Low smiled, taking another sip off the bottle. Then he continued. "I think she said her name was...Carmen...something like Karma, but she wasn't Spanish or anything. She looked kind a Haitian. Shit, wouldn't remember the bitches name if my life depended on it," Low chuckled with a drunken smirk. Then rubbing his baldhead, he continued. "She ain't even from 'round here, anyway. The bitch done flew up from Miami. She one of those college freaks," Low shrugged.

Red's left eye suddenly began twitching when he asked, "College freaks...? Say, what she look like again?"

"Man, I told you the bitch look just like that model-broad angel...just with green eyes," Low smiled, rubbing his crotch.

"C'mon man. You bullshittin' me..." Red said.

Red silently watched Low falling into a trance, reminiscing. Low's smile was a telltale sign of what was on his mind—the delicious sex he had earlier experienced. Pictures of her face, and body flashed in his memory banks. Low chuckled then said, "Shit, fuck around, and find out that it was angel. Nah, but this broad's ass wasn't as fat though."

Taking another swig, Low laughed, and said, "As a matter of fact, I remember that bitch had tats on her back coming down her spine."

"Yeah...?" Red asked, silently nodding.

"Yeah, my nigga. She had some red roses, and vines and shit. The bitch was riding my dick from the back. I was fucked on 'em pills, and them roses on her spine had a nigga feelin' like I was in the motherfucking Garden of Eden and shit," Low laughed.

He was the only one laughing. Red snapped impatiently. A violent surge of anger was rising deep inside him. His foot weighed down on the gas pedal. The Roadster speedometer hit two hundred and seven miles per hour, and climbing.

"Nigga, what's her name?" Red pressed.

"Ma-a-an, you know your boy ain't too good on names," Low muttered in a drunken slur.

The empty bottle of Haitian rum was now sitting idly in his lap. Low was completely oblivious to the heavy tension choking the air in the fast moving vehicle. Rum, along with the concoction of the ecstasy pills, and weed left him with double vision. Everything started to be blurry, and the world seemed to move in slow-mo. His rollercoaster ride reached the peak, and now it was time to go into a deep plunge. Suddenly, he felt the jolt.

"Matter of fact... I do remember that bitch's name... Low said, snapping his fingers. Glancing over at Red, he continued. "Yeah, the bitch told me her name's Karma, but I figured she was lying, and shit. So when she was rollin' up some exotic bud, I checked that bitch's wallet. She had a Miami U. ID. And that shit had Torri—"

"NIGGA WHAT!"

The car was moving at maximum speed driven by an impaired driver, who was under the influence of marijuana, alcohol, and Ecstasy. A surge of venomous anger exploded like a time bomb inside Red. The fiery output shot through his left leg, and it slammed against the brakes. Tragedy was a certainty.

Red's animated response activated the Roadster's four fifteen-inch Brembo upgraded brakes. The sudden halt in torque at such a great speed instantly elevated the Benz from the highway's pavement. Causing the coupe sized Roadster to lift up in a rapid, death-defying three hundred and sixty degree spin. The car hurtled through the air toward the highways four-foot guardrail separating the north and south lanes.

It happened too fast for Red and Low to react. Like a speeding bullet into on-coming traffic, the Benz shot across the highway, bumper smashing against the concrete guardrail. At the same time, a massive eighteen-wheeler Mack truck transporting three-dozen luxury vehicles in tow roared down the highway. Traveling at ninety–four miles per hour, it was headed in the same direction as the flying coupe.

The heavy-footed trucker behind the wheel of the Mack Truck noticed a spinning black object. Instinctively downshifted the truck's gear from fifth to fourth gear. This declension in speed prevented the unpleasant from occurring. The Roadster flew by the trucks massive front windshield, avoiding a head-on collision by fractions of a second. Maybe it was Divine intervention, but the Almighty couldn't prevent the next turn of events.

Thick smoke from its demolished radiator filled the car's interior. Slowly, Low raised his head from the dashboard on the passenger side. His face had smashed into the wood-grain trimmed air exhaust vent, he was feeling dazed, and felt the aches of a severe, neck-breaking whiplash. Low was also bleeding from his right eyebrow caused by a deep gash. Blood coursed freely down the side of his face.

"Ugh…ah shit! Ah…ugh!"

He let out an agonizing moan while trying to get into a sitting position. Feeling a sharp, burning pain from his shattered ribcage, Low grabbed his right side. Wincing, he collapsed backward against the passenger seat as the burning sensation intensified.

In the meantime, Red was in a nauseated state. Coughing, and desperately gasping for air, his head was spinning. Thick, toxic engine smoke engulfed his throat, and made it impossible to breathe. He was gagging uncontrollably, but Red did not suffer a scratch because he was safely secured in his seatbelt. Low neglected to put on the seatbelt, and suffered injuries. Other than a damaged bumper, punctured radiator, and a crack windshield, the Roadster was virtually intact. It was still running.

The Roadster crashed through a wooden gate that lined the residential backyard on the side of the highway, and landed on a manicured lawn. Red let down the driver's side window, and his dizziness began to fade. The toxic smoke seeped out into the late night sky. Red took a deep breath of fresh air into his lungs. He shifted his head toward the passenger seat. It didn't take long for his fogged mind to clear.

Low used both his hands to clutch his severely damaged ribcage. He glanced over at the driver's seat, and for the first time in his life his face was flushed with fear.

"You had my little sister doing drugs, Low…?" Red asked though clenched teeth.

"Your Sister…? What…? What you talk—" Low groggily began.

Red sharply interrupted, and said, "Shut the fuck up!"

All the drugs and alcohol left Low critically impaired, but his mind screamed danger. He was made leery of Red's emotion.

"My sister!" Red shouted.

Trying to shake off his heavy wooziness, Low's eyes instinctively grew wide. He was desperately fighting the feeling of being high while attempting to keep his focus on the driver's side. With every passing second, Red was clearly growing angrier.

"I'm a kill you!"

All seemed silent for the longest second of a gangster's life. Within that split second, Low locked eyes with Red, and saw what he already knew. Low's survival instincts took over, reaching for the gun on his waist, his heart sank. The realization that he wasn't armed hit him like a ton of bricks.

Watching Low's expression, Red firmly gripped the chrome handle of the.44. Low jumped at his only remaining option. He attempted to take flight, and even managed to get a foot out the door, but was ultimately seconds too slow. Red pulled the trigger, letting off two thunderous shots, and hitting Low in the left elbow. A second hollow tip slug tore through Low's side, shredding muscle tissues on exit. Low's arm was severely severed, and barely still attached to the rest of his body. His one hundred and eighty-five pound frame stumbled hard to the ground. Low attempted to break the fall with his right hand. It was just too much weight for his fragile wrist to withstand.

When Low hit the ground, his wrist broke in two places. Red let off another shot, missing by inches. Bullets exploded through the tinted glass window, sending fragments of glass, and plastic film flying everywhere. The deafeningly loud shot whizzed past echoing in Low's eardrum. He quickly realized if he didn't get away fast, his death was certain. Frantically making it to his feet, Low swallowed the pain. His only thoughts were now on survival. His adrenaline kicked into overdrive as he took off running toward the highway.

"Fuck!" Red seethed.

Low was making good on his getaway. Hastily distancing himself from the car, Low began really running for his life. Quickly reaching for the driver's side door handle, Red swung the cars door ajar, and attempted to hop out. His seatbelt restrained him.

"Fuck! Damn this motherfucker's getting away!" Red hissed, unbuckling the seatbelt in a rage, and hopping out the coupe.

Red's eyes adjusted to the late-night darkness located, and locked in on the back of his fleeing target. Low hit the highway's four-foot guardrail like Jesse Owens approaching the final hurdle at the Olympics. At thirty-six years old, Low deserved a gold medal the way he hopped over the guardrail. Low made it to the other side of the highway, dashing through a field of grass, and heading toward a backyard fence. Red took aim, trying to finish Low off. He squeezed off two shots in rapid succession hitting Low in the back.

His body jerked violently as the force of both shots sent Low flying into the fence. Low refused to die. Swallowing the intense pain, he managed to pull himself on top of the fence. He was now in the open, and Red had a clear shot at his head.

Red had one round left. Taking aim from fifty-five feet away, he zeroed in on the back of Low's skull, and was about to squeeze. The sound of sirens suddenly caught his ears, and he took his eyes off the target. Red glanced over his shoulder and spotted flashing cherry lights in the distance. They were closing in fast. His eyes darted back to the fence, but Low was nowhere in sight.

"Goddamn!" Red shouted, letting his last shot off at the fence.

Red figured he had twenty seconds to clear the scene. Turning, he dashed toward his Benz while silently praying that Low was dead. Quickly hopping back in the coupe's driver's seat, Red swiftly kicked the McLaren into gear, flooring it over the dismantled wooden gate. The Roadster's tires touched the highway's pavement, and Red was already in third gear. A cloud of dirt and smoke mixed in the air, Red was burning tires. Hitting a hundred and twenty in less than seven seconds making a smooth getaway.

✦ ✦ ✦

For the past hour, Low had been unconscious, and lying on his back in someone's backyard. Blinking twice, and glancing around him, Low was at a lost to exactly where he was. Low slowly began to regain consciousness. He realized that he had lost a tremendous amount of blood, and with each critical minute that passed, his life was slowly slipping away. His eyes opened to a full moon, and a sea of bright stars in the sky. His memory began to slowly kick in. Vivid scenes of the night's events started to swiftly flash through his mind. Then almost instantly, the sense that allows a person to feel kicked in, causing Low to let out an agonized-filled wail.

Low's body was on fire it felt like his flesh was burning. Someone must have held an extremely hot iron against his back. In a state of total panic, Low desperately tried to move. With great effort, he managed to roll onto his stomach, and was eventually able to stagger to his feet. Low quickly scanned his surroundings. He saw a big house ahead. The thought of knocking on the back door of the house wasn't an option.

The entire yard wasn't completely fenced in. There was a big space leading to an alleyway. Low took a step, and grimaced from the burning sensation that rattled his entire body. His legs ached painfully, and felt extremely heavy as he staggered forward. With greatly determined effort, Low managed his way to the open space. Glancing to his Left. A dozen or so family-sized trash bins were lined-up for a few yards on either side of the dark, narrow alleyway. About a hundred feet in the distance, Low saw the headlights of various vehicles speeding by on Highway I-85.

A renewed sense of hope washed over Low. Mustering all his remaining strength, Low winced as he began quickly hobbling toward the speeding headlights. Glancing further in the distance, he saw the other side of the highway. A convention of bright, flashing lights lit the skies. There were marked police cars, unmarked cruisers, and news vans parked alongside the highway by the large area of grass where Red crashed. Low knew why they were there. Being at the mercy of the law was like another heated slug penetrating Low's flesh. He needed medical assistance. In order to catch one of the cops, or reporter's eyes, Low made it as close to them as possible.

Low's body was weakening by the minute while struggling forward. Low was breathing hard, and feeling extremely fatigued. His chest and back were soaked with sweat. The warm, wet sensation Low felt caused him to glanced down at his shirt. Then his hope for survival turned into complete fear of dying.

His eyes grew wide, and panic set in when Low caught sight of his blood soaked, white Versace outfit. Low's gaze shifted back to the highway. Then staggering forward, Low raised his hand in the air, and waved it in a desperate attempt to get attention. The once vivid cars speeding by on I-85 were now blotches of white lights. His vision became blurred, and started fading. Desperation grew with each breath, Low tried to scream out for help. His weak voice was as faint as a whisper. All his senses began to slowly shut down..

Low wasn't conscious when his knees buckled. His body crashed face first into the dirt. Low let out a pain-filled moan on impact. But his hearing had long since faded, and his agony fell upon deaf ears.

He had shot many men in his lifetime. Low even got shot once when he was a teenager. However, he was not prepared to be on the receiving end of several pen-etrating bullets—until tonight. While losing conscious-ness, his mind turned to thoughts of his right-hand man, Rob. Low's past appeared to have finally caught up, and his Karma sure was an ugly bitch. Vividly, images of his life moved in a haste, flashing through his thoughts. It sped through his thirties. Moved into his twenty's. Then it was on to his teens when all the bullshit first started. Then darkness came.

CHAPTER

2

1989 MIAMI, FLORIDA

Rob was shaking his head, and laughing. Sitting comfortably in the reclined driver's seat of his dark tinted, stolen 1972 Buick Regal, he took a long deep drag on his weed filled Swisher Sweets cigar. Then he inhaled the smoke deeply into his lungs, and glanced toward the passenger seat. His partner, Low was putting the finishing touches on an E-Z Wider rolling paper that he previously packed with a mixture of weed and hash.

Reclining with a serious expression, Low fished in his black Dickies slacks for a lighter. He lit the tip of his joint, taking a few taste-taking tokes to ensure the weed was pulling right. Nodding his approval, he shook his head slightly to himself. It was as if he fully expected Rob 's reaction to him paying for a private phone line to be set up in Michelle's room.

"Yeah bro, I'm just keeping it real hood," Low repeated. After taking a toke, he continued. "I love her. So paying for a phone line ain't a big deal."

Again, Rob laughed out loud then said, "Man, you straight up tripping."

Puffing on the joint then exhaling, Rob shook his head while glancing at Low. A few years older than Low, Rob had already been through all the puppy love stages with girls in the hood. His heart was broken more than a few times by women that swore they loved him unconditionally. Then they turned around, and left him due to the condition that his pockets weren't as fat as the next man, or car wasn't as fly. Rob finally figured that part of the game out. He theorized that women were luxury items to be pursued only after he got his money right. This was viewed as an impossible achievement.

"Let me put you up on game, lil' homie," Rob said.

Taking a puff, Rob searched the armrest for a cassette tape to put in the tape deck. Then he continued. "First, these bitches ain't shit. Second, all they see is dollar signs. Shit...soon as you catch a case or take a loss in these streets, and you ain't on top of your game like when they first met you—it's on to the next one. Trust me, I'm telling you all this cause you my nigga, dig? Don't confuse good pussy for love. Bitches will have you doing some crazy shit when they know they got your heart, trust. Today, you paying for her to get her own phone line, and the next day you on child support like a muthafucka... All while your seed calling the next man daddy. Trust me. I've seen it a million times already. Don't fall victim, lil' nigga, thinking a phone bill is no big deal, cause you in so-called, love."

"Hmm, I hear you."

"How love starts...? The pussy always feels good until you nut."

Low respected Rob's expertise, and not only looked up to him but also valued his opinion. It was the only reason Low broached the subject with him. Low really needed Rob's blessing on this girl. He just had to make him see that Michelle was different. Low watched as Rob finally found the tape he was looking for, and pushed it into the tape deck.

"I feel where you coming from and all, but Michelle's different from all these hood-rats out here. I mean, she don't even care about my bread… She never asked me for money—be having her own. She's even offered to chip in, and pay for the phone line. Shit…it's the least I can do. I been living with her since I moved out of my Mom's spot—behind her parents back and shit. Plus, now you can reach me anytime… I really feel like Michelle's really in my corner—ride or die—"

"Really, that's all?"

"Remember when I was down for that ten-month bid at that juvie program…? Besides you, she's the only one I wrote. I'm just telling you cause I look up to you—she ain't just some other bitch I'm fucking. Dig?"

Rob nodded, and took a lungful of smoke from the Swisher Sweet. He exhaled, and seemed deep in thoughts for a beat. It wasn't that he was against Michelle, he just knew how badly women could cloud the mind of an over enthusiastic youth. He and Low had come too far. They couldn't get sidetracked now, and especially not by a hood rat. They were close enough to the prize for them to start tasting it. Rob just prayed Low didn't allow a bitch to distract him from them getting some real paper.

"I feel ya," Rob said.

Rob and Low had a business agreement. Michelle was now officially Low's girlfriend. This meant she was off limits. NWA's, *Fuck Tha Police* hummed through the speakers. Rob reached into the cars glove compartment, and pulled out a large envelope. He opened it and saw a color print of her driver's license.

Damn, she's pretty he thought to himself while admiring her hazel eyes, and bright smile. Rob had a weakness for light-skinned women. She was twenty-nine, and a dime.

LONNIE DAWSON

It was 2:04am when Lonnie Dawson drove her convertible, cherry red '71 Mustang Mach1 series into the drive-thru lane at McDonald's. Joining a long waiting line behind a green Toyota Celica, Lonnie's thoughts were on her bed. For the past twelve and a half hours she had been in her law office. Going through thousands of pages of federal motions, legal briefs, and criminal exhibits, she was preparing for her closing arguments in the morning.

Her entire body ached from sitting in the office chair for most of the day. She also noticed bags forming under her pretty hazel eyes. Lonnie glanced at her reflection in the rear view mirror. It was obvious the toll this case had taken on her. It wasn't just her social life, but also her physical appearance. Over the past three years, Lonnie worked on preparing for this particular case, United States vs. Alberto Acevedo.

In less than eight hours all her blood, sweat, and tears would be in the hands of a federal jury for deliberation. Her client was not only charged with capital murder—which carried the death penalty. Acevedo was also charged with sixteen other counts. These included drug trafficking, conspiracy, running an on-going criminal enterprise—kingpin charge, racketeering, and witness intimidation.

Even with Lonnie Dawson as his defense attorney, Acevedo's chance of walking on any of these counts was a long shot. Dawson, however, was currently on a successful run. Twenty-four of her cases received a not-guilty verdict. Dawson let out a deep sigh as the drive-thru lane began moving, only to come to an abrupt stop. The halt in her progress allowed her mind time to wander. It took her back to the day she was first assigned the case.

✦ ✦ ✦

Street Karma

Lonnie Dawson was two years out of Harvard University's School of Law, and she was already excelling tremendously as one of Miami's public defenders. Even though a rookie, Dawson was already showing signs of being a very good attorney. She had a tenacious work ethic, and her no-nonsense approach in the courtroom earned her the reputation of a winner. It wasn't long before coworkers, peers, and newshounds started to make her the topic of their daily discussions.

She continuously focused on errors in the police investigations, and uncovering loopholes in the judicial system. By the closing argument stages of her cases, it was clear that the backs of some of the most seasoned prosecutors were up against the wall before a jury even officially rendered a verdict. In the courtroom, the sight of defeat was painfully obvious on their faces.

Akbar Muhammad was a man who always heard Dawson's name mentioned in board meetings. A senior partner of Muhammad and Johnson LLC, Muhammad was always looking for fresh, capable talent to bolster an already prestigious criminal law firm, based in Atlanta. So he decided to fly out to Miami. Muhammad was extremely meticulous, and researched all recruits himself. He knew that in order for him to properly assess Dawson, he'd have to observe her.

It was her eighth murder trial. The Defendant Rico Gonzalez, a Cuban Immigrant was accused of killing a Miami-Dade Police, Officer Julian Suarez. Day one of the trial, all chatter in the courtroom seemed to immediately cease when Lonnie Dawson stepped into the courtroom with a man, charged with murder. The attorney and client went directly to their places.

Dressed in white Nike tennis shoes, blue Levi's, and a gray Southern University sweater with matching hat, Muhammad eased his way through the packed courtroom. Taking a seat on the prosecutor's side of the courtroom. He observed Dawson's stone cold demeanor. The two specially appointed prosecutors with over forty-two years of experience between them seemed quite uncomfortable. Fidgeting in their seats, they'd occasionally glanced over to the defense table. They tried nodding in that direction hoping to get a greeting, acknowledgement, but without luck. Lonnie Dawson remained poker faced. She was ready for war.

A sly smirk crept across Muhammad's face as he stood up along with everyone else for Judge Alana Rodriguez to preside. Muhammad believed that Dawson already had the prosecutors' hearts. When the trial began, Dawson went on the offensive attack, ripping the state's case to shreds. She stood firm on her client's plea of self-defense, pointing to accusations of police profiling, and corruption. By the time she was through with her opening statement, Dawson had vividly painted a picture of an envious dirty cop.

That was contrary to the officer's many years of service, and the numerous service medals he received for good deeds. Dawson explained why a routine traffic stop was turned into an opportunity for revenge.

"...Officer Julian Suarez, a Cuban native, pulled over my client Rico Gonzalez on that fateful night of March 15th, knowing exactly who he was stopping. Rico, on the other hand, didn't recognized Suarez, since it had been twenty years since he left his native country, Cuba. And he was obeying the law when he exited his work van, and consented to a full search of the vehicle. It wasn't until a sufficient amount of cocaine was discovered in Rico's van that he took a good look at Officer Suarez's face. He realized that he was being set up. He refused to be handcuffed. There was an intense scuffle. Rico managed to overpower Officer Suarez, grabbed his service handgun from its holster, and held him at gunpoint. Rico next attempted to report the officer to his superiors by alerting them on his work issued walkie-talkie. Rico held Officer Suarez at gunpoint while waiting for help. Officer Suarez reached for his chest, claiming to be having a heart attack. He fell to the ground, and Rico gave a warning for Officer Suarez not to move. He saw the officer reaching for his ankle. It was then that my client fired twice hitting Officer Suarez in the head, killing him instantly..."

The entire courtroom was completely silent. Dawson paused, took a deep breath, and glanced at the twelve members of the jury. She now had their undivided attention. Then she continued. "Rico Gonzalez had ample amount of time and opportunity to flee. However he chose not to. Instead he waited for the authorities to arrive then willingly gave himself up."

Picking up a plain white envelope, Dawson pulled out a document then said, "Your Honor, I would like to enter into evidence a certificate of death, for Yolanda Suarez."

She handed the document to Judge Rodriguez. It was carefully scrutinized. Then the judge nodded her approval, and passed it to the bailiff. It was then passed to the jury.

"Yolanda Suarez, ladies and gentlemen of the jury is Officer Suarez's first niece..." Dawson paused to pull out another document—a birth certificate of Julio Gonzalez. Then she continued. "Ladies and gentlemen of the jury, Julio Gonzalez is Rico Gonzalez's first born son with the now deceased Yolanda Suarez."

Dawson paused to let her revelation sink in before she continued. "Seeking revenge for his niece, Yolanda Suarez, who died tragically in the Atlantic ocean open waters after fleeing Cuba with her boyfriend, my client, Rico Gonzalez some twenty years ago. Leaving their only son behind, they sought a better life in the USA. Julio Suarez, still very much bitter about his niece's death took advantage of his chance encounter with Rico Gonzalez. He attempted to plant a large amount of cocaine on Rico so he could legally arrest him, murder him, and cover the entire thing up by making it look drug related..."

The team of prosecutors did their best to refute the defense claims, and tried to prolong the trial. Unfortunately Judge Rodriguez had already heard enough, and sighted the conflict of interest in the case as too overwhelming. The judge allowed Rico Gonzalez's plea of self-defense, and immediately *dismissed all charges. Attorney Dawson later filed out the courtroom with her client in tow to a mob of media personnel, and flashing camera lights. Fully convinced he had found his new recruit, Attorney Akbar Muhammad slipped out of the courtroom. The Rico Gonzalez case was Dawson's last as a public defender.*

✦ ✦ ✦

The sound of honking car horns brought Lonnie Dawson back to the reality of her situation.

"Hey lady what the fuck! Move it already!" A male voice shouted.

Glancing ahead, Dawson realized all the cars in front of her were long gone, and it was now her turn to order. Easing her foot off her cars brakes, she eased her Mustang up to the drive-thru window.

"Welcome to McDonalds. May I take your order…?"

"I'll have a six-piece Chicken McNugget meal, with a small Dr. Pepper."

It took a while, but finally Lonnie made a left turn onto Aventura Boulevard heading to her condo. While her career flourished to unexpected heights, her social life suffered severely, and was virtually non-existent. Other than a slight slip-up with one of her private investigators, a year ago, Lonnie relied on her vast collection of sex toys to bring her the most intense orgasms she ever experienced. But all that was still nothing, compared to the real thing. It had been three years since she had a good fuck. To a nymphomaniac like Lonnie, three years was beginning to feel like an eternity.

3 a.m.

Dawson made a right turn into the basement parking lot. She only had less than four hours to attempt to get some rest. Shutting off the engine, she reached in her backseat to retrieve her briefcase. An unfamiliar vehicle parked in her neighbor's reserved parking space caught her attention. Giving the black tinted, late-model vehicle the once over, she quickly pushed her suspicion aside. She was just too exhausted, and wanted to get in bed.

Briefcase and keys were in one hand, her meal and drink in the other, Lonnie stepped out her Mustang. She yawned while locking the cars doors with the remote sensor on her keychain, and made her way toward the building's basement elevators. Lonnie couldn't wait to get into her Condo.

"Excuse me Miss."

Lonnie could hear footsteps closing in fast. She rolled her eyes in aggravation at the sound of the male voice coming from behind her. She turned around, and found herself face to face with a masked gunman.

"Hand over the fucking keys!"

The gunman took a step toward Lonnie with the gun clutched tightly, and aimed dead center at her nose. The initial shock instantly turned into a state of fear. Lonnie's body temperature began to rise, causing sweat beads to form on her forehead and under her armpits. The Dr. Pepper crashed to the ground.

"If it is money you want you can have my wallet," Lonnie pleaded.

From her peripheral, Lonnie noticed a shadowy figure creeping. A second gunman approached. Cocking his Mossberg shotgun, he said, "Bitch, didn't you hear? Hand over the fucking keys!"

The second gunmen spat lifted the shotgun to eye level, sticking the cold steel barrel to Lonnie's temple.

"Bitch, hand over the fucking keys!"

The demands continued falling on deaf ears. Time was of the essence, and patience was wearing thin. It was now or never, and the gunmen were done talking.

Taking a step back, he angrily swung his Mossberg pump like Ken Griffey Jr. at Lonnie's head. The impact of the shotgun's one and a half inch, solid steel caught Lonnie just above her right eyebrow. It was lights-out before her fragile body collapsed to the parking lot's concrete surface. Her keys and all the contents in her hands flew through the air.

"What the fuck!" Low shouted, removing his mask.

He took a knee beside Lonnie's motionless body. Tucking his weapon in the waistband of his Dickies pants, he peered down at Lonnie. Blood was oozing from a deep gash above her right temple, and flooding her pretty face.

"I think she's dead!" Low muttered.

Low couldn't believe Rob hit her with that much force. Murder was not part of this plan. Rob saw the panic on Low's face. Rushing over to Low, Rob grabbed him by the shoulder of his hooded sweatshirt, and pulled him up.

"Get it together!" Rob said, giving Low a menacing stare. Then he continued. "Fuck that bitch! Stay focused. We gotta find the fucking car keys, and get the fuck outta here before one-time come. Or nigga we'll really be fucked. Now help me find the fucking key!"

Lonnie Dawson opened her blood-filled eyes to the echoing sound of Rob's voice. With her vigorous blinking, Lonnie was doing her best to focus her blurry vision. Surveying her surroundings, she noticed the robber with the shotgun frantically rummaging through her briefcase, dumping all its content onto the ground. Darting her eyes toward a row of parked cars, she saw the other assailant on his hands and knees beside her Mustang's rear bumper. Both gunmen were totally oblivious to what she was doing. With her mind racing, Lonnie painfully rose to a sitting position, and desperately began to reach for her ankle.

"Fuck!" Rob shouted in frustration.

Realizing the car keys weren't in the briefcase, Rob angrily tossed the leather attaché to the ground. With great effort, Lonnie managed to get a firm grip on her gun. Quickly pulling it out of her ankle holster. She immediately took aim at her car. Rob turned his attention in Low's direction, and his eyes grew wide with surprise at the sight of what was unfolding.

With one last strenuous effort, Low let out a sigh of relief. He grabbed a hold of the Mustang's keys.

"I found the keys!" Low smiled, lifting himself up off the ground.

"Low watch out!" Rob shouted, raising his Mossberg, and taking aim.

Lonnie squeezed the trigger of her gun twice in succession, letting off two thunderous shots. The first slug entered just below Low's neck, grazing his collarbone, and went straight through his flesh. The second bullet missed his head by mere inches, shattering the Mustang's rear taillights on impact. Lonnie took aim at the second assailant, but her attempt proved futile.

"You bitch!" Rob yelled.

He was running toward her. Then he squeezed the trigger of his shotgun. The pellets caught Lonnie dead center in her chest, lifting her petite frame off the concrete, sending her body flying several feet backwards.

"Yo, I'm hit!"

Low painfully stumbled to his feet, clutching Lonnie's car keys tightly in his palm. Blood flowed down his arm, and began to trickle onto the concrete. Low staggered toward Rob. He was hovering over Lonnie's body with a murderous look in his eyes. His Mossberg was aimed at Lonnie's tilted head.

"Don't do it! She gone," Low protested.

Handing Rob the keys, and tugging on his shirt, Low pulled Rob away from Lonnie's motionless body.

"Damn, you bleeding bad," Rob said.

"I'm good. Let's just get the fuck outta here."

The pair hustled toward Lonnie's car. Low hopped into the passenger seat, and Rob was in the driver's side. Low noticed an armed security guard emerging from the parking lot's elevator lobby. The sound of footsteps also caught Rob's attention. Rob cocked his pump, and took aim at the lobby. He squeezed the trigger, unloading a booming round in the direction of the security guard.

Low pulled the revolver from his waistband, and fired at another security guard getting off the elevator. Shards of glass were flying everywhere. Pellets and glass fragments got in the guard's face, blinding his vision as he tried to run. He dropped his handgun, collapsing to the lobby's floor, screaming in horror.

"Freeze!" Another security guard shouted.

He came around the corner running full speed from an emergency exit. His Beretta was clutched tightly, and aimed in Rob's direction. Low rose from the passenger seat of the drop-top, letting off three shots from his .44. The first two shots missed, but the third bullet dropped the guard.

Rob cocked his pump-action shotgun again, and took a few steps toward the screaming guard. He aimed with deadly thoughts. One more shot, and this fucker was silenced for good. The sound of sirens in the distance was closing in fast. Turning quickly, Rob made a dash for Lonnie's car.

"We gotta get the fuck up outta here!" Low exclaimed.

Rob jumped into the driver's seat, and quickly started the car. Tires screeching, Rob shifted into reverse, and burned rubber coming out the parking space.

"Watch out!" Low shouted.

Low's sudden warning caused Rob to make a desperate attempt to turn the cars steering wheel away from

Lonnie Dawson's body, but it was directly in their driving path, and he couldn't avoid the inevitable. The car sped over Lonnie's legs, snapping both her shinbones in half, and crushing every bone from her knees down.

Rob quickly zoomed out the condo's basement parking lot, floored the gas pedal, and made a getaway.

CHAPTER

3

LELA

4:40 a.m.

The late night sky over the city of Miami was fading. Rob was burning tires on I-95, speeding toward the city of Fort Lauderdale. In the past hour and a half, Low lost so much blood he was beginning to fall in and out of consciousness. His blood pressure was flowing at a dangerously low level. His words were slurred, and barely audible as he tried to communicate with Rob.

"I'm going Rob. I don't think I'm a make, man," Low muttered.

His head rested against the car's side door panel while his eyes were shut. Occasionally, moans escaped Low's parched lips. Glancing at his injured crime partner, Rob inhaled deeply, and let out a frustrated sigh. He returned his focus back on the road.

"Just hold on my nigga. We almost at Lela's," Rob urged.

Only ten exits away from his destination, Rob wanted Low to hang on just a little longer. A public hospital wasn't an option, and would only lead to a jail sentence. Rob's thoughts were going fast while he sped up I-95 toward his old neighborhood. His young partner's life was on the line, and there was only one person Rob knew could help him.

Downshifting speed, Rob exited the highway. Entering the city limits of Fort Lauderdale, he approached a turning red light, and prepared to take a right turn toward the beaches. Rob pushed a button on the car's electronic dash console retracting the roof, and made sure all the cars windows were shut. He made a right turn on Sunrise Boulevard continuing to the beaches. Rob finally arrived at Lela's veterinarian clinic.

The building was located on two and a half acres of privately owned land in the exclusive community of Sunrise Shores. Directly behind the animal hospital sat a five thousand square foot, seven and a half bedroom Creole-styled luxury penthouse. This was where Lela Shabazz, owner and head veterinarian of the animal hospital, and her daughter, Asani Lovely Shabazz resided.

Rob gazed in contempt at the multimillion-dollar home. It was a long two years now since Rob pulled out of this long, stone-floored driveway. He left the privileged lifestyle, and home of the only family that ever really cared about him, returning to the ghetto streets of Dade-County, Miami. Eventually, Rob reunited with his childhood best friend, Milow. Together they returned to fast-living and committing crimes. Maybe Rob should've forgiven Lovely, and continued his privileged life of attending the best private schools in South Florida. Lovely attended the best schools. Rob would've also. He even received an acceptance letter into a prestigious college, leading to a sure shot at the good life. Lovely's action was just too much to forgive.

The decision to leave Fort Lauderdale, and move back home with his Aunt in Miami was a sudden change. He knew he was leaving a promising future behind, but he left with his pride, and dignity. That was more important to Rob than being a fool. Pushing all thoughts aside of what could have been, Rob came to a screeching halt in front of the massive penthouse. He hurriedly exited the car, raced around to the passenger side, and pulled out the bleeding unconscious Low.

He carried the body up a stairwell. The alarm went off while he frantically rang the doorbell. Holding onto Low's body Rob felt tears welling in his eyes. Low wasn't breathing, and with every critical moment that passed, Low's life was slipping away.

Opening the front door, Lovely peered out onto her porch. She was immediately shocked with disbelief. Lovely jumped back.

"Oh my God!" Lovely exclaimed when she locked eyes with Rob.

She stared at him as if she was looking at a ghost. Since he left Lovely was totally unaware of Rob's whereabouts.

"Love, I need help," Rob said with tears in his eyes.

Hearing the commotion from the master bedroom, Lela made her way to the top of the stairwell that led directly to the front entrance. She saw Rob clutching Low's bloodied body, and immediately rushed downstairs to assist.

"Oh my God! Lovely, please get my surgical kit, dear," Lela exclaimed, making her way over to Rob, and helping him carry Low's body inside. Then she continued. "How long ago did this happen?"

Dropping to her knees next to Low, Lela immediately began undressing his bloody body.

"I've got to pinpoint his wounds. Rob, how long ago did this happen?" Lela asked.

"Um... Ah... About an hour or so..." Rob said in a solemn tone.

Lovely hurriedly retuned with the surgical kit. She handed the large clear box to her mother. Her wide eyes were filled with shock, Lovely just stood looking on. She appeared intrigued by the sight of Low's bloodstained body. She probably had never seen so much blood in her life. The amount of blood coming from his wound made it seem that Low wasn't going to make it.

"I don't understand you young brothers these days," Lela said with disdain.

She was just about finished cutting the rest of Low's clothing from his body. After pinpointing Low's single bullet wound, Lela realized that the slug went straight through. She immediately started looking for an exit wound. Blood was simultaneously leaking from two wounds. Once she found the exit wound, Lela applied pressure with a piece of large gauze. Lela securely taped around the bandage, she began to stitch up the front end of Lows' bullet wound.

"Young brothers just falling right into the white man's trap," Lela said with a frown. Then she glanced in Rob's direction, and continued. "Well at least you're breathing young brother. Cause unfortunately, this young soldier might not make it."

✦ ✦ ✦

Back to life, back to reality, back to life, back to reality,
Back to life, back to reality, back to the here and now yeah...
Show me how...decide what you want from me,
Tell me maybe I could be there for you.
However do you want me...however do you need me.

How however do you want me…however do you need me…

The music of Soul II Soul played through the AMI Rowe model 1100 jukebox speakers from a vinyl record. Low opened his eyes to a bizarre pattern of disco lights twirling in a circular motion all around him. He raised his body to a sitting position, and saw an intravenous needle inserted into a vein of his left arm. There were two liquid-filled medical IV plastic bags hanging from a pole above his head.

Quickly surveying his surroundings, Low saw that he was lying on a military-styled cot. It was located in the far corner of what seemed like a seventy's styled discotheque. Then he spotted Rob standing beside a pool table, puffing a cigarette, and chatting with a broad. This all seemed like it was a dream, he thought eyeing the caramel complexioned girl next to Rob. At first glance, Low didn't recognize who she was. Then she leaned over with her pool stick in hand preparing to take her shot. He got a good look at her face, and recognized Lovely, Rob's ex.

Designed like a nightclub from the seventies, the place was equipped with a full-length bar, two professional-sized pool tables, and a large bulls eye dart area. The massive AMI Rowe Model 1100 Jukebox played hit singles from the seventies through the eighties. A large crystal disco ball hung above the freshly polished, hardwood dance floor. There were also hundreds of pictures, and posters of iconic Black men— Malcolm, Martin, Marshall, and women—Baker, Coleman, Davis—to name a few—adorning the walls. His location began to slowly make sense, and a sigh of relief escaped Low's parched lips. Low wasn't dreaming, he was actually in Lovely's basement.

Low didn't recognize the black hooded sweat-shirt, Dickie's pants, and black British Knights sneak-ers he wore the night before. He was now wearing a pair of thin, orange basketball shorts, a white tank top, and green and white Adidas slippers. Vivid scenes of the shootout started flashing through his mind. Low stared at his left shoulder, and silently counted his blessings. The sight of the wounded area was covered with white sur-gical bandage.

Memories of last night's events replayed in his head. Rob was speeding on I-95. He was in the passenger seat soaked in his own blood. Low remembered the excruci-ating pain of the bullet wound. He was unsure if he was going to live, but was still breathing because of Rob's quick thinking. Low was grateful.

Placing his feet on the hardwood floor, Low attempted to get up. An intense pain shot through the left side of his body. He lost grip on the side of the cot, and his body crashed to the wooden floor. Low let out an agonizing wail then rolled around in pain. His entire left side was on fire. The loud commotion caused Lovely and Rob to stop their game of nine-ball. They imme-diately turned their attention to Low. Rob dropped the pool stick, and ran across the room.

"Low, Low... You up, my nigga?" Rob exclaimed.

There was a big smile on Rob's face as he helped him to his feet. Making her way over to assist, Lovely placed the cot that Low tipped over in the upright posi-tion.

"Sit him back down. He may still be weak from all the blood he lost," Lovely said.

Rob helped Low to a sitting position, and Lovely began to examine his left arm and shoulder. The intrave-nous bags, and stitches were still intact.

"I think I should go tell mom he's awake," Lovely said.

Lovely saw that one of the IV needles was out of place, and quickly exited. Rob took a seat on the cot next to his wincing partner in crime.

"I thought you had fucked around and died on me," Rob said, smoking a Kool cigarette.

He offered it to Low, who quickly declined with a wave of his hand.

"Rob, if it wasn't for you bringing me here I probably would've died," Low muttered, looking at his bandaged shoulder. Shaking his head in disbelief, Low continued. "That bitch really tried to take my fucking head off."

"Damn sure did," Rob said.

Easing his right hand over his wound, Low felt the stitches underneath the bandage. Then he said, "Damn, who would've thought that a broad so fine would be packing that type of iron."

"Yeah, she was strapped, and was definitely going for the kill," Rob solemnly agreed.

"Yesterday don 't even exist no more. Ya dig? We made it. You alive, breathing, and still in one piece… That's all that matters. And we just one more car from the prize… Ya dig? Live for today. Fuck the past. One more car, and we cashing out."

Low surveyed the basement walls adorned with all the many pictures of iconic Black faces. He took a deep breath, gathered his thoughts, and sighed. Then he contemplated last night's events clouding his head. The security guards that were shot—fair game, but the thought that they killed a Black woman in the process wasn't sitting well with him. Low was about to voice his opinion, but kept silent. His eyes locked in on a poster-sized picture of U.S athletes, Tommie Smith, and John Carlos. The gold medal winners were on the medal podium raising their fist skyward.

Low took a deep breath, nodded his head, and said, "Yeah Rob...one more car and we out."

✦ ✦ ✦

Sitting in the backseat of Lovely's Infiniti Q45, his head resting comfortably on the luxury vehicle's beige, leather headrest, Low was lost in a daydream. He gazed out the car's window, glancing at all the luxury homes lining I-95. Lovely was driving south headed to Miami while Low was thinking of what his life would've been like if he was born to a wealthy family. The ruminations caused Low to shake his head. His thoughts were nothing more than fantasy. Low turned his attention back inside the car. Public Enemy's new hit, *Fight the Power* played as Miami's 99 Jamz 5 o'clock Traffic-Jam was in full effect.

This was the first time he heard the song from his favorite rap group, and Low wanted the song louder, but Rob was asleep in the passenger seat. He decided not to, and just listened intently while bobbing his head to the lyrics. Low caught a glimpse of Lovely's face, and she was nodding her head to the beat as well. She was enthusiastically mouthing the lyrics to the song.

Low chuckled at the sight. Glancing in her rearview, Lovely locked eyes with Low, and smiled. Low asked her with an amused grin.

"What you know 'bout P.E.? I thought squares don't listen to rap," Low joked.

"What you mean square? Negro please... Best believe I'm hip. Have you forgotten who my mother is...? Don't let the fact that I live in the 'burbs fool you. I know all about P.E, KRS1, Rakim, and Lords of the Underground, N.W.A., Pete Rock, and Rob Base, LL Cool J... What!"

"Okay then. I guess your mother raised you well."

"She sure did," Lovely smiled.

Turning her attention back on the road, Lovely activated the turn signal, and prepared to make her exit at the 54th Street exit.

"What your cripple-ass laughing 'bout?" Rob muttered, yawning.

"Oh, so sleepy-head got jokes?" Low smirked, throwing a fake punch at Rob.

"I can dig it, lil' homie," Rob smiled, nodding.

Rob turned his head to the scenery in the heart of Lil' Haiti's streets. There were loose chickens all around, and Botanical shops on every other corner.

Lovely made a left to NE 2nd Terrace, and stopped in front of a big white two-story house. Rob extended and gave Low their signature handshake—the web between their right ring finger and pinky came together.

"Low, you sure old boy ain't home?" Rob asked.

"Yeah, shit straight Rob. I'm good," Low said, reaching for the door handle.

"Okay then pimping. Just make sure you on time in the morning," Rob smiled.

"C'mon Rob. I know the routine by now. Thanks for the ride, Lovely," Low smiled.

Then he exited the car. Tomorrow they were set to meet with Tony to give him the location of Lonnie's car. Parked in Lela's garage, Tony could tow it to his chop shop, and assign them their next, and final Job. Lovely sped-off down the street. Low took in a deep breath, as he contemplated his next move.

Michelle's father wouldn't be home until later, but her mother was another issue. She was always home. With one of Low's arm out of commission, and in a sling, he knew there was no way he was going to make it through Michelle's small room window like he always did. Michelle's father was an old school Haitian man. Notoriously known for dealing harshly with past boyfriends of his daughter.

CHAPTER

4

MICHELLE

After an hour-long bubble bath, Michelle stepped out of her Jacuzzi styled bathtub, and made her way to the shower area. She began to rinse her body. Ten minutes later, she stepped out the glass enclosed shower booth, and walked dripping wet out of her bathroom. Michelle stepped into the carpeted master bedroom, made her way over to a Magnavox stereo player, and popped in her favorite cassette by Michael Jackson. She set the volume to a low tone then went to the vanity dresser. *Human Nature* played through the speakers.

She poured some body oil into her palm, rubbing it evenly into her hands, and down the entire length of her body. After oiling every inch of her mocha complexioned body, Michelle walked over to her underwear drawer, and picked out a leopard pattern set. She slipped into them and walked to her bed. Taking a seat on the edge of the queen-sized mattress, Michelle sang along to Michael Jackson while wishing Low was over to put oil on the rest of her back.

A loud sigh escaped her lips when it suddenly dawned on her that Low didn't spend the night. It was the first time since he moved in Michelle's room that Low neglected to do so. She knew about the plan for him to meet up with Rob last night, but didn't know why. Michelle was worried and concerned for his safety. Then she heard the sound of a whistle from outside her bedroom window. It was music to her ears, and brought an instant smile to her face. She quickly made her way behind the vanity dresser to her window.

Michelle eased the Victorian-styled curtains aside, and peered outside. The joy she felt instantly faded at the sight of Low's condition. His arm was in a shoulder sling, and his left shoulder was covered in a huge, white surgical bandage.

"Oh my God! Baby, what happened?" Michelle exclaimed. Her wide eyes were filled with anxiety.

"I'll fill you in when I get inside," Low said, trying not to shout.

Then Low quickly raised his finger to his lips, silencing Michelle before asking in a hushed tone.

"Where's your mother?"

"She's asleep," Michelle said, gesturing for Low to go to her front door.

"Okay…"

"Baby…" Michelle said with a worried smile, and planting a wet kiss on Low's lips.

He stepped inside her house, and Michelle shut the door behind them. A sly smirk crept across Low's face as Michelle sashayed back to her room. The sight of Michelle in her underwear, and smelling like freshly cut roses caused Low to bite down on his bottom lip. Following closely behind her, Low's dick hardened as she led the way. His eyes were fixated on Michelle's glistening behind.

Her backfield bounced up and down with each sexy stride. By the time they made it to her room door, Low's dick was rock hard, and bulged through the thin mesh shorts he was wearing. They entered Michelle's room, and Low made his way over to the bed. He took a deep breath and slowly exhaled, feeling drained, and exhausted.

"Well baby, I'm happy you're home," Michelle said.

Carefully shutting her bedroom door so as not to awake her mother, Michelle placed the chain lock on.

"What the hell happened to your arm, Milow?" she quizzed, raising her eyebrow.

Michelle walked over to her stereo system, and began to scan through her collection of R&B cassettes. Meanwhile, Low took in another deep breath, kicked off his Adidas slippers, and eased onto Michelle's bed.

With his bald dome resting on her arrangement of silk covered pillows, Low said, "Honestly Chelle, it's a long-ass story, and I don't even feel like getting into right now."

Then yawning, he gazed up at Michelle's crystal light fixtures hanging from the ceiling above her bed. He glanced at her, and saw that she was rolling her eyes at him. Content with the fact that Low was safe and sound, Michelle put a Tina Marie cassette in the player.

"Okay baby," Michelle said, walking to the bed.

By the time she got to the edge of the bed, she was naked. The sight of Michelle's big, perky, breast, and chocolate colored nipples, immediately caused Low to recline against the headboard.

Michelle slipped her thong from around her ankle, and tossed it at Low. Her panties landed on his chin, and Low raised the underwear to his nose. Watching him closely, Michelle said, "You know you can't leave me for too long. I need you on the regular. Last night I felt lonely I had to pleasure myself to sleep. It felt soo good. I wanna replay that scene for you right now. You wanna see what I did last night, baby?"

Michelle didn't wait for a response. Placing two fingers inside her moist pussy hole, she started massaging her pussy while playing with her clit.

"Ah...I'm getting soo wet, Low," she moaned.

Low watched with a huge smile, loving the show. Sliding his right hand under his shorts, he began stroking his erection. Her head was tilted back in pleasure, and she moaned, squeezing her thighs together. Her body slightly jerked, releasing an overflow of juice over her hand.

"That one felt better since you were watching," Michelle smiled.

Then raising her hand to her lip, she began to seductively lick her manicured fingers, one at a time.

"Come here, girl," Low said.

Their lovemaking was intense and lasted a long time. Low was exhausted and fell asleep with a satisfied look on his mug.

CHAPTER
5

HOMEWORK

Low was already an hour and forty-five minutes late for his meeting with Rob and Tony. He knew Rob hated when he was late, but more so when Michelle was the cause. He got off the Jitney bus on N.W 2nd Ave. and 79th Street. Crossing Opa Locka Blvd's busy intersection, Low power-walked the five and a half blocks. Miami's afternoon sunshine was having no mercy on him.

"Damn nigga! It's about time," Rob said, frowning.

He was sitting on the hood of a cocaine-white '89 Chevrolet Corvette, and clutching a forty-ounce. Rob took the last swig of Old English then tossed the bottle to the concrete.

"My fault, Rob," Low said, embracing Rob, and offering a handshake. Then he continued. "Fucking Jitney bus took forever. You know how them old-school Haitians get—trying to jam fifty muthafuckas in a van that only fit twenty?"

"Yeah, sure nigga," Rob said, reaching in his red Nike sweatpants.

He pulled out a pack of Kool's cigarettes, and a lighter. Then removing two cigarettes from the pack, Rob lit one for Low before lighting his own.

"It don't take two hours to get from Lil' Haiti to Opa Locka—not even in traffic. If your face wasn't all up Michelle's ass you would've been on time. Time is money. You just gotta learn how to separate business and pleasure. It's money over bitches, and not the other way around. And it gets even more critical when we trying to eat off the same plate, ya dig? Cause, not only did I have to feed Tony a bullshit story as to why you didn't 't show, but what if something would've went wrong when Tony came through? I keep telling you, bitches will fuck up your focus bro. Shit... I bet you anything you didn't 't even bring ya license, huh?"

"Damn... My bad. I'm a tighten-up."

"I ain't even tripping. I took care of Tony, and got our new job. Time for us to go do our homework..."

"Fuck!"

Shaking his head, Rob said, "The good news is I already took care of all that. I got everything we gonna need. A pair of binoculars, and just in case we gotta clock in some overtime, I got some good weed. I knew once you was late you was gonna forget to bring ya tools. So I have my own, and got us a car too.

"What's the bad news?"

"Since you was late, and unprepared, your crippled-ass is driving," Rob smiled.

Tossing the car keys to Low, Rob made his way to the passenger side door of the Corvette.

"Damn. I can't believe Tony actually let you take his new ride for us to do our homework," Low said.

He gripped the Corvette's red, leather steering wheel, and hit the gas. The two hundred and forty-five horse powered, V8 engine effortlessly climbed to ninety-four miles per hour. While Low was switching lanes on Biscayne Boulevard, heading toward Biscayne Bay, Rob used a terry cloth to clean the weapons. First, he took care of the Mossberg shotgun, sitting on his lap. After making sure it was free of fingerprints, he gave Low an incredulous look, and said, "Let me put you on to something. There's one thing about business and negotiating you need to understand. Tony didn't let me get his ride. I gave that muthafucka no other choice."

Rob then picked up Low's .44Magnum, and starting with the long chrome barrel, he began wiping it clean.

"I can dig it. That lawyer bitch was high profile like a mutha, and we taking all the risk. It's about time we ridin' clean for a change," Low said.

After thoroughly wiping down both weapons, Rob placed it next to the Mossberg. He zipped the duffle bag, and cracked the passenger side window. Then he tossed the terry cloth rag, and latex gloves onto the street. Reaching in the glove compartment, he pulled out a large envelope, and skimmed its contents. He removed an enlarged DMV photo of the next target, and showed it to Low.

"If you thought Lonnie Dawson was high profile, you should peep this assignment right here! Take a look at this muthafucka," Rob declared.

Low rolled to stop at a red light, and glanced at the photo of a middle-aged white guy, shrugged his shoulders, and made a left turn on Biscayne Bay Bridge. Then he said, "Looks like a regular-old-cracker to me. What makes him so high profile?"

"This regular-old-cracker is Alex Daoud."

"Alex Daoud… Oh shit…! Mayor Daoud…?"

Rob nodded his head. Low shook his head, and said, "Nigga, that's the fucking mayor of Miami-Dade County! What the fuck!"

It was Low's turn to incredulously stare at Rob. He glanced back at traffic before he said, "That Lawyer bitch alone could've earned us the death penalty. Imagine the fucking mayor…? They'll fry us. Bury our black-asses, dig us up, and fry us again. Ain't he gonna run for governor or something?"

"Exactly," Rob said, nodding. Low was finally getting the point. Then Rob continued. "That's why when Tony handed me this packet I told his bitch-ass. 'Ain't no fucking way we doing our homework in no stolen car first off. And fuck twenty G's! Nigga. If he wanted us to deliver on this last car we needed a forty-stack bonus or all bets were off—period. And we still want the twenty thousand he owes us. Or…he already know!"

Low made a left turn to the bridge connecting the exclusive Miami-by-the-shore community with North Miami. Half mile later across Biscayne Bridge, they were deep in the Bay. Then he activated the Corvette's emergency signal, and slowly merged to the bridge's emergency lane. The he pulled over.

"Let me get this straight. You convinced Tony to pay us an extra forty stacks?" Low asked, hoping he understood Rob correctly.

Cracking a wide grin, Rob snapped his fingers together, and said, "I almost had 'em all in too. My poker face was strong. I was dead serious with that fucka. But in the end he didn't quite agree to forty. We got a twenty thousand cash bonus. He added these to the deal to sweeten the pot.

Then he reached in the glove compartment, and grabbed a small, black, plastic jewelry bag. Rob pulled out two identical, gold wristwatches. Handing one to Low, he said, "These Chopards worth ten stacks a piece."

Low took the watch, admired it for a few beats then said, "This watch's hard as fuck!" His eyes were brightened following the moving diamonds flooding the face.

"See all it took was a little hardball negotiating with Tony. And now payday will be that much sweeter," Rob said in a braggadocios tone.

Low nodded in agreement as Rob's words began to sink in. He began envisioning all the possibilities with some real money at their disposal.

"Yeah, I can dig it Rob. Man, with forty plus G's to play with—sky's the limit."

"Exactly," Rob said, tossing the envelope in the glove compartment. Reaching for the duffle bag between his feet, he continued. "Nineteen down, one more to go. Now let's stay focused."

Rob turned his attention to the passenger's side rearview mirror, and waited on Low's signal. While Rob watched the traffic lights behind them at the beginning of the bridge, Low kept his eyes on the lights at the end of the bridge. His right hand was on the Corvette's door handle, and his left was clutching the hundred and fifty pound duffle bag. It was weighted with dumbbells.

The lights at either end of the bridge went yellow, Rob took a deep breath, and said, "One, two, three…"

The traffic lights turned red. Rob jumped out the passenger side door. Running like an all-pro tailback toward the side of the bridge, he tossed the heavy duffle bag over the bridge's side rail, and into the Bay. Then he did a quick sprint back and hopped into the car. The passenger door shut, Low floored the V8 engine, hitting the changing traffic lights for a smooth getaway.

✦ ✦ ✦

Coconut Grove with its high-end boutiques, luxurious gated communities, and professional golf courses was also the home to some of Florida's most elite. From actors and entertainment moguls to retired sports legends, and even a few heavy politicians. For the residents in this wealthy, small-knit, suburban community, life was mostly full of joy.

But as he drove down Main Street entering the heart

of the Grove, a frown was plastered on his face. Showing his contempt for this part of the city, Rob said, "Man I hate this cracker-ass town."

Low looked at Rob fuming in the passenger seat while breaking down a Swisher Sweet Cigar. Low chuckled then said, "What's your beef with this city?"

"Ever since I used to work with my father on his paper-route when I was younger, I always hated this racist-ass town."

Low momentarily took his eye off the road and stared at Rob. He thought of a joke about the discovery of Rob being a paperboy. There was serious look in Rob's eyes and Low quickly decided against it.

"The police out here are so foul they use to pull us over on the regular. One morning, some old Nazi super cop pulled us over. That muthafucka had one o' them ol' soup bowl haircut with the little mustache and all. Hitler in the flesh!"

"Yeah?"

"Hell yeah! Once I saw that fucka step out the police car in my rearview I just knew he was gonna be on some bullshit. You would've thought since we were in a neon blue company van with Miami Herald Newspaper sprawled all over it that at least he would've spared us the stupid questions. We were obviously on the clock working, but first thing that comes out this pig's country-ass is 'Why all the frequent stops fellas?'.

"Ha, ha…" Low chuckled at Rob's impersonation of the cops redneck drawl.

"I'm serious, Low. Muthafucka had us out there a whole hour—searched us, went through the whole damn van like we had some keys stashed up in the newspapers. Then when he discovered pop wasn't an American citizen, and was in the country on an expired visa…that muthafucka locked the both of us up."

"Damn, that's fucked up," Low said with sympathy in his voice.

Low approached the ·intersection of Main Street and Palm Coast Boulevard. He gazed up at a billboard showing an advertisement for an open house viewing.

"What that sign say up there?" Low asked, pointing at the billboard.

"Next right, Sunshine Village. A stone's throw away from paradise."

"That's it," Low said, and pulled into the parking lot of a shopping plaza.

The parking space provided the perfect view of the security-patrolled gate of Sunshine Village's main entrance. Low shut off the engine, and reached into Rob's book bag, retrieving a pair of military-issued binoculars.

"What kind of car is it?" Low asked, adjusting the lenses.

Low focused on the vehicles of residents and visitors, coming and going. He studied the movements inside the armed security booth.

"It's a royal blue '68 Ferrari GTO," Rob said between tokes on the Swisher.

He was reading a piece on the mayor's and his teenage son's love for classic sports cars in a Car and Driver magazine article.

"Damn, that's a classic," Low said, taking his eyes off the security booth to glance down at a color picture of the classic Ferrari in the magazine.

"I know. Says here, it's been twenty-one years since the last Ferrari was even produced. And since Enzo Ferrari died last year, the value of all Ferraris from '68, or prior models have skyrocketed. There are only eighteen GTO's still intact in the world... Ten in Europe, four in Asia, four in the U.S., and only one in the state of Florida... Owned by non-other than Mayor Alex

Daoud," Rob smiled, sucking on the Swisher.

"Damn. That means this car's worth some serious muthafuckin' bread," Low said, quickly calculating the math.

"One point six million dollars just for this one car. I'm shocked that muthafuckas ain't lined up on this fool's lawn tryin' to jack his ass," Rob chuckled.

"That's cause it's guarded like a muthafucka," Low said, turning his focus back on the main entrance before he continued. "Check inside that envelope, and see if there's any info on Sunshine Village," Low said, zeroing in on the security booth.

An armed guard was chatting it up with a middle-aged blonde in a silver BMW M3. Low watched carefully while the security guard checked her in through the security gate. Meanwhile, Rob scanned the mayor's file, and came across a real estate pamphlet.

"It says here they asking a hundred and fifty thousand for a two-bedroom—"

"Only one fifty thousand, huh?" Low muttered in a sarcastic tone.

Low's eyes followed the M3 going through the security gate then focused back on the security booth.

"Tell me about it. Daoud's living in straight up luxury," Rob said, reading through the pamphlet.

Finally Rob found something in the pamphlet that hit his eyes, and he read it aloud.

"Residents of Sunshine Village can choose to enjoy their days golfing, playing tennis, and diving in one of our three Olympic-sized swimming pools. By nightfall residents can also enjoy fine dining at our on-site five-star Italian eateries. Or just enjoy the scenery of our lavish landscape taking a night jog, or long walk around our twelve acres, and feel completely at ease knowing that our hired security officers are there twenty four hours a day. Their presence ensures our residents of Sunshine

Village are always safe and sound."

"Damn! We probably got a better chance catching this fool when he takes his car out on the town or some shit. Cause security seems pretty much on point," Low said.

"I know," Rob sighed, and closed the pamphlet then replacing it in Daoud's file.

He sat back in the passenger seat, and let out a deep sigh then shook his head. Staring at the mayor's file, Rob began to feel defeated.

"I thought about that scenario already. First off, it's way too risky. We just got lucky with Lonnie Dawson. I mean, look at your arm. If we're put in that situation again it'll be with real police. A cop won't miss like that bitch did. And besides, Daoud may only drive that car once or twice a year. So waiting for him to decide if he's in the mood to take the antique out on the town for a test drive is not an option. We don't have the time for that," Rob said, tossing the mayor's file inside the glove compartment.

"I don't see how Tony expects us to pull this off," Low said, shaking his head.

"Shit, me neither. But fuck that! I didn't get this close to the prize to quit. We just gotta figure this shit out between us—and fast. If there's a will there's gotta be a way. So we can't leave here 'til we figure out a successful plan of attack."

"Since you put it that way. Sounds like we gonna be here for a while. So why don't you roll another one of those Swisher Sweets up. But this time, pass the shit," Low said, adjusting his seat, and reclining to a snug position.

CHAPTER

CUBAN TONY

Antonio 'Tony' Morales was born in 1949 to Cuban parents who eventually migrated to the United States from Cuba in the late fifties. Tony's parents were very outspoken against communism, and were forced to flee their native homeland when Fidel Castro rose to power. They settled in a predominantly Cuban section of Miami, Florida, dubbed 'Little Havana'.

Hector and Maria Morales, Tony's parents were established bankers in Cuba, and used their entire life-savings to launch a Cuban-styled restaurant in the heart of Little Havana called, 'Havana Heaven'. The eatery served-up home cooked dishes that made customers feel like they were back home in Cuba, and was an instant hit. Business was great, and by 1962 the family-owned Havana Heaven restaurant flourished into a franchise with two restaurants located in the prestigious part of the downtown area. Hector and Maria Morales pursued the American dream and succeeded.

For their first ten years living in the U.S., life was perfect for the Morales, especially for Tony. In 1971, he was a full-time party animal. Moving into his own condo in Miami Beach, Tony purchased two luxury sports cars. He was young, good-looking, and living the high-life—all on his parent's dime. Being the only child of two wealthy business moguls, Tony lived a very entitled life. His parents made sure he received the best in everything their money could buy. He was the sole heir to their accumulating fortune.

They also made certain Tony was well educated in the field of business. Enrolling him in one of the most prestigious business schools in South Florida, they equipped Tony with all the knowledge, and credentials he needed. His parents wanted him to be capable of operating the franchises, and carry the torch of his family's namesake and legacy.

Unfortunately for Tony that time came sooner than anticipated, and was completely unexpected. 1976, tragedy struck during a botched armed robbery attempt. Hector and Maria were in their office going over the company's financial books. They, along with two other male employees, were shot and killed.

It didn't take long for the assailants—two teenagers from the neighborhood—to be apprehended. Their fingerprints were all over a time activated safe. However not even their timely capture, and subsequent convictions for the homicides was enough to ease the pain Tony endured. He grieved the loss of the only family members he knew. For the first time in his life, Tony felt depressed, alone, and scared. In an effort to pacify his pain, his partying lifestyle increased tenfold.

From the bars on Ocean Drive to the Salsa clubs in Miami Beach, Tony lived it up with the top business executives, entertainers, and even a few underworld crime figures. It was during these partying binges that

Tony met, and began to build a real solid friendship with Papito.

He affectionately called Tony 'Cuban Tony', and was a high-ranking member of the Mexican mafia. Taking a strong liking to Tony over a course of time, Papito began to view Tony as his own blood. The two men began referring to each other as brothers. By 1981, Tony had blown through hundreds of thousands of dollars and was dealing with serious financial issues.

The restaurant franchises he had inherited from his parents were experiencing a revenue crisis, and weren't attracting as many customers as before. This was partly due to the horrific shooting that took place inside the main restaurant that still left an unpleasant stigma with the once loyal, and potential customers, and the fierce competition by many Spanish fast-food chains quickly springing up all over the city of Miami.

With the franchises becoming unprofitable, and his net worth declining, Tony went to Papito for advice. Papito was an expert in insurance scams, and convinced Tony to burn down the main Havana Heaven restaurant in Little Havana, and the one in Hialeah. He advised him to shut down the remaining three restaurants, and utilize the properties to build three storage warehouses.

Papito told him to use the insurance money from the burned down restaurants to invest with him in a luxury vehicles VIN scheme. Papito assured Tony that his car scheme was a guaranteed multi-million dollar investment, and Tony would be rich beyond his wildest dreams. Papito also told Tony he would vouch for him so he could officially become an affiliate of the Mexican cartel. This affiliation would guarantee Tony, and all his future business ventures security, and the freedom to network throughout the underworld. Trusting his comrade, Tony agreed.

CHAPTER

7

TRANS

A stolen vehicle with all the serial and identifying VIN removed was known as a 'trans'. The old numbers were replaced with the serial and VIN numbers of an identical vehicle that was totaled, deemed not repairable, or undrivable. The vehicle's model, and year being the same would most likely be sent to a junkyard to be chopped down for parts.

After tearing down the remaining three Havana Heaven restaurants, and building three huge storage warehouses on the properties, Tony used the land of his parents two other restaurants as empty lots. Then with some of the large lump sum of money he received from his small business insurance check, he along with Papito set their multi-million dollar heist in motion. They rallied up thirty teenage kids that were known for stealing cars in their neighborhoods and put them on the payroll.

Papito and Tony targeted luxury vehicles exclusively. Hundreds of junkyards, and towing companies around the counties of Miami-Dade, Broward, and the

Palm Beach areas supplied them with lists of cars they needed.

Their inventory of totaled luxury vehicles coming into their shops were from various car accidents across the state. Papito was very specific in the type of cars he needed. His interest was centered on exotic sports cars like Porsches, Maseratis, and Ferraris, but he also took BMWs Mercedes Benz, and Jaguars.

Tony and Papito paid a dirt-cheap base price for the titles of all the totaled exotic, and luxury cars sent to the junkyards. If Porsches, with retail value of sixty thousand dollars, were available, they'd pay a base price of five thousand dollars for title and ownership of the wrecked car. Then they would arrange to have the car transported on a flatbed tow truck to one of Tony's storage warehouses. An envelope filled with color printouts—including make, model, year, and pictures of all the crashed vehicles they purchased were passed out amongst the thirty teenage car thieves. They were split in six groups of five, and sent out across the city to retrieve all the targeted vehicles by any means necessary—usually stealing, and carjacking.

The stolen vehicle would be taken to Tony's storage warehouse. It would be matched with an exact totaled duplicate make, model, and year. Then the transformation process would begin. All serial and VIN numbers would be stripped from the stolen car, and replaced with the serial and VIN numbers from the wrecked vehicle.

After that process was completed, a fresh paint job would be provided. Papito would then have one of his many connections within the Department of Motor Vehicles erase all prior history of ownership for the crashed vehicle. The status of the crashed car was changed from totaled from the DMV database. The new VIN and serial numbers would be reactivated in the computer system, making it appear as if the car had been in operation for years without any significant damages by the original owner.

Then the car would be brought to one of Tony's car lots. He had two substations built on the lots. The cars would be priced for lease, or for sale at a huge discount compared to all the other competitive car dealerships in the city.

Papito and Tony would make thirty thousand dollars profit collectively for each 'trans' car they sold. Tony's business savvy allowed the used car dealerships to immediately take off. The cheap price tags for high-end, late model, exotic, luxury vehicles were too low for any other dealership in the city to compete. The clientele for their dealership was so great that they were forced to buy four more car lots just to have enough supply for the growing demands.

1985 was the first year the dealerships sold two hundred 'trans' cars, and raked in over six million dollars in profit. Two and a half years into their illegal venture, Tony and Papito's car dealerships were well known around the South Florida area. He was the front man of the car dealerships, and Tony's name rose in status, and power. With his dealerships flourishing, Tony started thinking long term, and use his money to purchase truckloads of legit luxury cars at wholesale prices. Then he added the legit cars to his dealerships existing inventory while selling less, and less 'trans' cars by the year. Slowly making the transition, to legitimizing his corporations. Tony was now a staple of success. Finally in 1986, Papito and Tony officially halted their entire car operation. Within a year they were multi-millionaires, with a collective net worth of over twenty-two million dollars.

CHAPTER
8

Michael O'Connell

In 1987, Papito received a promotion to captain in the cartel. He relocated to Texas to oversee an underground tunnel drug smuggling operation. Before he left Florida, Papito co-signed an agreement between Tony and the cartel. Tony became an official affiliate of the Mexican Mafia. With his newfound alliance to the Florida based cartel, Tony was assured security, and the freedom to network throughout the underworld with any person, or organization of his choice.

From the Russians to the Chinese, and even the Italians, Tony now had the backing of the Mexican Mafia, if warranted. This new, and privileged position came with a hefty price tag. Tony was obligated to contribute a monthly percentage to the cartel. In order to satisfy his affiliates, and expand his business empire, he was forced to come up with new moneymaking schemes without direct assistance of Papito.

In the winter of 1988, Tony met an Irish man by the name of Michael O'Connell at an exotic sports car show in Key West, Florida. Tony jumped at Michael's offer to partner up on another heist. Michael O'Connell was the son of Arthur O'Connell, an Irish immigrant who was a millionaire in the car dealership business back in the early seventies. When Arthur became gravely ill, and could no longer run his local car dealership franchises, Michael became the president of his dad's company. Michael handled all operation of the businesses, and seemed well prepared for the unexpected opportunity. He immediately used the company's money and expanded the car dealership franchises far beyond the city limits of their hometown of Huntington, Long Island.

O'Connell Wheels now owned dealerships in New York, Florida, California, Texas, and Nevada. It became one of the largest, and most flourishing car franchises in the nation. Michael O'Connell went on vacation to Dubai, and told Tony about a Saudi billionaire who was into Arabian antiques.

"He's trying to acquire twenty specific classic sports cars to add to his personal collection. He's very resourceful, and located the owners of these vehicles, but was met with great resistance."

"Did he sweeten the pot or—"

"Everyone of the owners weren't too interested in selling their beloved classic sports cars, even at double the market price."

"Well I'll be damn—" Tony began, but Michael cut him off.

"Don't be. He's now willing to pay up to five times the market price to anyone who could acquire the vehicles for him."

"He's really sweetening the pot."

"It gets sweeter. He's providing an info packet for each owner...their addresses, work schedules, DMV photos, to pictures of the targeted vehicles, and even a monthly agenda tracked by his private investigators."

"All right. He's really on his game," Tony said with enthusiasm.

"I'll say. When all twenty vehicles are retrieved, he'll make all arrangements for pickup, and transportation to the port."

"Here in Miami?"

"Yes, Miami. All the cars will be shipped to an estate in the Middle East. The wire transfer of twenty-five million dollars will immediately be deposited in an offshore account of the payee's choice."

"You're right. It is a very sweet deal," Tony smiled, nodding.

This was a chance to forge a new partnership with a well-known business mogul, Michael O'Connell, and rake in an easy twelve and a half million dollars. Tony needed to expand his business empire, and this couldn't be more perfect. He could easily prove his worth to his new-found affiliates with the two and a half million-dollar payday they were set to receive. It would prove that he was a good earner, and could be trusted to take part in other schemes that would eventually arise. It didn't take long for Tony to assure Michael O'Connell that he could deliver.

"I'm sold. I'll immediately get busy on the delivery of those cars," Tony said, shaking Michael's hand.

The two agreed to a fifty-fifty split. Michael gave Tony a copy of the list of all twenty vehicles and their owners' information packets.

Tony set out to hire a team of car thieves. He needed a team well skilled, and fully capable of carrying out such a diligent task without any significant mistakes being made. Out of thirty potential car thieves from Tony and Papito's original heist, two guys that met his strict standards stuck out to Tony. Robertocito and Milow. Three years passed, and Tony wasn't sure if those two were still in the business of stealing autos, but he certainly knew where to find them.

CHAPTER

STAKEOUT

At midnight the twenty-four-hour Winn Dixie super-market was the only remaining business still opened. The Main Street Plaza in Coconut Groves was virtually empty. The handful of employee's cars scattered about the huge parking lot made it look bleak. Tony's white tinted Corvette sat idle beside a large Winn Dixie shipping truck. It was the only vehicle that had been there since sundown. Five long hours passed by as Low and Rob sat in the two-seated sports car, passing the sixth Swisher Sweet between them.

Any hope of coming up with a successful plan was almost as dead as the conversation between them. It trickled down to small talk.

"So what you, and Lovely kissed and make up?" Low asked, taking a long pull on the weed-filled Swisher Sweet.

"Lovely huh?" Rob repeated her name, chuckled, and continued. "Man, fuck that bitch!"

Low took another hit off the weed, allowing the smoke to linger in his lungs a bit. Then he passed the Swisher Sweet to Rob and gathered his thoughts. He had never discussed Rob's relationship with Lovely before. Low knew that at one point, Rob and Lovely were inseparable. Rob used to drive her in her mother's Benz around the hood, showing Lovely off. That was when he was living with her at her mother's house. Then before long it was like Lovely was an afterthought, and Rob was back in the hood with him, drawing up the blueprint for the next come-up.

"What the hell ever happened to y'all two anyway...? Thought that was your baby-girl...? Shit, the way you used to floss her around, I would've sworn you loved her. What happened?"

Rob smoked the Swisher Sweet. Sucking the smoke deeply into his lungs, he exhaled loudly. Then sighing, he chuckled, "Man, fuck that bitch."

Then he passed the cigar back to Low who then raised the Swisher Sweet to his lips, and took a pull. A loud sound of a damaged vehicle's exhaust pipe caught both of their ears. They turned to see a Chinese delivery van zooming by on the road in front of them. It wasn't until Low and Rob noticed the delivery car making a right turn, and heading for the Sunshine Village main entrance gate that their interests were piqued. Quickly sitting up from their reclined seats, they watched.

"Ain't that one of those City Wok Chinese-food delivery cars that be in the hood?" Low asked, eyeing the yellow and red shining sign on top of the delivery car.

"Hell yeah! That's the same ones that be delivering to the crib. What the fuck they Chinese asses doing all the way in this cracker town?" Rob said.

"Shit, you don't know who the hell be ordering Chinese takeout this time of night anyways," Low wondered aloud.

They watched the delivery car making its way through the main entrance pass the security gate, and drove into Sunshine Village. Ten minutes later, it was on its way out. When the delivery car zoomed by Low and Rob, a Kool-Aid smile swept across Rob's face. A light bulb went off in his head.

"Start the car," Rob instructed.

"What you want me to follow him?" Low asked, revving the engine, and pulling out the parking space.

"Nah, let's just get outta here. Drop me at my crib. It's been a long day, and we need to rest up. I got an idea though."

✦ ✦ ✦

Low heard his phone ringing, and groggily opened his eyes. Clearing his throat, Low answered it on the third ring.

"Damn fool. It's six in the evening, and you still sleeping?" Rob asked.

"Man, after dropping you off in Opa-Locka, it took me about an hour to find a decent spot to park Tony's car where it wouldn't be stolen. Then I had to walk from damn near downtown to Michelle's crib. I didn't get home 'til 'bout four something in the morning."

"My fault. Get all the rest you need. It's on and poppin' tonight."

"Speak to me."

"Okay, remember when I told you I had a plan?"

"Yeah…"

"Well a cousin of mines works the third-shift as a Manager at Dominoes over on one-twenty-fifth and sixth in north Miami."

"Okay…"

"After doing a little research, I found out that Mayor Daoud ain't even in town this week. He's in Boston attending some type of mayor's summit or some shit."

"Okay…?"

"The Car and Driver magazine article said that Mayor Daoud's son, Ryan Daoud, is seventeen. That's around the same age as us. And his info packet says the mayor's currently separated from his wife, and they have one son that the mayor has full custody of."

"So what's the point?"

"Ain't no seventeen year old gonna be home alone while his dad's out of town, and not have at least a girl over for company. Ya dig?"

"Okay…"

"I convinced my cousin to let me borrow one of his uniforms and a pizza-delivery car for a few hours tonight."

"Oh, so you really think that plan's gonna work?"

"It should get us through the main entrance, at least. So you riding with me on this or not?"

"Fuck it. That may be the only shot we got at getting pass the security. I'm with it."

"Okay, that's what I like. My cousin should have a delivery car ready for us by eleven. I'm a call your phone once I'm ready for you to go get Tony's car. Then pick me up from my aunt's crib. Ya heard?"

"I got you," Low said, hanging up the phone.

He turned and saw that Michelle was no longer lying in bed with him. She was sitting in a rocking chair by the window, preparing to rollup a joint.

"Damn, you just gonna smoke without me, babe?" Low asked, making his way over to Michelle.

There was love in his eyes, and Low planted a wet kiss on her temple. Michelle wiped his saliva from her face with attitude, and said, "Boy, please! You were knocked out once you got here last night. Slept all day…and from what I just heard, seems like you, and your badass counterpart will be ripping and running the streets again tonight."

Low watched as she sucked her teeth. Michelle licked the joint, and began twisting it. Then Low took a seat next to Michelle, and said, "Aw c'mon Chelle. You know…? Rob and me just taking care of some business. Tonight should be our last night doing it."

Michelle lit the joint, took a pull, and exhaled. A floor fan quickly helped the evaporation of smoke fumes. She passed the joint to Low, and walked to a wooden dresser. Michelle opened her top drawer, pulled out a bottle of Tanqueray, and made her way back over to Low.

"Look at what I got," she smiled with a devilish grin.

After opening the pint of gin, Michelle took a swig then passed it to Low. She sat next to him, watching him sip.

"You know gin brings that super freak out me, girl," Low joked, raising the bottle to his mouth, and taking a few gulps.

"Hmm maybe that's the plan," Michelle purred.

She began to seductively massage Low's crotch, causing an immediate erection. Michelle smiled and said, "You took-off your shoulder sling, huh?"

Reaching her hand underneath his boxers, Michelle gently caressed him. Smiling, she said, "That means you're gonna be able to smack my ass with both hands this time, daddy?"

His dick was out, and Michelle showered it with soft, wet kisses. Low's dick was into her warm, wet mouth, and she stroked his bulging penis between her soft, pillow lips. Low took in a long, deep toke on the joint then washed it down with another gulp of gin.

"Uh hmm…" Low hissed.

A tsunami of sounds escaped his lips while he rested his baldhead against the rocking chair's cushion. Michelle continued to suck his dick. After her toe-curling head-game, Low realized he drank the entire bottle of Tanqueray, and was feeling excellent.

Taking a breather from her oral escapade, Michelle took a pause, gazed up at Low, and said, "You know what I want right now, baby?"

She moaned between light, teasing flickers of her wet tongue around the head of Low's massive tool.

"What's that, babe?" Low muttered in total bliss.

Michelle's soft palm was slowly jacking the head of his penis. With a seductive smile, she said, "I want you to fuck the shit out of me right now."

Her eyes were sex-filled, and she rose from the seat. Michelle sashayed her way over to her bed. Low placed the empty bottle of gin on the carpeted floor. He was feeling nice and woozy as he slipped-off his boxers, and followed behind her. By the time he reached the bed, Michelle was lying on the edge of the mattress. She was completely nude, and both her legs spread-eagle. Michelle rubbed her fat, Brazilian-waxed, pussy with manicured fingers. Her pussy was dripping wet in anticipation.

"Turn on your stomach," Low ordered, standing at the edge of the mattress.

"Anything you say, daddy."

With a girlish giggle, Michelle swiftly turned around, and got on all fours, her plump backside raised high in the air. His stiff cock inches away from Michelle's glistening wet pussy. Low leaned forward, and began teasing the outer walls of Michelle's pussy. Rubbing the swollen head up, down, and around her moistened pussy lips. Her love-juices dripped while he teased her.

"Oh daddy! Stop teasing me like this and stick it in. Please…"

Her pussy pulsated in anticipation. With a sly smirk plastered across his face, Low immediately dropped to his knees. Michelle's plump, wet pussy was staring at him. Low dove in face first and devoured her love box.

"Oh daddy! Yes!" Michelle cried.

Low's tongue eagerly explored the inside of her warmth while Michelle's fingers rubbed her clit. Low feasted on her pussy lips, sucking her moist twat. Occasionally she felt his stiff tongue plunging inside her goodies. He was tongue fucking her pussy so good, Michelle lost control.

"Oh-oh-oh daddy! Yes! Keep it there! Right there!"

Low's oral antics drove Michelle crazy. Her eyes were rolling to the back of her head, and her body writhed in ecstasy.

"Oh God! Yes! Ah I'm—"

The volcanic eruption was building inside washed her voice away. Low lips continued their assault on her pulsating clit. Then the intensity of her orgasm took over her entire body. Michelle grabbed a hold of her tits, squeezed her eyelids shut, and bit her bottom lip.

"Hmm…hmm… Oh God I'm cumming!"

Moaning loudly, her pussy lips overflowing with juices, Michelle shoved Low's face deeper between her ass cheeks. His nose was knocking on her backdoor when her body shook and squirmed.

"Oh my God!"

Michelle collapsed on the bed panting for air. Low gave her no time for recovery, he immediately saddled Michelle's plump, round ass from the behind. He spread her ass cheeks apart, and plunged his cock inside her gushing, wet twat. With each long stroke, his massive tool stretched her inner-walls, giving Michelle exactly what she wanted.

"Oh-oh… Yes daddy! Give it to me! Fuck me!"

Throwing it back, Michelle squeezed her ass cheeks while tightening her pussy muscles. She gloved his huge cock, and became more demanding.

"Fuck me daddy! Faster! C'mon, give it to me hard!"

Low felt his erection pulsing. A massive explosion

was building. His hips moved faster, and his breath got shallow. Michelle felt his cock pulsating inside het tight pussy, and knew it was time. Squeezing her ass cheeks together, she gyrated her hips, meeting his pounding dick.

"Cum for mama, baby!"

Reaching his ecstatic peak, Low's body froze. Then he busted off inside her pussy before collapsing on top of her.

"Hmm daddy, that was the best!"

Michelle's smile was seductive watching Low rolled onto his back. Clearly exhausted, he wore a satisfied grin.

"Damn, you're something else."

Michelle got up, and grabbed a facecloth out of her pantry. Soaking it in warm water, she went back to her bed and wiped all her juices from Low's body. By the time she was done, Low was fast asleep. Tossing the wet face-cloth inside her laundry basket, Michelle crawled into the bed. After making sure Low was fully knocked out, she reached over to the nightstand, and unplugged the phone cord. Then laid her head on his chest, shut her eyes, and drifted off to sleep with a satisfied smile on her face.

CHAPTER
10

PLAN B

"Hi, you have reached Michelle Jean… I'm currently unable to come to the phone right now. Please leave your name, and number… And I'll get back to you. Thank you."

The outgoing message of Michelle's answering machine greeted Rob for the umpteenth time.

"Fuck!"

Rob was fuming. He slammed down his phone's receiver, and glanced at the time. It was now eleven forty-five. For the past forty-five minutes, Rob had been calling Michelle's phone without getting any answer. Picking up the phone's receiver he pressed re-dial, and heard the same outgoing message.

"Hi, you have reached Michelle Jean… I'm currently unable to come—"

"What the fuck!"

Rob slammed the receiver again, and was at a total loss as to why Low wasn't picking up. He had specifically instructed him to be ready for this call. This wasn't making sense. Low would never leave him hanging at such a critical moment. Thinking of possible unexpected scenarios, he decided to try another number.

"Yes, hello…!"

An agitated tone greeted him. Rob cleared his throat, and spoke.

"Umm yes. Bonsoir Ms. Pierre. Milow La s'il vous plait…?" Rob asked in Creole, hoping the answer was yes.

"No! Milow don't live here no more!"

Low's Haitian-born mother was clearly pissed, but she gave Rob her best English. There was a short pause then she said, "Who dis? What's your name…? You calling too late… It's midnight. You must be crazy…!"

The sound of her dial tone quickly jolted Rob back to the reality of his situation. Quickly, he summed up his options. It was already too late to knock on Michelle's window. Her pops was at home, and Rob would risk get shot. He didn't know where Tony's car was parked. It was impossible to steal another car, find Tony's car, and try to locate Low. Time was too critical for all that work.

With no other options left, Rob was left shaking his head. Then he made the most fateful decision of his life. Picking up the phone's receiver, Rob's sigh was filled with frustration. Forty thousand dollars was on the line, and he started dialing.

"Dominoes Pizza, hello. This is Daniel speaking. Pickup or delivery?"

"This Rob, cuz. I don't need no pizza, fool. But I damn sure do need a favor right now big cuz."

"What the hell Robinson…? Man, you were supposed to come pickup a half hour ago. I got everything ready as you ordered. Man, are you coming to get it or what? I really need that money."

Taking a deep breath Rob chose his words wisely then he said, "Check it, big cuz. Our deal's still on, but something came up with my partner. So I'm gonna need you to fill-in for him."

"Fill in…? What you talking 'bout, cuz?"

"A little bit of driving. But I really don't wanna talk 'bout it on the phone. I'll double up on what we already agreed on."

"Hmm…" Daniel said, pausing for a second. Then he continued. "Sound to me like more than a little driving, lil cuz. I wasn't born yesterday. You know…? I know what you into. If you wasn't blood, it would be a straight up 'hell no'. Nigga, you know I just got out."

"I know, I know, but I ain't had no one else that I can really trust like that…"

"Alright cuz. Since it's like that I'll ride. It's gon' cost you more than four hundred fool."

"What you talking 'bout…?"

"Throw me a G., and you got the deal."

"Damn cuz!"

"Fucking with you might have me violating my parole. So throw me a G., or…"

Rob took a deep breath, and shook his head in disbelief. He had no choice. No way was he leaving forty G's on the table. After silently cursing Low in his head, he made a mental note to deduct this G from Low's share of the money. Rob reluctantly agreed.

"A'ight cool we got a deal… How long is it gonna take you to get here?"

"About twenty minutes tops."

"A'ight. Remember to have your work uniform. And make sure you bring a few boxes of pizzas and some sodas wit' cha."

"Shit, for a stack, I'll make sure I bring some side orders too."

"Funny… Just make sure you get here in twenty minutes."

With a ride on the way, Rob made another call.

"Sunshine Village… Main gate…" A security guard with a thick country drawl said.

"Um yes, is this Bill?" Rob asked in his best White boy voice.

"No… Chuck, who's this…? Sorry kid, Billy's off tonight."

Silently releasing a sigh of relief, Rob felt ecstatic the name-dropping trick worked. Smiling ear to ear, Rob continued. "Oh hey, Chuck. It's Ryan. And I'm in need of a major favor, buddy."

"Oh, Ryan Daoud…? I don 't know, kid. Last time I did you a favor, I almost got my ass handed to me by the mayor."

Rob could hear Country music playing in the background. Easing the phone's receiver from his ear, he shook his head and smiled. This was way too fucking easy. Rob took a deep breath, and got back into character.

"Oh gosh. C'mon Chuck. I was just about to order a few pizzas, and was hoping you could just let the delivery-guy through without logging him in. My dad would kill me if he finds out I had company over this late."

"Oh…? Who's the lucky gal this time? Wait…let me guess. Is it that councilman's daughter, Sara McLaughlin again?"

"You know it," Rob smiled.

"Okay, so long as you swing one of those hot pies my way, we got a deal, kid. I'm starving."

"Aw geez, awesome! Cheese or pepperoni, buddy?"

"You know I gotta have my pepperoni, and a two-liter Pepsi."

"Absolutely, Chuck. And thanks, man."

"No problem, kid."

Rob hung up the phone, clapped his hands, and burst out laughing. He hadn't used his *Brady Bunch* tone in a while, but it still worked like a charm. Making

his way to his closet, Rob pulled out a black Oakland
Raiders hooded sweatshirt, black Reebok Classic sneakers, and threw them onto his bed. After getting dressed,
he made his way to his dresser, and pulled out a pair of
black leather batters' gloves—from his glory days in high
school—and slipped them on.

Walking over to his bed, Rob went underneath, and
pulled out a black Jansport book bag. Placing it on top
of his bed, he unzipped it, and did a quick inventory of
his work tools. Starting with a twenty-five pound handheld dent-puller, a massive flathead screwdriver, and his
binoculars, Rob removed each item. He placed a black
ski mask in his pocket, and examined a change of light
colored clothing, a small box of spark plugs. He put the
Olympic track and field stopwatch around his neck. Then
he checked out his two prized possessions, two military
nine-millimeter handguns. The day before, Tony gave
him these two weapons to replace his Mossberg pump
and Low's .44Magnum.

Rob armed with one of the nines comfortably in the
small of his back, tightened the waistband of his sweatpants, and returned all the tools back inside his book bag.
The second gun was the last thing. He planned to give it
to Daniel, just in case. Zipping the book bag shut, Rob
took a deep breath, faced the east, and prayed.

Rob wasn't much on his dean, and was doing much
dirt, but still feared Allah. By praying for his safety, Rob
knew one day he would be blessed, and would no longer
have to lead a life of crime. Rising to his feet, he heard
a car's horn coming from outside his room's window.
Daniel had arrived.

✦ ✦ ✦

Coconut Grove was a ghost town. Daniel drove down
Main Street in his pizza delivery car with Rob reclining

in the passenger seat. The only other soul on the entire four-mile strip was the bright headlights of a large eighteen-wheeler tractor-trailer behind them.

"A'ight, so you sure you know what to do, right?" Rob asked, tightening the straps on his gloves, and slid his ski mask over the top of his head.

Rob had never executed a mission with anyone else but Low. He was going over the plan with his cousin for the sixth time.

"Come on, lil' cuz! I've been doing this job for a year now. I know how to deliver a damn pizza! One large pepperoni for the security guard, and two large cheese pies for Ryan Daoud… I got it under control," Daniel said in an aggravated tone.

"And you're sure you got everything else down packed too right?" Rob asked.

"I'm positive lil' cuz. Trust me. I got this."

"A'ight cool."

"For all my troubles you might as well let me keep this gun," Daniel said, admiring the large pistol in his lap.

"Those models go for fifteen hundred dollars. You can keep it, but it'll be your payment," Rob said.

"Nah, I'd rather the cash," Daniel said, putting the gun in his waistband, and covering it with his uniform shirt.

"I thought so. Pullover, and let this truck behind us pass. We almost there," Rob said, getting ready for the mission.

Daniel pulled over, and the tractor-trailer zoomed by. They were two and a half blocks from Sunshine Village.

"A'ight big cuz, its muthafuckin' show time!" Rob said, pulling the ski mask completely over his face. After retrieving the book bag from between his legs, he continued. "A'ight, on three pop the trunk."

✦ ✦ ✦

"It's about time, boy. I'm starving!" A security guard frowned.

Daniel pulled to a stop at the main gate of Sunshine Village, and let out an exasperating sigh. The security reference of boy bothered him, but Daniel set his emotions aside, and quickly jumped into character. Smiling, he said, "So sorry, big fella. I had to make two other stops before this one."

Without acknowledging the apology, the security said, "Whatever boy. You got my pie or what?"

"Sure do. One large pepperoni and a two-liter Sprite," Daniel said.

"Sprite…? Boy, I'm sure that Daoud kid specifically told your simple-ass I wanted a Pepsi!" The guard angrily barked, snatching the meal from Daniel.

"Oh…he did. But unfortunately we ran out of Pepsi sir," Daniel lied, relishing the guard's anger.

"Yeah, yeah, you people always run out of something," the guard muttered then went back into the security booth.

After putting the pizza and drink on top of a small foldout table inside the booth, the guard activated the entrance gate. It slowly slid open. He waved Daniel on, and said, "Make it quick, boy."

Daniel drove down Flamingo Way in Sunshine Village, checking the house numbers as he went by the. Rob was lying in the trunk with his tool book bag clutched tightly over his chest. He took slow, deep breaths, trying to stay calm. His anticipation and adrenaline were in overdrive. When the inside of the trunk illuminated red from the brake lights, Rob took another deep breath, exhaling slowly, and waited for Daniel's signal.

Finally Daniel saw Daoud's driveway. He located the mayor's royal blue Ferrari parked beside a black late-model 964 Carrera 2 Porsche. Slowly, he pulled over on the opposite side of the street, one house down as instructed. Daniel quickly scanned the house, trying to get a sense of any activities on the inside. Then he gave Rob the signal.

The brake lights illuminated once, twice then a third time. Daniel then activated the left turn signal to let Rob know what side of the street the house was on. After glancing in the rearview mirror, assuring that the coast was clear, Daniel popped the trunk.

Rob carefully eased out the trunk with his book bag in his hand then quietly shut the trunk. Using the darkened street to his advantage, Rob made his way to the driveway. Creeping to the driver's side door of the Ferrari, he dropped to a knee, and immediately unzipped the book bag. Then he pulled out the large flathead screwdriver, preparing to forcefully unlock the driver's side door. As a precaution, Rob pulled on the door handle. To his amazement, the door clicked open. With a satisfied grin on his face, Rob sprung to his feet, swung the door open, and hopped into the driver's seat.

Tossing his book bag in the passenger seat beside him, Rob started the stopwatch laced around his neck. Then he put the flathead in his lap, reached back in the book bag, and pulled out his handheld twenty-five pound dent puller. He screwed in the front end of the pulley into the Ferrari's key ignition. Rob inserted the pulley's screw into the Ferrari's ignition, and gave the twenty-five pound weight on the dent puller a hard tug. The car's ignition was completely destroyed, sending all the inner metal contents flying everywhere. Rob ecstatically halted the stopwatch at twelve seconds. Rob tossed the pulley in the passenger seat, retrieved the flathead, and stuck the massive screwdriver into a now hollow hole of the car's ignition. The Ferrari's 3.4liter V8 engine started. Rob pressed the brakes three times in succession. It was his signal for Daniel to take off.

Shifting to reverse, Rob slowly backed out the driveway. He was careful not to rev the Ferrari's engine, and shifted into first. Then with his headlights off, Rob slowly followed behind the delivery car. They made their way back toward the main entrance gate.

"Well it's about time, boy!" The security guard angrily spat.

Daniel approached the exit side of the main entrance gate, and stopped in front of the security booth. He said, "Sorry, boss. I got lost back there for a sec."

"Yeah, right," the guard frowned, and activated the security gate.

He waved the delivery car through. Shaking-off the guard's ignorance, Daniel kept up the act, and smiled.

"You have a good night now, boss."

Releasing his foot off the brakes, and slowly easing forward, Daniel began to make his exit. He was halfway through the security gate when suddenly the engine of his delivery car shut-off.

"Hey, what's the fucking hold up, boy?" the guard snapped, stepping from behind the confines of the security booth.

He made his way toward the driver's side door of Daniel's delivery car.

"Um, I don't know, boss. The engine just stalled out on me."

Daniel frantically tried to restart the car's engine. Unclipping his heavy-duty flashlight from his utility belt, the guard shined the bright light on Daniel, completely illuminating the inside of the delivery car.

"I don't know what to tell you, boy. Next time don't make your deliveries in a fucking lemon," the guard said, shining the flashlight on Daniel's face.

"Uh…huh…"

"I don't give a damn how you're going to, but you do need to get this piece of shit started, and off this damn property, or I'll have it towed off this property, and have your Black-ass arrested for trespassing!" the guard angrily warned.

The security guard continued to beam his bright flashlight on Daniel's face. While Daniel frantically attempted to restart the delivery car's engine, the guard saw two pizza boxes and a two-liter soda that was supposedly for Ryan Daoud.

"Say boy, why the hell are there still two pizza boxes in that damn car?"

His hand inched closer to the service-issued Smith & Wesson.38 revolver on his waist.

"I got it!" Daniel shouted when he heard the engine start.

"Oh no you don't, boy! You hold it right there!"

Immediately the security guard pulled out his service pistol, and took aim at Daniel's head. The loud revving sound of a car's engine caught the guard's ears. Rob flipped on the Ferrari's high beams, and floored the sports car's gas pedal, sending a thick fog of burned tire fumes flying into the night sky.

All seven hundred and twenty horsepower were released, accelerating the Ferrari forward in the direction of the guard. The security guard 1etoff two successive shots from his.38 in Rob's direction, but his attempt proved to be futile. Daniel pulled out the military M9 from his waistband, returning fire from the delivery car. Peppering the guard with five shots—one of the slugs entered just above the guard's left calf, sending the guard crashing onto the concrete—face first.

Daniel sped away, making a sharp right turn. The Ferrari blasted through Sunshine Village's main entrance gate at sixty miles per hour. Rob raced passed the dying guard, making a death defying left turn. Shifting gears, he hit ninety miles per hour effortlessly down a desolate service road, making his getaway.

CHAPTER
11

SHOTS FIRED

Rob drove the Ferrari to the back of the three-story building, and stopped at a massive steel service gate. Tony's car dealership storage complex on N.W. 2nd Avenue and 79th Street in the heart of Opa Locka was his final destination. After honking three times in slow succession, Rob took a deep breath, and waited. The huge steel gate began to lift up as Tony, and his lead mechanic Bolo stood smiling on the other side of the gate.

Easing the Ferrari onto the platform of the complex's detail and repairs area, Rob heard a roaring applause. Tony, Bolo, and two other mechanical staff began to clap and cheer him on. Rob drove the GTO all the way onto the brightly lit floor, and stopped beside a partially painted Jaguar. He hopped out the Ferrari with his book bag clutched tightly over his shoulders. Rob did his best to keep his facial expression calm, but couldn't help but crack a smile.

"You did it!" Tony exclaimed with glee.

He made his way over to Rob saluting him with a firm handshake, and a congratulatory pat on the back.

"Yeah Rob, you the man," Bolo said, extending his hand.

"Thanks," Rob smiled, letting out a deep breath.

The realization that the mission was finally accomplished began sinking in. Collecting the money was the only thing left to do.

"Say, where's your partner Milowcito?" Tony asked, snapping his fingers at his staff of mechanics.

After directing them to immediately get to work on the Ferrari, Tony motioned for Rob to follow him to his office.

"You'll see him in the a.m. when he drops off that Vette," Rob said.

"Okay, no sweat," Tony said in his thick Cuban accent.

The two entered a glass-enclosed office, and Tony continued. "You guys really pulled it off. Tony sat on a leather office chair behind an oak wood desk, and continued. "I must say, I was a little reluctant at first to give you two such a heavy workload. But I had faith you guys could do it. And you did! And for that, I am grateful."

Reaching under his desk, Tony pulled out a black duffle bag. He placed the duffle bag on top of the desk in front of him then slid it across the table. Stepping forward, Rob reached for the duffle bag, unzipped it, and took a look inside. It was completely filled to the top with crisp new, rubber-banded rolls of money.

"Fifty thousand dollars in cash," Tony smiled.

"What? Why?"

"Si, you and Milowcito have been nothing but loyal and efficient workers. So I decided to add an extra ten as a token of my appreciation."

Rob never saw so much cash in his life. Smiling, he whispered, "Hell yeah."

Then he glided his fingers over the crisp bills, admiring the fresh currency. For a whole year, Low and him put their lives on the line. They took some lives in the process. In the end, the risk was worth the reward.

"It was a pleasure doing business with you Robertcito," Tony said, rising, and extended his hand to Rob.

"Same here, Tony… Whenever you need us—you know how to reach us."

"My mechanics should be done repairing the Ferrari's ignition shortly. Care to stick around? I got a few bottles of the finest champagne for us to celebrate. And I got some excellent exotic marijuana, straight from Cuba."

Glancing down at his Chopard wristwatch, it was closing in on four in the morning. Tony's offer sounded pretty tempting, but Rob had major plans for him and Low in the afternoon.

"Sounds pretty tempting papa, but I'll have to pass. Been a long night, and I need some shuteye."

"Okay, no problem. I'll just catch up with you guys later when you and Milowcito stop by to return my car."

"Cool," Rob agreed, and made his exit.

Once he reached the doorway of the office, Rob stopped, and looked at the duffle bag in his hand. Turning back toward Tony, he said, "On second thought, I think it'll be best if we come get this cash when we drop off your car. A black man with a book bag on his back, and carrying a duffle bag in his hand walking down Opa Locka Boulevard ain't too smart."

"Whatever's works for you. I'll just put it away in my safe 'til you're back in the afternoon. Your money will be safe here," Tony shrugged.

"A'ight cool, see you 'round two," Rob said.

✦ ✦ ✦

N.E. 79th Street near Biscayne Boulevard was known as
'The Cayne'. During the day, the place was like any other
major boulevard in Miami, but at night it was totally
different. Afterhours 'The Cayne' was home to most of
the cities prostitutes and overly aggressive pimps. It was
a place for transvestites, and some of the most ruthless
crack heads around. There were dope fiends, willing to
do any and everything for their next hit, and a few crews
of late-night Jack boys, riding around 'The Cayne',
making their usual drive-bys in hopes of catching someone slipping. Walking on 'The Cayne' Rob's eyes were
peeled, looking out for the 'night strollers,' better known
as Miami-Dade's third-shift police squad. They were on
patrol up and down 'The Cayne' all night long.

Their presence added more conflict to an area that
was full of chaos. They were considered to be the nastiest
shift on the force, and were infamous for not playing
by the rules. Making his way down 'The Cayne', Rob
hoped none of the above crossed his path. He was almost
home, and just wanted to end such a good day on a high
note, without having to shoot somebody.

Finally, Rob reached his block on the corner of
Biscayne Boulevard and 3rd Street. He made a quick
right turn onto his street, and his pace quickened when
he saw the headlights of a Miami-Dade patrol car coming toward him. The patrol car was cruising on the other
side of the street, and Rob wasn't sure if the cops in it
saw him. He continued to power-walk down his block,
silently praying that they indeed didn't see him. Suddenly
the squeaking of the patrol car's brakes as it made a left
turn behind him pierced the early morn's air.

"Fuck!" Rob hissed.

The bright headlights from the patrol car shone behind him confirming his worse fear. His gut feeling was screaming for him to run, but his house lay in full view about a dozen yards away. He resisted the tempting urge, and decided to just keep cool for the moment. Rob saw that the patrol car was a K-9 unit, and there was hysterically loud barking coming from the German shepherd in the backseat of the patrol vehicle. Rob's adrenaline kicked into overdrive. His heart began pumping a million beats per second. Rob was doing his best to keep a calm facial expression. He sighed loudly, but a couple yards in front of him the patrol car stopped, and the dome lights were activated. Both doors swung open, and Rob swallowed hard while silently cursing his luck.

Two officers stepped out the patrol car, and approached him. Rob wasn't familiar with the fat black cop. He was a sergeant. Rob quickly glanced at the white cop approaching from the driver's side with a flashlight in one hand. His other hand was intimately close to the gun holster on his waist. It was officer Demarco. In the hood, he was known as 'Robocop'—a straight-up asshole.

"Kinda late. Where you headed, son?" The Black cop asked in a fatherly tone.

"Um, just coming from my girl's house down the street," Rob said nonchalantly.

"That's not what he asked you!" Robocop spat in a menacing tone. Lifting his flashlight to eye level, he shined the beam on Rob's face then he continued. "I think he asked you where the fuck are you headed!"

"Well sir, I'm heading to my house."

"Where moron?" Robocop sarcastically spat.

He was getting closer when suddenly the officer's radio sounded off before Rob could answer.

"Three-eight-niner... Officer Demarco, come in please..."

"This is three-eight-niner, go ahead…"

"Three-eight-niner, the shift commander would like a word with you on frequency channel 4."

"Ten-four…" He rolled his eyes in frustration. Then he turned to his partner, and said, "Fucking captain's on my ass. That's the second time tonight!"

Returning to the squad car, Robocop was fuming. The sergeant pulled out his pen and note pad then said, "The reason why we stopped you is because there's been a lot of complaints of armed robberies in the area. So we have to do a lot of random inquiry stops. But let me have your name and birth date. If I run it and you're clean then I'll let you go?"

Rob nodded in agreement, but his mind immediately began racing. He was wondering if he had any outstanding warrants he was unaware of. The amount of dirt him and Low had done in the past year, it would be a miracle if he were clean. This was a roll of the dice.

"My name's Christopher Paul, date of birth, six-sixteen-seventy-one," Rob lied.

He gave the name and birth date of one of his cousins who was around the same age as him. Rob was certain there were no warrants on the name he gave. Sergeant Williams walked away to check the information, and Rob waited on the sidewalk clutching each strap on the book bag tightly. He glanced around while mentally tossing around a few possible routes of escape.

"NCIC all clear."

"You're all set. Get home safely, kid," Sergeant Williams said, tucking away his pen and pad. After a short pause, he turned toward his squad car, and started to leave.

"Okay then," Rob whispered under his breath, walking away as fast as he could.

Williams reached for the patrol car's door handle, and was preparing to get in. Officer Demarco was stepping out. Making his way over to the patrol car's passenger side, Robocop was stunned that his sergeant was finished.

"He came back clean, huh?" Demarco sighed, glancing in Rob's direction.

"He did," Williams said.

"What the hell was in the book bag?" Demarco wondered aloud.

"I wouldn't know," Williams shrugged, and stepped inside the patrol car. He sat down, and continued. "I didn't 't search him."

"What…? How could you not?"

Robocop turned in Rob's direction, and shouted. "Hey kid, hold it right there!"

There was only two blocks separating him and his house. Rob ignored the officer's demand, and increased his pace.

"Hey, didn't you hear me? I said stop!" Officer Demarco shouted.

Only a few feet from the stop sign on the corner of N.E. 3rd Street and 3rd Court, Rob knew he if was going to make it to his block on 4th Avenue then he had to move now.

"Freeze!" Demarco shouted.

Rob broke into a sprint around the corner. Robocop dashed for his squad car, swung open the car's back door, and sprung his K- 9 loose. Racing to the front of the patrol car, Demarco hopped into the driver's seat, and floored the gas pedal. Activated sirens lit up the early morning's air, and Demarco gave chase.

Dipping down a long, dark, dirt-filled alley behind his house, Rob sprinted until he reached the wooden fence separating his backyard. Quickly, he slipped his book bag off his shoulders, and slipped easily through a small space. Then he made a dash for the gated back door of his house. Motion-sensor lights instantly illuminated the entire backyard. Rob frantically reached for the gated door handle. Swinging the steel gate open in desperation, he reached for the second door handle. It was then that he felt the razor-sharp teeth of the police K- 9 piercing his flesh.

"Ah…ah… Ugh!" Rob hollered.

The rigid jaw of the police dog clamped down on his fragile wrist, leaving him in excruciating pain. Rob collapsed to the ground in agony while the K- 9 attempted to rip his hand from his body. Rob tried to pull his wrist free, but only made it worse. The dog tore deeper into his flesh.

CHAPTER

12

DECEPTION

"I'm standing in the alleyway behind the suspect's house—just off Biscayne Boulevard and Eighty-third Street. Where a horrific, early morning incident took place. The scene here, as you can see, is the aftermath of a bloody shootout between two police officers, and suspect, Robinson Matayer..."

The female newscaster mentioning Rob's government caused Low to immediately open his eyes. He was jolted awake from a deep slumber, and listened carefully to the television.

"Matayer, known to Police in the area, has an extensive juvenile record. He was shot in the head after he opened fire on two officers, and their patrol dog. The police dog was killed, and both officers were injured. Matayer was also shot..."

Low glanced at his Chopard wristwatch. It was 9:15 am. He turned toward Michelle, sitting up, and hugging a pillow. Tears were freely flowing down her face. Low was totally dumbfounded. His eyes locked in on the screen.

"Both Officer Richard Demarco, and the suspect have been taken to Jackson Memorial Hospital. Where they're both reportedly in critical condition at this hour. We'll have more on this developing story at noon. Live from Biscayne, Miami. I'm Sherri Cooper..."

He was now in complete panic mode, Low leaped out of bed so fast he scared the shit out of Michelle. She jumped back against the bed's headboard, letting out a startling yelp. They locked eyes, and Low instantly saw the guilt in her eyes.

"What the fuck did you do?" Low shouted.

His tone was laced with venom, and his eyes shot bullets when he saw the phone sitting on the nightstand. Michelle quickly rose to her knees on the bed.

"Baby, I just didn't want you to get in no trouble!"

Ignoring her tearful plea, Low dashed for the phone. When he picked it up, his suspicions were confirmed. The phone's cord wasn't connected to the jack in the wall.

"What the fuck!" Low snapped, releasing his grip on the phone.

It crashed loudly to the floor. He stared at Michelle, and said, "I'm a kill you, bitch!"

Then leaping onto the bed, Low struck Michelle with a backhand. The vicious blow sent her crashing onto her bed's wooden headboard.

"I'm sorry, Low..." Michelle shouted.

Low grabbed her by her hair, and his brutal punch busted her bottom lip. Cocking back, Low swung again, but his punch never landed. The striking force from the butt of a shotgun smashed against his skull. His body tumbled off the bed, and crashed to the carpeted floor. Landing awkwardly on his unhealed shoulder, Low cringed in pain. He staggered to his feet, trying to regain his focus. The room was spinning, and Low felt the crunch of a hard kick that caved his chest. His body flew backwards, crashing into Michelle's glass vanity dresser, and Low could hear Michelle begging for his mercy.

"Daddy, please stop! You're gonna kill him!" Michelle screamed hysterically at her father.

Giving him no time to recover, Michelle's father pounced on Low like a wild lion attacking its prey.

"He deserves to die!" the man with dreadlocks roared.

He angrily struck Low again with the butt of his shotgun. Then he grabbed Low's neck, and hoisted Low's slumped body in the air.

"I can't breathe!" Low gasped.

His body was dangling in the massive arms of Michelle's angry father. Low's vision became darker with each critical second that passed.

"Oh my God! Daddy, stop please!" Michelle pleaded.

Blood oozed from the sides of Low's busted mouth. Cocking the shotgun, her father said, "Give me one reason why I shouldn't blow this muthafucka's brains to the ceiling?"

"I love him…" Michelle tearfully said.

"That's not good enough!" Michelle's father said, tightening his grip around Low's throat.

"I'M PREGNANT!"

Her father released his grip, and Low's body collapsed onto the floor. Low immediately reached for his throat, and gasped loudly for breath. Michelle's father turned, stared at her, and silently exited the room.

Rushing toward Low, who was laid out on the floor, Michelle helped him up onto her lap, and buried her tearstained face against his.

"I'm sorry, baby… I'm soo sorry…"

CHAPTER

13

IN SEARCH OF ANSWERS

Low sat in the driver's seat of Tony's Corvette, waiting on the stoplight to change. The events of the past hours were hastily racing through his mind. Michelle was pregnant, her crazy-ass father almost killed him, and Rob was in critical condition.

The news reported that Rob was transported from Jackson Memorial Hospital in Overtown to Miami University Hospital downtown. Rob had undergone emergency surgery, and the doctors removed a portion of his skull to relieve swelling in his brain. The procedure caused Rob to fall into a deep coma. He was currently lying in critical condition in the hospital's Intensive Care Unit.

Rob was given a thirty percent chance of survival. He was facing two counts of attempted murder, and would immediately be charged, and transported to Dade County's main jail if he survived.

A deep sigh escaped Low's parched lips. He was at a total loss as to what happened that led Rob to shoot it out with the cops in the first place. The news didn't say anything about stolen cars or mentioned Cuban Tony. Low gave Tony a call, but he just wanted to know what time they were dropping off his car. Tony didn't sound the least bit knowledgeable that anything went wrong with Rob. Nothing was adding up.

Could Tony be trusted? Did he setup Rob with the police, and now had some trick up his sleeve to get rid of him too? Maybe he didn't want to pay them. Low needed answers. His search would start with Tony. He reassuringly tapped the gun on his waist, and made a left turn on NW Seventy-Ninth Street. Then after a sharp right, he pulled onto the property of Tony's storage complex.

It was two in the afternoon, and Low knew the business hour routine. Since potential customers, clients, and business personnel would be out and about throughout the huge three- story warehouse Tony had a strict routine that Rob and Low must follow whenever they went to meet with him during his office hours.

Tony made sure Rob and Low were familiar with who was involved in the illegal aspect of his operation. Low parked in one of Tony's three reserved parking spaces. He hopped out the Corvette, and made his way toward the main entrance.

Walking along the sidewalk leading to the main entrance, Low saw a huge tractor-trailer equipped with two ten-slot, vehicle cargo-carriers in tow. The tractor-trailer was going toward the rear of the warehouse complex, where the vehicle loading and unloading docks were located. The vehicle carrying slots on the massive truck were all empty, and Low figured that a large amount of Tony's vehicle inventory were set to be loaded onto that cargo truck, and hauled off to one of his many car dealerships.

"Damn," Low sighed.

Tony was very fortunate to own such a lucrative

corporation, Low thought while entering the waiting area, and making his way to the reception window. Gloria, Tony's niece was sitting behind a desk. She was twenty-one, a few years older than Low, but he had a thing for her.

When she looked up from her work, and saw Low approaching, a smile framed her pretty face. She set aside her typing, stepped from behind her desk, and waited at the reception window.

"Hello, how may I help you today, sir?" Gloria asked with a sexy Cuban accent.

Returning her smile, Low knew she was being formal because someone was in earshot sitting in the waiting area. He kept it professional, and stuck to the business hour routine while their eyes did all the flirting.

"Yes, I'm here for my scheduled job interview," Low said, letting Gloria know he was here to see Tony.

"Oh yes. He's expecting you," she said, reaching for the office's conference phone before continuing. "Have a seat, and he should be with you shortly."

She dialed Tony's office extension. Low went to the waiting area, and took a seat next to a White guy, dressed in an expensive looking Italian suit. Picking up a Time magazine, Low skimmed through the pages. The man wearing a pair of dark Armani shades glanced at Low. His eyes grew wide with awe at the watch that adorned Low's wrist.

"Nice watch you got there, kid," he said, giving the moving VVS diamonds that flooded the face of Low's Chopard an in depth examination. Then he asked, "How'd you get your hands on that sucker?"

Low's facial expression grew into a sly grin. Looking up from the magazine, he said, "It was a gift."

"I see."

"Why...? What do you know about Chopards anyway?"

"Oh, I know all about Chopards," the man smiled, pulling back the sleeve of his Armani suit just a bit. Then he continued. "Had two or three last year, but Chopards are played out. These are what the nineties bring."

He flashed an eighteen-carat yellow gold, Cartier Calandre on his wrist. It was flooded with so many diamonds that Low could hardly make out the watches Roman numerals.

"Nice," Low nonchalantly nodded in admiration.

"But it's nice to see that you've got good taste, kid," the man said, extending his hand before continuing. "I'm Michael O'Connell."

Gloria suddenly stepped into the waiting area, and said, "Excuse me. Mr. O'Connell, Mr. Morales would like to know if it would be okay with you if he conducted a quick job-interview before meeting with you?"

Glancing at his watch, Michael O'Connell said, "No problem."

"Thank you," Gloria said.

Then she nodded, and signaled for Low to follow her. Smiling he obliged while closely watching the sway of her ass.

✦ ✦ ✦

"Milowcito!" Tony greeted with a rueful smile as Low entered his office.

"Hey Tony…"

"We missed you last night. We had a little celebration here with the fellas. Roberto said you had a personal issue to take care of. I hope everything's alright."

"Yeah, everything's cool," Low said, sitting down. The he continued, "So Rob was here celebrating last night?"

"Oh no, Roberto was too tired to party," Tony chuckled then continued. "He passed… Said he had to get some shuteye. Such professionals. I will greatly miss you guys' loyalty and hard work. You two have really come through in a major way for me. I wanna thank you."

"Damn…" Low sighed.

"I know papi. Everything must eventually come to an end. We had a wonderful ride though. But hey…"

Tony smiled, walking to a huge safe mounted in the far corner of his office. Then he continued. "You two are now fifty thousand dollars richer."

Flabbergasted, Low struggle for something to say, but before he could, Tony continued.

"If you guys invest correctly then you two won't ever have to look back. I mean look at me. I wasn't always the biggest car dealer in Miami, you know?"

Low unzipped the duffle bag, and peeked inside. It immediately became crystal clear that Tony was not only oblivious to Rob's predicament, but he definitely had nothing to do with it.

"Fifty thousand…?" Low asked in confusion.

"Oh yes, papi," Tony smiled then continued. "I see that you and Roberto haven't spoken yet. Just a little bonus—a token of my appreciation."

"Okay…"

"Now don't go spending it all on the mamacitas," Tony joked.

"Nah, definitely not." Low said, standing.

He reached into his pockets, and pulled out Tony's car keys. Then Low zipped the duffle bag, and tossed the keys to Tony.

"Thanks for the ride," Low nodded.

"No… Thank you," Tony said, extending his hand.

Low grabbed the duffle bag, and left to continue his search for answers. He was walking away when Gloria came into the waiting area.

"Mr. O'Connell… Mr. Morales will see you now," Gloria smiled.

"Thank you," O'Connell smiled.

O'Connell followed Gloria down a long hallway. They headed to the complex's main vehicle storage area.

"Manito, come on inside" Tony greeted, looking up from the platform.

Michael O'Connell entered through a side doorway behind Gloria. They slowly came down the steps, leading down to the platform of the massively huge main vehicle storage area. Tony excused himself from a conversation he was having with one of his mechanics, and made his way toward O'Connell.

"Hey, hey! My Cuban compadre," O'Connell beamed.

The two men embraced. Then O'Connell wore a huge grin when he said, "I thought you were going to leave me out in that waiting room to rot."

"Oh no, no. At least not in such a fine looking suit," Tony laughed.

The two shared a laugh, and O'Connell said, "Today's a big day for me. Had to pull out the best for the occasion. But you're not dressed so bad yourself, Rico Suave.

Tony was wearing a silk rose-colored Versace shirt, with matching Versace pants, and shoes. Smiling Tony said, "Just like you…today is also a very big day for me."

Tony nodded at Gloria, and she went back up the steel staircase. Tony motioned for O'Connell to follow him, and continued. "You see my friend, in business presentation is everything.

Leading the way to a section of the platform where twenty vehicles sat side by side, parked in a long row. They were covered, concealing the cars' bodies. Tony pointed to the covered vehicles, and said, "A year ago, we met and agreed to a fifty-fifty partnership. In that agreement my friend, I promised you twenty sports cars within a twelve-month span. I gave you my word that I would be able to deliver on time, and not a day later, right? Well…"

Tony paused and called out to two of his mechanics then he continued. "Today, making good on my word, I present to you the fruits of that agreement."

After snapping his fingers, two technicians started removing the coverings from all the cars, and O'Connell's eyes immediately lit up.

"Wow!" O'Connell smiled.

While O'Connell surveyed the fleet of stolen cars, Tony wore a satisfied grin. Putting his arms around O'Connell's shoulder, Tony said, "Take a good look. We're a wire transfer away from becoming twenty-five million dollars richer." Turning to his mechanics, Tony continued. "Bring me my cigars and a bottle of champagne."

Within a minute the mechanics returned with a box of Cohiba cigars, and a chilled bottle of Dom Perignon, along with two flute-shaped champagne glasses.

One of them poured two glasses for Tony and O'Connell while the other mechanic brought the Cohiba.

"A taste of Cuba's finest cigar," Tony smiled.

The mechanic held a matches for them. Tony and O'Connell prepared to toast champagne while puffing on cigars.

"A small token of my appreciation," Tony said, taking a puff on his cigar, and extending his champagne glass. Then he continued. "And a toast to a new found partnership, and more business to come."

"Here's to a new partnership," O'Connell said with a wide grin.

The beeping horn of a truck disturbed the fiesta, and O'Connell continued. "Sounds like the ride for the cars is here." O'Connell then drank the rest of his champagne, and handed the glass to a mechanic.

"Buenos!" Tony chimed.

Stepping into action, Tony began barking orders in Spanish to his entire staff of mechanics and technicians, directing them to prepare the sports cars for loading.

"I'm going to tell the driver that we'll be ready to roll shortly," O'Connell said.

Tony watched O'Connell making his way toward a side exit door, leading to the back of the storage complex where the loading docks were located.

"Okay, sure," Tony said, and continued giving orders to his staff.

Everyone was at work preparing the sports cars to be loaded, and Tony called out to his lead mechanic Bolo.

"Oye Bolo. Activate the service gates," Tony ordered.

One of the mechanics revved the classic cherry red Tesla Roadster, and waited for the signal to proceed.

"Right away, boss," Bolo said, making his way over to the control panel of the loading-unloading docks.

The massive service gates simultaneously began to rise. Miami's afternoon sunlight instantly darted inside from under the gates. The intensely bright sunlight temporarily blinded Tony while he attempted to gaze outside. When his vision adjusted, his eyes locked in on the caravan of unmarked cruisers on the other end of the loading docks, and Tony instantly realized he made a grave mistake.

"FBI FREEZE!"

The next several minutes seemed to play out in slow motion. Four masked federal agents filed through the side exit door. Nine large aluminum cans were simultaneously shot onto the platform from outside. The element of surprise was highly in the federal agents' favor. Tony and his crew of mechanics attempts at fleeing were short lived. The four flash bombs exploded temporarily blinding everyone. Smoke was everywhere. Dressed in full tactical gear, equipped with gas masks, and armed with fully automatic submachine guns, the fifty-man crew of federal agents from the FBI's Grand Theft Auto Division filed into the storage warehouse.

"Get down on the ground. Everyone! Down on the ground!"

Each member of Tony's staff dropped to their knees in surrender, but Tony wasn't going down without a fight. The butt of an agent's MP5 sub-machine gun made contact with the back of his head. Tony gave up, and allowed the feds to do their work.

"Make sure everything's tagged, and lets take everyone downtown!" the lead FBI agent shouted.

CHAPTER
14

ICU

Low walked through the sliding doors, and entered the emergency room entrance. He was visiting Rob at the University of Miami Hospital. The intoxicatingly strong, sanitized smell brought an instant frown to Low's face. He hated hospitals because they brought back bad memories of when his father was killed.

His recollection of these dark moments was locked away in a corner of his brain, and never revisited. Low stepped into the waiting room of the Intensive care Unit, and saw the same grim facial expressions of all the people scattered about the room.

Her back was to him, and she stared out a rectangular-shaped window, but Low immediately spotted Rob's Aunt Lucile. He saw her signature black and yellow Pittsburgh Steelers fitted-cap that she always wore backward. All the neighborhood drug dealers called her 'Lucile the Steel'. She got her heroin-bundles from them to support her, and her lesbian lover, Precious', extensive needle-itch on the daily.

Lucile turned in time to see Low approaching. The beginnings of a warm smile spread quickly across her face when they shared a heartfelt hug.

"Hey you," Lucile greeted with a grin that was toothless and wide.

"Hey Aunt Lu," Low affectionately replied.

His somber mood made it difficult to even fake a smile. Placing the duffle bag on a nearby foldout chair, Low asked, "How long you been here, Aunt Lu?"

She motioned for them to sit, and said, "Well the whole thing went-down right in my backyard. So I've been with him ever since the paramedics arrived. Them pigs didn't let me ride up here in the ambulance with him. So as soon as they took off, I hopped in Precious' car and immediately hit the road behind them muthafuckas, you know? Been here waiting on word of his progress."

"Damn... How's Precious taking it?"

"Oh man...she's taking it pretty hard. She was soo distraught by the whole thing... She was the first one to look out the window after the shooting stopped. When she saw Rob laid out like..." Her voice trailed, and tears flowed freely down Lucille's cheeks.

Low rose from his seat, and grabbed a box of tissues that sat in front of them on a coffee table. For a couple of minutes, all was silent. Low consoled Lucille by rubbing her back. The only sounds were of Michael Jackson's, *Billie Jean* music video playing at a low volume on a small black and white television in the far corner of the waiting room.

"You know, Rob loves this damn song soo much," Lucile sobbed, wiping away the moisture from her face while gazing at the television screen. She had a faint smile when she continued. "Caught him singing this shit at the top of his lungs in the shower last week."

Her comment brought a smile to Low's face. He knew that Rob was a down-low fan of Michael Jackson.

Low inhaled, and slowly exhaled. He was preparing to ask the question he was dreading.

"So you think I can see him?" Low asked.

"He's in police custody, and the hospital's policy is only immediate family can, but I went to high school with the cop guarding his door. He's cool. Plus, ain't no family member more immediate than his brother, right?"

"Yes, we thicker than blood."

"I know, baby," Lu said. Then standing, she continued. "Follow me. I'll take you to him."

Lucille led the way out of the waiting room, and they walked to the room where a middle-aged police officer sat guarding the door. Lifting his head slightly from the magazine he was reading, the officer glanced at Low. Then his eyes hit the duffle bag in Low's hand. He was about to say something, but instead his eyes darted to Lucile.

"Family...?" The officer asked with his eyebrows raised.

Reaching into his shirt pocket, the officer pulled out a pen. Then started scribbling on a clipboard on his lap.

"Brother," Lucile said.

The officer nodded, and made a notation on his clipboard. Then he went back to reading his magazine.

"Go ahead, he's in there. Tell him I said hi," Lucille softly smiled then walked away.

"Hold on, you're not coming in with me?" Low asked.

"I can't. But I know he's been waiting to speak to you. Just tell him I said hi. I'll be in the waiting room."

Taking a deep breath, Low reached for the door handle. He exhaled slowly, mentally preparing for what was awaiting him on the other side. After quietly shutting the door behind him, Low found himself in a short hallway. To his left was a bathroom held open by a small aluminum trashcan. A candle shaped nightlight shone from atop a porcelain sink, and straight ahead, he saw light from a small color television. It was on a wall-mounted stand facing the foot of the hospital bed. A rerun of a *Yo! MTV Raps* could hardly be heard over the loud beeping sounds coming from a large cardiac monitoring machine. It sat just below the television, and beeped every few seconds.

Low stood in the doorway, and was unsure if he wanted to go any further or turn around and just leave. His heart was beating at a rapid pace, and the feeling of anxiety to leave was becoming overwhelming, but turning around wasn't an option. Rob was his right hand man, and not speaking to him would be like turning his back and abandoning his brother. All the homework, plotting, and scheming they did together over the years never prepared them for this moment. Low slowly made his way down the hallway until Rob's body came into view. An intense feeling agitated him, and stopped Low dead in his tracks.

In an effort to calm his nerves, Low took another deep breath, and willed himself forward. Then he saw Rob's face, and Low lost all composure. His emotions completely took over, and he burst out crying.

"Damn, what the fuck...?" Low tearfully grimaced.

The duffle bag slipped from his grasp, and crashed to the hospital room floor with a thud. The sight of Rob lying there with his whole head bandaged, and all kinds of tubes attached to his body brought an intense burning feeling to Low's heart. He had never felt this way before.

Reaching the edge of the bed, Low peered at Rob's motionless body with his left eye shut. The entire right side of his face was covered with surgical gauze. Low cried harder, and tears flooded his eyes, flowing freely down his face. The clear tubes coming from Rob's mouth and nostrils were connected to a clear circular oxygen machine with a pump moving up and down inside with every breath that Rob took.

"I feel fucked up," Low said, feeling guilty, and wiping tears from his eyes with the back of his hand. Shaking his head, Low continued. "Man, if I would've been more on-point, and stuck to the game plan you wouldn't even be here." Low reached for Rob's hand, and taking a knee beside the bed, he said, "Tony paid us. He even threw in an extra ten stacks to our cause. We did it, my nigga. We fifty up."

Letting out another deep sigh, Low gathered his thoughts then continued. "Best believe, just because you laid-up right now, shit don't stop. I'll hold us down. You got my word Rob. We brothers 'til death, ya heard me?"

Low felt one of Rob's fingers twitching in his hand. Nodding he said, "I know you hear me, Rob." Then he stood, and said, "Stay strong Rob. We been through worse, feel me…? So fight, my nigga. Show these crackers that they can't kill you cause you ain't ready to die. Nigga, we warriors, and warriors die on their own time."

He glanced at the leather duffle bag on the floor then Low said, "I don't even know what's next, Rob. But I do know we done with this car stealing shit. Just know that whatever I decide to do I'm a do it for us, and go hard. We grinded too much not to succeed…ya dig? Trust me Rob, I'm a do what it do with that fifty. Believe that! Ain't no fucking looking back. When you do wake up, my nigga we'll be up. I put my soul on that."

Low intertwined his fingers with Rob's. He brought the web between their pinkies and ring fingers together, and held Rob's hand firmly in their signature handshake.

"I love you, my brother. But now it's time for me to get back to work."

Leaning close, Low kissed the gauze on Rob's forehead. Then he walked away. Picking up the duffle bag, Low made his way to the door. He reached for the steel doorknob knowing that a chapter in his life was officially closed.

PART 2
THE GAME

CHAPTER
15

RAZOR

The bright sunshine beamed on him as he exited the hospital. Low's eyes immediately squinted as he gazed across the street at the Metro bus stop. The thought of waiting in the scorching heat for a bus made perspiration trickled from his forehead. This was an activity he wasn't looking forward to doing.

Only a few feet away, there was a taxi stand with plenty cabs available. The fare from downtown to Lil' Haiti was not cheap. Low was considering spending the extra cash to hop in a cab, and escape the heat. To his relief, he saw a bus coming. Low hurriedly stepped onto the bus, and was preparing to pay his fare. Suddenly the realization that he didn't have any change hit him.

"Damn!" Low said in frustration.

The duffle bag contained only large bills, and unzipping it in public wasn't an option. Low was about to get off the bus when he heard his name being called.

"Milow…?"

Low stared skeptically at the dreadlocked man making his way from the back of the bus with three Macy's shopping bags. At first glance, Low couldn't identify the person. But staring intensely at the man, he realized it was his cousin, Riche A.K.A. Razor.

"Oh shit, Razor… It's been a while."

"Yeah nigga, I see you can't even recognize your own blood," Razor said with a wide grin that was accented by a diamond cut grill.

"Man, honestly for a second there I didn't," Low said.

"I know," Razor chuckled.

They embraced then Low asked, "Damn, when the hell did you grow your hair that long?"

"Excuse me, I hate to break-up y'all family reunion, but ya need to hurry the hell up, and pay ya damn fare so the bus driver can drive!" an old lady said with an indignant tone. Giving Razor and Low an evil look, she continued. "Shoot, I've been working all day, and my feet hurt!"

"Whoa! Slow ya roll, grandma," Razor chuckled. Then reaching into the pocket of his Gucci shorts, he paid the fare, and continued. "We don't want problems."

"Damn Milow, it's been like two years since we've seen each other?" Razor said.

The two sat down across from one another. Then Low said, "Yeah cuz. Damn near three."

"For real?"

"Last time we spoke I was in the ninth grade at Edison. Your mom had just moved out the hood to Miami Springs, and transferred you to Jackson Senior High."

"Damn, the old Edison High days, huh…?" Razor said, reminiscing.

"I remembered all that…"

"Whatever happened to that kid you use to always be with?"

"Who you talking 'bout?"

"You know…the one who stole the principle's Benz that time, and y'all ended up putting the school police on a high-speed chase through the hood. What's that nigga's name again?"

"You mean Rob…?"

"Yeah, Rob…" Razor quipped, snapping his fingers. Then he continued. "Damn, I haven't seen that fool in a minute. What's good with Rob? Y'all still into cars and shit?"

"Rob straight. We left that splak game alone," Low said.

"That's good. So Milow, what you be into nowadays? You nine to five, or just grinding?"

"I'm getting by," Low nonchalantly shrugged, returning Razor's smile.

"The watch you wearing says you beg to differ…"

"Shit, you ain't doing too bad yourself, I see. Got the hair going, the grill shining, and jewel game on point, Gucci shorts…a few Macy's bags… Damn nigga, put me on!"

The two men nodded, sharing knowing smiles. Then Razor nodded, and shifted the conversation. He said, "Say little cuz, my stop's coming up next. You're free to roll with me if you ain't busy. I'll make sure you get a ride home."

"Okay…" Low said without a second thought.

✦ ✦ ✦

Located in the Ti-Mache shopping plaza, Sunny's Electronics Shop was a few blocks outside Lil' Haiti. From the latest in beepers and sky-pagers to the most recent innovation in communication, the cellphone, Sunny's offered the best in electronics and accessories. The store also boasted an extensive jewelry section, and a music section with the latest albums and chart topping releases.

However the entire establishment was a front for the main headquarters of South Florida's most notorious crime syndicate, the Zoe Pound. Razor and Low entered the shop to the sound of jingling bells hanging above the glass door.

The owner, Sunny Fats was seated in his custom leather cushioned stool. A large amount of cash, a small pile of thick white rubber bands, and an electronic money counting machine sat on the glass display counter in front of him. Looking up from behind the jewelry section, Sunny peered toward the front of the store.

"Goddamn! It's about time, Zoe! I was a few minutes away from closing for the day, and sending a squad of goons out to look for you."

"I paged you like five times with no response, Zoe. You could've at least paged me back. You got to check in… Got a nigga thinking all types of shit."

"My fault, Sunny," Razor said, extending his hand, and greeting Sunny with a firm handshake.

"Fucking Zoe-Man was bullshitting. Honestly I'd have been back an hour ago. But you know how that old muthafucka likes chattin' 'bout Haitian politics, and sports back home and shit. Zoe-Man held a nigga hostage all day talking."

Razor placed three Macy's bags on top of the display counter next to the money. Then he continued. "This my lil' cousin, Low—Low, this is Sunny Fats, and that pretty, young thang right there is his stuck-up-ass niece, Lavisha."

Sunny and Low greeted each other with handshakes. Low nodded politely to the woman standing next to Sunny. She was holding a Texas Instrument desktop calculator, and wearing a floor manager's tag. Lavisha rolled her eyes at Razor, and continued to punch figures into her calculator.

Surveying the stacks of money on top of the glass counter, Razor said, "But say Sunny, you tripping counting all this money out here like this, Zoe. Shit, me and lil' cuz could've been Jack-boys out this bitch."

"Ha! Jack-boys...?" Sunny chuckled.

Sunny Fats then grabbed a black Heckle & Koch M4 machine gun by the shoulder strap, and placed it on the counter in front of him.

"Don't let this big belly fool ya. I'm Karma to the bone! I don't workout, but my trigger finger stay in shape."

"Okay then, playboy. Just making sure y'all on point 'round here," Razor smiled.

Razor already knew the deal, but anytime he could get Sunny riled up he jumped at it. This time, he got to Sunny.

"Jack boys!" Sunny said, looking at the shop's half-opened basement door. "Walter, you hear this shit? Razor think we scared of some Jack boys!"

Footsteps were heard racing up the wooden steps. A man wearing black fishnet tank top with thin cream colored linen shorts, black Ferragamo shoes, and a blue and red Haitian flag bandanna wrapped around his head came upstairs. Walter was looking truly Haitian, and the black submachine gun dangling from his neck made him dangerous.

"That nigga said what?" Walter exclaimed in thick Haitian accent. His gold grill was gleaming when he smiled as he continued. "Come on, Zoe, why you trying Sunny like that?"

"Oh, oh..." Razor jokingly said as he reached out to Walter.

Embracing Razor, Walter said, "You know we never slipping 'round here, Zoe."

"I just love to get Sunny going. But when you get back from Ayiti?"

"Me and King Zoe got back this morning. I'm tired as shit from being on that damn plane. Shit, soon as King Zoe dropped me here. I headed straight downstairs to take a snooze. Just woke up."

"Okay then, Zoe. This my lil' cousin, Low. This is Sunny's nephew, Walter," Razor said to Low.

Walter and Low nodded in acknowledgement. Then Sunny rose from his seat, made his way from behind the display counter, and said, "Well since we all here, we've gotta tighten up cause King Zoe will be here in about an hour. And I don 't even wanna hear Zoe mouth if we ain't got everything ready for him.

"Me neither. So let's get this done," Walter said.

Razor grabbed the Macy's shopping bags off the counter. Sunny placed a five thousand dollar stack into the Louis Vuitton bag, and zipped it shut.

"Lavisha, go lock up the shop for the day, and clean the rest of this place up," Sunny instructed.

Then grabbing the LV duffle bag, Sunny led the way to the basement's door. Just before walking out, Razor pulled out a hundred dollar bill, turned to Low, and said, "Say lil' cuz, here…buy yourself a few tapes, a new beeper or something. I'm 'bout to go handle something… Be about fifteen to twenty minutes."

Low was walking around the store, checking out the merchandise when Lavisha came up behind him, and asked, "So you're Razor's cousin huh?"

Low turned his attention away from a huge Public Enemy album release poster adorning the wall behind the music section, and gazed at Lavisha's pretty face. Her light brown eyes sparkled as she stared back at him.

"Um, yeah that's big cuz," Low smiled.

His eyes drifted from Lavisha's pretty face to the massive submachine gun as she effortlessly lifted the weapon off the glass counter, and placed it out of sight.

"You two don't get along or something?" Low asked, surveying all the varieties of beepers, and sky pagers on display.

"Razor is a Zoe. He's cool. But sometimes he just gets on my damn nerves," Lavisha said, rolling her eyes.

She returned to cleaning off the counter. Low immediately concluded that Lavisha and Razor must have had something going on in the past. Her tone and facial expression made him certain of that.

"So where you from?" Lavisha asked.

"Lil' Haiti," Low said.

"Oh really…? I've lived in the hood my whole life. Never seen you before though," Lavisha said.

"It be like that in the hood," Low shrugged.

He glanced at a money-green sky pager. The sound of footsteps, and loud laughter was heard. The basement's door swung open.

"Nigga, stop joking! Zoe, you for real?" Razor asked, laughing.

"Nigga, I put that on Zoe Pound," Sunny said.

"I hear that," Razor smiled.

"I told that rat-bastard, J-Blaze, you got two options. Either you take this gun and put a bullet in your head or jump out the window… Take your chances out there… He must've not respected them ten floors. Maybe he thought he was superman or some shit. Me an Walter couldn't believe he really jumped!"

The three men shared the joke, and burst out in laughter. Then Razor said, "Man, y'all two are something else. Now 'em Zombies gonna trace that kill back to us, and be on some revenge shit, right?"

Razor's warning seemed to fuel Sunny, he said, "Muthafuck them Zombies! If they wanna ride for that rat...so be it! Every last one of them fucking niggas can get it."

At forty-seven, Sunny was twice Razor's, and Walter's age. Sunny was of King Zoe's generation. They had over twenty-seven years of thug life under their belts.

"Fuck it," Razor shrugged. Then he continued. "Sunny you remember to get my car washed, right?"

"Yeah, took care of that earlier," Sunny said, reaching in his pockets, and tossing Razor the car keys.

"Okay. So what time y'all boys heading over to Silk's tonight? I got a few stops to make, and I'm tired as hell. I might need to get some rest at the crib before I head over."

"'Round midnight," Walter said, glancing at his gold Presidential Rolex.

"When the fuck niggas start making early appearances at the club?"

"Ever since Silk told us we can't get in strapped if we show up at his shit after one. He don't want his security team dealing with the added stress," Walter said.

"When did that shit start?" Razor asked.

"A few nights ago, we got there 'round one-thirty... Had to go back to the parking lot, and leave our guns in the car," Sunny said.

"That's that bullshit. I'm the one that put the security team together! Silk done fucked around, and let this club ownership get to his head. King Zoe put the club in his name. And this nigga think he can start making up rules now?"

"That's it..."

"You know what...? Y'all niggas don't even sweat that shit, man. I'm gonna have a chat tonight with Silk," Razor said. Then he waved at Low to follow him, and the two walked out.

✦ ✦ ✦

The entire sky was illuminated to orange as the sun
began to set, leaving the entire Northwest side of Miami
calm. During this serene thirty-minute period separating day from night, law-abiding citizens of the city were
approaching the driveways of their homes after a long
day of work.

Around this time, the city's prostitutes, pimps,
thieves, dealers, and users were just waking up. They
were preparing themselves for a night of adventure.

Razor led the way to a corner of the parking lot.
Low noticed that the three Macy's shopping bags Razor
entered Sunny's shop with earlier had been replaced
with a Louis Vuitton duffle bag. They walked-by several
parked cars, and continued toward the far corner of the
lot. Razor pulled out his car keys, and deactivated the
car's alarm. Then he instantly activated his car's headlights. Razor's Beluga black, 964 Porsche Carrera 4 came
into full view.

Low's eyes instantly sprung wide-open in awe, and
he said, "Oh snap! That whips hard as fuck!"

Low peered inside the two-door sports car, illuminated with bright-red dome lights that set off the interi-
or's beige leather, suede-trimmed seats.

"This the newest model… These bitches ain't even
being sold yet!" Low exclaimed, sounding like a sports
car expert.

"Yeah, you know your big cousin gotta stay up to
date," Razor said with a wide grin.

Pressing another button on his keys, Razor popped
the Porsche's trunk, and said, "Don 't just stand there.
Throw your bag in the trunk with mines, and get in."

Public Enemy, *Don't Believe The Hype,* blasted
through the four fifteen-inch speakers of the Porsche's
Pioneer stereo system with explosive bass. Low sat

securely behind the passenger seat's red colored racing seatbelt, puffing on a hash filled Garcia Vega that had him coughing. Razor gunned it down N.W. 32nd Avenue, heading in the direction of Carol City. He had already made four other quick stops to collect money. He made a right turn on N.W 182nd Street. Before he could head home, Razor needed to make one other stop.

"Damn cuz, don't kill yourself. You a'ight?" Razor chuckled.

"Yeah, I'm straight," Low said, passing Razor the cigar.

"Yeah cuz! That's Haiti's finest for ya!" Razor chimed with a wide grin. "Then Walter snuck a whole pound of that shit on the plane with him. Walter's crazy."

"That shit got a nigga straight! I'mma need a lil' of that shit to take to the crib… I never been so damn high in my life!" Low exclaimed.

"Ha, ha. Yeah, no doubt cuz!" Razor said, passing Low the cigar.

Reaching inside the glove, Razor pulled out a chrome Magnum Dessert Eagle, and placed it on his lap. Then he grabbed the magazine, and continued. "Put that out so you can come with me. This my last stop before we head to my crib. Let's ride."

Opening the driver's side door, Razor got out. Low followed behind him. They made their way through a broken down fence into the yard of the shabby gray painted trap house. Low quickly examined the thick wood riddled with bullet holes. Suddenly a couple female crack heads emerged, scaring Low.

"Hey Zoe!" The crack heads greeted Razor.

Razor nodded then sucked his teeth in aggravation. He went around the corner to the side, and saw the reason why the crack-heads were walking out the wrong fucking way after they finished copping.

The sight of one of Razor's lookouts reclined on a black milk crate, fast asleep, and snoring greeted them. The lookout's head was leaned up against the side of the trap house.

"Fuck! This idiot, Streets is sleeping…?" Razor hissed, and his blood pressure seemed to rise.

Desert Eagle in hand, and his eyes glued to the sleeping lookout, Razor inched his way closer. When he was in the lookout's face, he shouted, "Rise and shine!"

Razor's order immediately startled the lookout. Then Razor leaned forward, and stuck the barrel of his gun into Streets' open mouth. Streets came to life, his eyes bulging. The sight of Razor's scowl made him visibly shook. Streets tried to swallow, but the massive gun in his mouth prevented him from doing so.

"Fuck you doing, Streets?" Razor angrily asked.

While struggling for an answer, pee began slowly trickling down Streets' thighs. Then gagging, he said, "My fault, Zoe. I just drifted off for a quick sec—"

"Shut the fuck up!" Razor snapped.

He angrily snatched Streets by the collar of his black T-shirt, and forcefully lifted him to his feet. Then he said, "Muthafucka, this the second time I caught you slipping! You supposed to be the lookout! Do you know what the fuck lookout means?"

Streets stayed silent. Tears were running down his face, and his moist eyes begged for mercy.

"Answer me!" Razor ordered.

Streets quickly nodded his head up and down. Then Razor said, "I can't fucking tell! Not only do you have crack-heads going the wrong fucking way after they cop, but you're totally oblivious to anything going on cause you're fucking asleep. What if I was a jack boy? Matter fact…where's your fucking gun?" Razor asked.

Razor turned around to Low, and waved him over. When Low walked to where Razor and Streets were,

Razor said, "Cuz, search this fool!"

Streets found himself pinned against the side of the house, and Low patted around Streets' waistband until he felt a bulge in the small of Streets' back.

"Here it goes, cuz," Low said, reaching under Streets' long, black T-shirt, and pulling out a nine millimeter Berretta. He handed it to Razor.

"Nah, that's you, cuz. Keep it. This muthafucka doesn't deserve to carry no fucking pistol!"

Razor removed his gun from Streets' mouth, and struck him with a vicious backhand to the face. Streets grimaced in pain, and let out an agonizing yelp while spitting out a mouthful of blood.

"Nigga, since you can't stay awake sitting down. From now on, you keep lookout while you jog around this whole fucking block. Until you learn how to stay up, and alert for an eight-hour shift. Now get the fuck out my face!"

Streets' facial expression registered displeasure, but he valued his life. He away without so much as a verbal protest. Then reluctantly, he started running.

"Can't believe that young nigga," Razor said, shaking his head then continued toward the trap house.

With a joyful smirk, Low tucked away the new piece in his waistband, and followed Razor to the back of the trap house.

✦ ✦ ✦

Ghost and Gunner

Twin brothers, Ghost and Gunner—Razor's most trusted workers were born October 1st. '74. Their mother, a dope fiend, sold her body on Biscayne Boulevard to support her heavy drug addiction that ultimately led to her demise from a heroin overdose in '85. Their father, a well-known pimp on 'the Cayne', watched his money, and status fade once he caught the 'dope-itch' himself. He allowed his hungry habit to get out of control, and a few months after his twin's mother died, he did.

Ghost and Gunner inevitably became products of the crime-ridden environment—the streets of Carol City—at a very early age. During 1987 when Razor officially became a member of Zoe Pound, he brought the young Ghost and Gunner along with him. As he began putting his narcotics operation in motion, Razor took them under his wing as protégés. By '89, Razor had established a great drug empire—over twenty-five trap houses set up in, and around the city of Miami. His operation sold everything including weed, cocaine, crack, and heroin.

Business was quite lucrative, raking in over three hundred and fifty thousand dollars in weekly revenue. Now Razor mostly played the background. He stayed off the radar as he tried to network with more established connections locally, and internationally to sufficiently supply his narcotics enterprise.

While Razor did all the networking, he gave his protégés the positions of lieutenants. Ghost and Gunner provided direct supervision to the workers, and played the roles of enforcers. Within two years, Razor had molded the twins into a pair of heartless, cold, calculated killers. Razor fed, clothed, and housed the brothers, raising them like his own siblings.

Over the years Razor grew in power and status, and so did the twins. They were loyal to him, and willing to do anything, even kill on-sight. Unlocking the gated back door of the trap house, Razor and Low stepped into a pitch-black hallway. The only light illuminating from inside the trap was coming from the screen of a small thirteen-inch black and white television that sat atop of a bunch of folded blankets in the far corner of the desolated living room. Music video from *Yo MTV Raps Spring Bash* blared.

"Who goes there?" A voice shouted.

Suddenly an infrared beam instantly reflected off the wall in the hallway, and lit their position.

"One tough-ass Zoe," Razor said.

Razor and Low entered the living room. Ghost sat on a metal foldout chair behind a cheap plastic table littered with cigarette butts, and beer cans.

"Big homey! What it do, Zoe?" Ghost greeted.

Then Ghost turned off the infrared laser attached to the top of the sub-machine gun clutched in his hands. He placed the high capacity weapon on top of the table.

"Everything's, everything," Razor said, extending a closed fist to Ghost, and giving him dap. Then he continued. "Other than the fact that I just caught Streets sleeping again. This my lil' cousin, Low."

Ghost and Low greeted each other with daps. Razor heard a muffled moan coming from the kitchen area.

"So where the hell is Country at?" Razor asked.

A toilet could be heard flushing, as Gunner emerged from the bathroom. A black nine-millimeter was tightly clutched in his hand.

"Man, I'm a let him tell you, Zoe," Ghost said.

"Come see what I got for ya," Gunner said then signaled for Razor to follow him into the kitchen.

Razor and Low followed Gunner. Ghost immediately rose from his seat, and followed as well. The sight of Country lying on the kitchen's dirty tile floors greeted them. Country was butt-naked, and hog-tied with duct tape covering his mouth. Stretched out on the floor alongside Country were a man and woman. Razor recognized them as customers from the area. They were stripped of all their clothing, hog-tied and duct-taped.

"What the fuck is this?" Razor asked, glancing at Gunner for an explanation.

"It seems like we have an infiltrator on our hands, boss," Gunner said.

Making his way over to Country, Gunner grabbed him by his locks and forcefully lifted him up to his knees. Then he said, "Not only is this bitch-ass nigga an undercover crack head that's been shortening the packs we've been giving him so he could get high on the side." Gunner stuck the barrel of his.9mm to Country's temple, and continued. "But word on the street is this fat mutha-fucka's a paid informant for Miami Vice."

Gunner ripped the duct tape from Country's face, and Country immediately began to plead his case to Razor.

"Please, please don't believe it, Zoe. It's not true. I ain't no snitch," Country begged, tears flowing freely down his chubby cheeks.

Easing his hand under his Polo shirt, Razor pulled out his Desert Eagle, and calmly asked, "How'd you find out this information?"

Gunner smiled, released his grip on Country, and made his way over to the female crack head. Naked, her hands and feet were bound. Pulling her up to her knees, Gunner said, "This Omi. She'll tell you all you need to know, boss."

Gunner ripped the duct tape covering Omi's mouth. When she saw Razor, her eyes widened as she licked her lips. She couldn't wait to start yapping.

"It's true, Zoe. He's a fucking thief, and a snitch!"

Scratching his temple with the barrel of his Desert Eagle. Razor inhaled loudly, and asked, "And how are you so sure of this accusation?"

"Because Sergeant Foley, the head of the third division drug task-force is one of my tricks, and he told me so. I wasn't even going to put his business out there, but he tried to fucking play me! I suck his dick in here every night, and we got high together. But today he tried to kick me out without breaking me off. Fuck that!"

"That bitch is lying, Zoe! I fucking swear to God!" Country pleaded.

Unfortunately his trial ended quickly. Razor lifted his Desert Eagle, and pumped one deafeningly loud shot into Country's head.

"Damn boss. I just bought this fucking outfit!" Gunner said, looking at his brand new all white Karl Kani sweat suit, now ruined with blotches of Country's blood.

"So what does he have to do with this?" Razor asked, pointing to the other male crack head.

"Nothing really. He was just with her when we pulled up, and saw her blitzing on Country," Gunner shrugged.

"Y'all clean this shit up," Razor said, tucking the gun back in his waistband.

Both Razor and Low walked down a dark hallway leading to the trap's back door. They were just about to exit when they heard Gunner asked, "Boss, what the fuck we 'pose to do with these two?"

"Do what you want," Razor said without turning around.

CHAPTER

16

I WANT IN

Razor pulled to a stop at the security gate of Biscayne Bays' exclusive Palm Bay Luxury Villas, and punched his seven-digit pass code into the security gate's keypad. He waited as the gate slowly began to slide open, and drove onto Palm Bay's property. Razor pressed a small button on his Porsche's electronic dash console that activated one of the gates on his five-car garage to open up. He pulled into the garage, and stopped beside a car that was concealed under a black, silk car cover.

Blam and Haze, Razors two large Rottweiler dogs emerged from inside the huge house through a slide door with a square dog chute custom built into it. Razor shut off the Porsche's engine, and the two dogs began barking loudly in anticipation of their owner's arrival. Low immediately jumped up from his nap. He quickly surveyed his surroundings, and realized they were no longer on the road.

"Rise and shine sleeping beauty, we here," Razor said, getting out the car, and greeting his dogs.

The inside of Razor's garage was very big. Low walked into a mini car show. Many cars were lined up including a Porsche, a chromed out '79 Monte Carlo rag top, a rose colored '90 two-door Nissan 300ZX twin turbo sports car, and a classic blue-white striped '70 Shelby GT 500 convertible.

"Damn cuz. These whips tight as fuck!" Low beamed, admiring Razor's inventory of automotive eye-candy.

"A lil' sump'n…"

"So what's under this car cover?" Low asked.

Low's inquiry only brought a smile to Razor's face. He let out a slight chuckle, and said, "Grab the bags out the trunk and come on. Let me show you the crib. You remember Mildred right?"

"Yes, I do…" Low smiled.

"She's inside."

✦ ✦ ✦

Razor and Low entered the living room. Mildred, had just returned from her Lamaze class, and was taking a nap on a cushioned paternity rocking chair. She awoke smiling with joy at the sight of her fiancé's arrival. "Hey Baby!" She whispered with a warm smile.

"Hey, how was your Lamaze class?" asked Razor, greeting Mildred with a kiss on the lips.

Taking a knee beside her, Razor planted an affectionate kiss on Mildred's swollen stomach.

"Fine I guess. Other than the fact that you missed another class mister," Mildred said, playfully nudging Razor's chin.

"Sorry babe. Today was pretty hectic for me. You remember my lil' cuz, Milow, right?"

Mildred glanced at Low, and he nodded. She smiled, and said, "Oh the quarterback at Edison High, right?"

"Yeah," Razor chuckled.

"Hey, haven't seen you since the tenth grade. Good to see you," Mildred said.

"Time flies," Low said.

"A lot has changed since high school lil' cuz. Come with me Low," Razor said, heading to the stairs.

Low and Razor went upstairs, and went into a colossal-sized master bedroom. Suddenly one of the two sky-pagers clipped to Razor's waistband began to vibrate. After checking the call, Razor pulled out his gun, and tossed the large pistol on the king-sized waterbed.

"Low, you can just put the bags on the bed, and make yourself comfortable," Razor said.

Razor picked up a cordless phone, and dialed. Then he disappeared behind a sliding glass door, leading to an outdoor balcony. Planting both his and Razor's duffle bags at the foot of the bed, Low took a seat on the edge of the bed. He turned on a large Zenith television, and flipped through the channels. The sight of a familiar looking building on the news caused Low to listen intently to the news.

"Of all the owners of the twenty Classic sports cars obtained by the FBI earlier today, no name is more notable than Alex Daoud. He's the seasoned fifteen-year Republican politician, and mayor of Miami-Dade County. The car has become a centerpiece of the FBI raid. It was learned that the classic 1968 Ferrari GTO sports car was stolen from the driveway of his estate, located in the upscale community of Coconut Groves' Sunshine Village. This brazen heist took place while the mayor was attending a National Mayors summit in Boston. The alleged ringleader of this botched heist is a well known exotic car dealer, Antonio Morales..."

His stomach was in knots, and his heart sank when the mug shot of Cuban Tony flashed across the screen. Low felt like a ton of brick had just fallen on top of him.

The bottom fell out when the news reporter said, *"Authorities reported that Mayor Daoud's sports car is worth an estimated nine million dollars on the black market. Investigation is ongoing so authorities have not released all the details in this case. However the authorities are on the lookout for a man who has been seen on the building's security monitors leaving the establishment with a duffle bag moments before it was raided. He has been identified as Milow Pierre, an eighteen year old Black male—"*

A still photo of him walking out of Tony's warehouse flashed across the screen, and Low quickly turned off the television when he heard the balcony's sliding glass door. Razor walked into the bedroom with a fat grin on his face. Nodding, he was still speaking on the phone.

"A'ight, I'm 'bout to hop in the shower, and get ready right now!" Then Razor made his way to the bed, unzipped his LV duffle bag, and continued. "Cool, y'all just make sure y'all get in that muthafucka."

Hanging up, Razor tossed the cordless phone on the bed. Low stayed frozen, his mind and heart rate were racing faster than a Motor Cross Speedway. In an effort to calm his nerves, Low inhaled deeply, and tried to let it out slowly. His action only seemed to intensify his anxiety as the reality of his current predicament became quite evident in the frown lines of his expression.

"You alright, Low?" Razor asked with a raised eyebrow, staring at his cousin.

Low looked like he had just seen a ghost. He stood, took another deep breath, and locked eyes with Razor. Then Low said, "I want in."

His bold declaration brought a smirk to Razor's face. Chuckling, he reached into his duffle bag, and tossed out big rubber banded stacks of cash onto the bed.

"What you talkin' 'bout, Low?"

"Man, you know what I'm talking bout. I'm no

baby to this shit. I see how you and Zoe Pound getting down. Y'all getting major dough... I wanna roll like y'all, big cuz."

Razor shook his head then said, "It ain't that simple lil' cuz."

"What you mean?" Low asked.

"I mean this shit ain't like no fucking street gang! Being a Zoe isn't that damn simple. This shit takes sacrifice. Plus this street shit ain't no game, Low. It's some real life gangster shit. The money you see right here's dirty—filthy. We done shed blood for this... What you know 'bout that huh?"

Low tossed the remote on the bed, and unzipped his Filson duffle bag. Then he turned the bag upside down, and dumped all fifty thousand dollars on the waterbed.

"Here's my sacrifice. Keep it. I just want in."

"Bombo-claat!" Razor shouted in his best Patois accent. He paused then his eyes grew wide with amazement at the sight of the big pile of cash. After a few beats, Razor continued. "How the hell did you get all that?"

Low picked up the remote, and turned the television back on. The news report was still being aired.

"The authorities say that due to his alleged ties to the Mexican cartel, he is considered to be a flight risk. Morales will be held without bail, pending a special hearing. As for Milow Pierre, he has not yet been named an accomplice in this operation. He is still considered to be a person of high interest... And again, I would like to remind viewers that due to the violent circumstances surrounding this unfolding investigation, Mr. Pierre is currently being considered armed and extremely dangerous. So remember if you see or happen to come across this man, please call 911... Reporting live from Opa Locka, I'm La' Shauna Williams. Back to you Tom..."

Low turned off the television then tossed the remote onto the waterbed. He gazed up at Razor, and said, "Like you, I've shed blood for mines."

Razor smiled, looking his little cousin dead in the eyes, he saw that killer instinct inside him. It was the same look he'd seen in the eyes of Ghost, Gunner, and every other member of Zoë Pound.

"You're really serious about this, huh?"

"As a heart attack."

"A'ight then... I'll tell you what, lil' cuz, put that money up in the closet," Razor said, pointing to a door beside the television.

"Okay..."

"In there you'll find some of my clothes that you can change into. Tonight, all the head Zoes are gonna be at Silk's Lounge for the Yo MTV Rap's Summer Bash After-Party. Trust me, I hear your hunger for more, young cuz. And trust, I know your current predicament got you all in, but there's still a lot more to becoming a Zoe than meets the eye. Your desire has officially been noted and will be forwarded to King Zoe. Your actions from now on will determine if you're truly built for this shit. In order for you to be recognized, I'm a have to vouch for you. From now on, every move you make is not only a reflection of the family it's now a direct reflection of me. So you're now officially under my personal microscope too, ya dig? I'm a give you one last chance to think about this move."

Taking a deep breath, Low nodded his head. He was absorbing everything Razor just told him.

"I'm all in, so ain't nothing else to say," Low said.

"Well alright then. The gloves are officially off. Welcome to the game."

Razor extended his fist out to Low, and gave him a pound that he brought to his chest signifying his introduction was from the heart. Razor put all his money back into his LV duffle bag, and made his way to the door.

"What's mine is yours. Just make sure you're dressed to impress. Tonight, all eyes gonna be on you. Rule number one…always look the part. I'm about to take a shower, and get dressed in the guest room. We leave for Silk's Lounge in an hour. Be ready."

CHAPTER
17

Silk's Lounge

Dressed from head to toe in Salvatore Ferragamo, Razor was looking every ounce of success. His beige three-piece linen suit, lightly tinted shades, and leather almond loafers on his feet were offset by the car Razor unleashed when he pulled the black silk cover off. The apple-green '90 Lamborghini Diablo was sparkling.

"Now this is how a Zoe hits the town. In style…" Razor said.

Low's eyes grew wide with awe, and he said, "Oh yeah! This shits fucking crazy!"

Razor wore a wide grin as he pressed a button on his keys activating both the car's suicide doors.

"Rule number two, never let anyone outshine you on your own turf," Razor smiled, making his way to the driver's side door.

Low was dressed in a silk cinnamon colored Armani shirt with diamond cuff links, accenting the diamonds flooding his Chopard watch. A pair of cinnamon colored Armani linen slacks, Ray-Ban aviators covering his eyes, a Borsalino fedora over his freshly shaved head, and Cole Haan loafers on his feet, Low felt like a million bucks.

"I usually don't bring her out, but there's gonna be a lot of out-of-town bitches and wanna-be-Willie's at the Lounge tonight. It's a must we make our presence felt in that bitch, and let these muthafuckas know they in the city of Zoes."

"That's right, cuz."

Low walked to the passenger side, and hopped in. Razor started the sports car, and revved the V-10 Turbo engine. He shifted into first gear, and zoomed out the garage. Placing the fedora on his lap, Low rested his freshly shaved head against the luxurious silk leather headrest, and smiled. If this was the life of a gangster then he wanted to be a gangster for life. Low's thoughts traveled as fast as the car flying down the highway.

They were headed to South Beach—better known as 'the strip' to locals. With its multi-million dollar high-rise estates overlooking the tropical Atlantic Ocean with breath-taking views, the endless miles of its flawlessly lavish, white sandy beaches, and carefree atmosphere, this was home to Miami's rich and famous.

The sunniest city of the Sunshine state, it was a place where women and weed were exotic and flavorful. Because of its hot, sunny days filled with surfing, jet skiing, and sunbathing things locals and tourists easily enjoy, South Florida drew millions of tourists from around the world. However, the nightlife was the cherry on top.

A smile of anticipation crossed Low's grill. They turned on Collins Avenue on the strip, and the nightly festivities were already in full swing. Scantily clad, beautiful women were everywhere. The streets were crowded with men dressed in their finest summer gears scrambling to find parking. Everyone seemed eager to experience a hot summer night in paradise.

They stopped at a gas station just around the corner from Collins Avenue. After fueling up on gas, and packs of Swisher Sweets, Razor walked to the passenger side.

"Low drive," Razor said, hopping in the passenger seat.

Razor started slipping a bulletproof vest under his shirt. He chuckled and said, "There's gonna be a lot of out-of-town muthafuckas in this bitch tonight." He fixed his Ferragamo dress shirt over his vest and continued. "Just in case shit goes down…"

Nodding his head, Low's eyes were on the road. Razor popped open the Lamborghini's glove compartment, pulled out a two-slot shoulder holster, and slipped it on. Reaching back in the glove he pulled out two black Glocks. Then he slipped both guns into the holsters on each side of his ribcage before putting on his linen vest, and jacket.

"You brought that gun I gave you earlier with you right?" Razor asked.

"Yeah, got it right here."

Lifting up the right side of his silk shirt, Low revealed the gun on his hip.

"You know how to use that bitch, right?"

"Yeah…"

"A'ight then. Get ready to make this next left into that parking lot. We here."

A fleet of private, luxury super-yachts were docked on South Beach's Grand Marina. There was a spectacular view of the futuristic nightlights of Miami's breathtaking skyline of luxurious upscale condominiums and high rises. Many of the yachts were unoccupied, but a small get together was being held on one of the two yachts occupying the private Marina. A bar mitzvah was being held for the thirteen-year-old son of a Jewish billionaire real estate agent. The private gathering was calm and serene with occasional outbursts of laughter. On the largest yacht docked at the private Marina, the atmosphere was totally different.

The biggest hip hop party of the year was taking place on a massive four-hundred-and-fifty-foot, three-story yacht, better known to the South Beach party crowd as Silk's Lounge. Hosted by DJ Ron G., Ed Lover, and Dr. Dre of MTV, and Vibe magazine, the *Yo MTV Raps* Summer Block party was in full effect. Pulling into the packed parking lot, Low and Razor glanced knowingly at each other. It was on.

"Damn, this bitch's thicker than a mutha!" Razor excitedly exclaimed.

The crowd in the parking lot was making their way toward the entrance of Silk's Lounge.

"Man, I don't think we gonna be able to find parking," Low sighed in frustration.

Glancing around at the hundreds of mostly luxury parked cars lining every row in the lot, Low didn't see a vacant spot.

"You must not know who you with, lil' cuz. This our city. Zoes don't wait to park," Razor said, pointing in the direction of two stocky men dressed in tight black 'Big Dawg Security' t-shirts.

The security guards were standing in front of a purple velvet rope that led to the valet parking area. "That's their job," Razor declared.

"My nigga, Razor. What it do, Pimp?" One of the valet attendants greeted.

Low and Razor stepped out of the car, and made their way toward him.

"Ice, you know…'nother day, 'nother dollar," Razor smiled, and exchanged daps with the valet.

The other valet attendant grabbed the keys from Low, and hopped in the driver's seat. Ice unhooked the velvet rope, letting the car through. He motioned for Razor and Low to follow him, and escorted them through a private walkway, leading to the platform entrance of Silk's Lounge.

"You just missed Janet Jackson," Ice smiled.

"Damn, I did...?"

"Yeah, she had a whole entourage of beautiful girls," Ice added.

Another security guard with a metal detecting wand in his hand stood in front of the private docking ramp that led to an exclusive entrance onto the massive luxury yacht.

"You better find her quick before another nigga snatch her up," Ice laughed.

"You know that!" Razor chimed, pulling a fifty-dollar bill out of his pocket.

Ice winked at the guard with the metal detector, and he quickly stepped aside letting Razor and Low onto the yacht. Silk's Lounge was filled to capacity. Every floor of the three-story yacht was rocking. Heavy bass of dance hall reggae pounded from the first floor. The massive dance floor was overflowed with scantily clothed women, grinding against sweaty, overzealous male dance partners.

Loud rap music rocked the second floor. DJ Ron G was mixing things down something fierce. His skills on the turntables had the crowded dance floor hopping in frenzy. The V.I.P. Lounge overlooked the huge dance floor in a U-shaped balcony setting. Hip-Hop and R&B royalties from the east to the west coast were there. The crème de la crème of the entertainment industry dressed to impress in their finest linens. Razor and Low made their way up to the staircase to the Lounge and entered the V.I.P. floor.

The head of security approached Razor, and said, "Its about time, playa! All the rest of the other Zoes here... They been wondering where you were at—"

"Oh yeah…? Well I'm here, Big Gizz!" Razor said, sharing hugs with Gizz. Then he continued. "Where my niggas at?"

"They in one of the private booths. Follow me," Gizz said, and made a path through the crowd.

Gizz, Razor, and Low approached a private booth where Gunner, other members and affiliates of Zoe Pound were sitting around a long table laden with Champagne bottles. They puffed weed filled cigars, and sipped ice-chilled Dom Perignon.

"Yo, what up ma…? You banging, girl!"

"You wanna drink some Dom with some real niggas…?"

"You got that fatty, ma. Can I get you a glass of Dom, boo?"

"You smiling… Come fuck with the Pound baby…"

Rowdy as usual, members of the Pound were busy hollering at every fine woman with a fat ass walking by the booth. Then Gunner spotted Razor.

"If it ain't the biggest dawg in Miami! Razor!" Gunner greeted Razor with a wide grin.

"What up Gunner? You know a party ain't a party 'til I walk in!" Razor chimed, giving Gunner an enthused handshake.

Gunner passed the weed-filled Optimo he was puffing to Razor. Sitting at the booth along with Gunner were his brother, Ghost, dapper in Gucci from head to heel. Sunny, and Walter wore cashmere and silk Polo shirts. T-Zoe was hands down, one of the freshest on the yacht. He was wearing off-white Versace linen shorts set with matching goat skin loafers, and Caine, second in command of Zoe Pound, was fresh home from jail after posting a two hundred and fifty thousand dollar bond for a pending murder case. Rocking Karl Kani black label suit, his facial expression was all business.

After introducing Low, Razor asked, "Why y'all just sitting around...? Ya'll don't see all this pussy in this bitch? I don't know about y'all, but me and lil' cuz bout to hit that muthafuckin' dance floor. Ain't that right lil' cuz?"

"We gangsters, nigga, and gangsters don't dance," Sunny said, gulping champagne.

"Zoe, with broads like that headed to the dance floor. I'm gangsta, but I'm a dance tonight!" Razor exclaimed, grabbing his crotch as he and the entire table watched the beautiful chick walking by.

"I'm wit'cha, big homey," Gunner said, standing then continued. "I heard that Janet Jackson's fine ass is in this bitch somewhere. I'm 'bout to go try and bump into her."

"Gunner, I love you dawg, but we gon' have an issue if ya go next to my girl," Razor said with a serious face.

He couldn't keep his expression straight long enough as he and Gunner stared each other down then burst out in laughter.

"A'ight Zoe, finders keepers. Don't let me find her first," Gunner laughed.

An event waiter dressed in a tuxedo, and white service gloves approached the booth carrying several bottles of Dom Perignon. She replenished the empty silver bucket of ice sitting on the table with the two chilled bottles of champagne, and walked away.

"Damn, muthafuckas ain't playing, y'all getting it straight poppin' with the drink huh?" Razor said, looking at all the empty champagne bottles.

"All compliments of the house... Ever since we told Silk you wanted to have a chat with him when you got here. He's been on some extra friendly shit all night. This 'bout the tenth bottle he sent so far," Sunny said.

"Oh shit! I almost forgot all about that bitch-ass-nigga. Where he at?" Razor asked.

"Beats me," Sunny shrugged, popping a bottle.

"Hmm…"

"He around somewhere. Haven't seen him in 'bout an hour, but the bottles keep coming like clockwork," Sunny said, offering the bottle of Dom to Razor.

With a wave of his hand, Razor said, "Nah Sunny, you know a nigga only fuck with dat yak."

"True dat," Sunny smiled.

"But when you see Silk, tell him I'm looking for him. I'm 'bout to hit the bar, and make my rounds in this piece… I'm a see y'all in a few. Lil' cuz, Gunner, let's ride," Razor said motioning for Low and Gunner to follow him.

"Alright y'all, our first performance of the night, coming to you live all the way from the city of bright lights, the ladies love, L.L. Cool J!"

A thunderous applause from the capacity crowd greeted L.L. to the V.I.P. stage. He broke into hit after hit. Razor and Low were at the wet bar scoping out all of the gorgeous women on the dance floor. Gunner stood close by a couple of feet away spitting game in the ear of a pretty, young Spanish girl.

"Keep 'em flowing, sexy!" Razor said, throwing back another cognac filled shot glass.

He slapped a fifty-dollar bill on top of the bar, tipping the longed haired exotic looking bartender. She smiled graciously, and kept the double shots of Hennessy coming his way. Razor was throwing back double shots of liquor like water while Low nursed a bottle of Heineken.

"See Low, this is the life of a Zoe, my nigga. We work all day, and ball all night! The game is all about enjoying the fruits of your labor. But to get to where you need to be in this game, you need lots of money. It takes two things to get your hands on that type of money. Ambition and sacrifices... You gotta have the ambition to put the necessary work in to get your hands on that money, and be willing to sacrifice the lives of anyone— no matter who they are— that tries to stand in your way. Ya dig? The money always comes first... Big cars, mansions, expensive clothes, and women all become luxuries... Ya dig?"

Nodding his head thoughtfully, Low soaked up every bit of what Razor was saying. He sipped the beer and watched the dance floor. He saw an attractive girl with smooth ebony complexion staring at him from a far off corner of the room. Low and the girl locked eyes. Then her inviting smile made him stare when he saw her approaching.

"There that bitch-ass-nigga go!" Razor spat.

His mug became mean when he spotted Silk chatting it up with a white girl in a corner of the dance floor. LL was wrapping up his performance. Thanking the fans, he headed off stage.

"I'll be right back. I'm 'bout to go holla at this fool," Razor said, and quickly broke away from the bar.

"I thought that was you!"

Low almost didn't recognize Lavisha, but those big light brown eyes of hers were truly unmistakable.

"Hey what's up, girl?"

Low saw her earlier at Sunny's shop in jeans and t-shirt, but Sunny's niece was now all dressed up, and looking fine as hell. Low stood speechless admiring her curves under the gold see-through shoulder less Valentino mini that barley covered up much of her thick dark chocolate thighs in the front.

"You don't remember me...?" Lavisha asked with a mischievous sneer.

Low saw her lips curled, and she posed with her hands on her hips. Then with a devilish grin, he said,

"Nah, that ain't it at all. Damn, you looking truly awesome!"

"Thank you. You have good taste," Lavisha smiled.

"Your uncle knows you wearing that dress, girl?" Low joked.

"Please, boy. I'm grown," Lavisha giggled.

Then she softly traced the outer rim of Low's Bersolino Fedora with the tip of her manicured nails, and continued. "I bet all the girls in here been sweating you."

"Not even," Low smiled coyly.

"Yeah right..."

"But as fine as you are, I guess that explains why you can't keep the stalkers away," Low smiled, nodding in the direction of a man looking at them.

"Shut up, boy," Lavisha said, and playfully punched Low on his shoulder.

"Who's that then?"

"That's my ex. I don't even know why he's here," Lavisha said, shaking her head in frustration. Then she continued. "Forget him. You're buying me a drink or what?"

"Seems like I don't have much of a choice," Low said.

"No, you don't," Lavisha smiled.

"I didn't think so. What you drinking, girl?"

"Sex on the beach..."

"You sure you can handle that?"

"Play your cards right, and you might find out."

Low ordered Lavisha's drink, and another Heineken. Gunner made his way over with a mixed drink of his own in hand, and a newly acquired beautiful Spanish girl was two steps behind him.

"Okay then Low! I see ya pimp!" Gunner exclaimed, sounding tipsy.

"Damn, where you been?" Low asked, paying for the drinks.

"I've been over here spitting tech to this bad ass bitch! Where Razor at?" Gunner asked.

"Over there," Low said, pointing Razor out on the dance floor.

Gunner glanced in the direction, and saw Razor in Silk's face giving him an earful. Then he said, "Guess he finally caught up to Silk, huh?"

"Oh yeah."

Low grabbed his Heineken and Lavisha's drink off the bar. He turned to hand it to her. The sight of her ex-boyfriend caught Low kind of off guard. His first thought was to step in and say something, but knowing better than to butt into another person's relationship issues, Low calmly placed her drink back on top of the bar and stayed quiet. He watched the scene between Lavisha and her ex unfold.

"Who dat fool?" Gunner asked.

"Her ex trying to get back in her good graces," Low replied.

"What you trying a do? Shit, just let me know."

Before Low could respond, Gunner's new Spanish girl grabbed him by the hand, and pulled him toward the dance floor.

Lavisha allowed her ex to pull her away from the bar without saying anything. Low took a few gulps of Heineken, shook his head, and chuckled. Even though he was itching to intervene and say something to Lavisha's ex, Low knew he still had to mind his business. He drank the rest of his beer, and summoned the bartender over for another round.

He kept an eye on Lavisha, and her ex as they returned to the far corner of the dance floor, not far from where Razor stood. They were clearly arguing. Low tipped the bartender and grabbed his third Heineken. He was about to head back to the V.I.P. when Lavisha seemed to have had enough of her bickering ex, pulled herself free from his grasp, and attempted to walk away. A vicious backhand slap to her face sent her crashing to the floor.

Low immediately started rushing through the crowded dance floor. Lavisha attempted to get off the floor, but her ex-boyfriend quickly followed up with a brutal kick to her ribcage. Then he reached for his waistband, pulling out a gun. Dropping the Heineken, Low pulled out his Berretta. The angered ex-boyfriend took a step closer toward his intended target. Low's eyes sprung wide with horror as he sprinted toward his cousin.

"RAZOR...!"

Lavisha's ex-boyfriend unloaded his Glock into the back of Razor's skull. Blood and brain fragments splattered all over Silk and dozens of partygoers' clothing. Razor's body crashed onto the wooden dance floor. Complete pandemonium followed. Hundreds of frantically screaming revelers began scrambling for the exits. Standing over Razor's body, the man fired two more slugs into Razor's lifeless body before fleeing.

"NO!" Low screamed, wildly firing in the fleeing gunman's direction.

He missed his mark. An innocent partygoer was caught in the crossfire. A bullet lifted him out of his Travel Fox sneakers. He collapsed face-first to his death. Another bullet ricocheted off the caged metal of a huge speaker, penetrating an emergency water pipeline instantly activating the yacht's fire sprinklers. Water was raining everywhere.

Clutching the gun in his sweaty palm, Low crouched, his eyes rifling through the faces of the crowd. His search was in vain. Low couldn't locate the shooter, he had made good of his escape. Lowering his weapon, Low turned to where Razor's dead body was sprawled. Collapsing to his knees, Low was in complete agony.

Taking a deep breath, he crawled over to his cousin, and immediately began to weep.

"Damn my nigga… What the fuck Razor…?"

Tears streaming down his face, Low pulled Razor's lifeless body into his arms. Blood oozed from Razor's skull. Low stared into the glazed eyes of his cousin. Razor was staring back, but Low knew he was gone. The sound of the fire engines and police sirens could be heard in the distance. The dozen or so people remaining were either frozen in shock, or so severely injured from being trampled during the chaotic melee they couldn't move.

Low's face was buried in Razor's chest. Crying his eyes out, he felt a hand on his shoulder. He looked up, and saw Gunner.

"Come on Low!" Gunner shouted, pulling Low to his feet.

Low's reluctance to let go of Razor's lifeless body caused Gunner to shake Low's shoulder, and said, "Come on my nigga!"

Tugging on Low's blood-soaked shirt, Gunner continued. "We gotta go now!"

After unclipping both beepers from Razor's hip, Low remove Razor's gold chain, and placed the Cuban link with a big diamond encrusted R medallion around his own neck. Low leaned, and planted a farewell kiss on Razor's forehead. Then he shut his lifeless eyes with two fingers.

"Warriors don't die," Low whispered, gently placing Razor's head on the ground, and quickly left with Gunner.

CHAPTER

18

Sent for

Razor's funeral was held at the famed, Notre Dame Church, located on N.E. 2nd Ave and 54th Street in the heart of Little Haiti. Low was still wearing the same bloody Armani outfit he had on the night of the shooting. The service came to an end, and he was feeling way too distraught to follow the funeral procession to the cemetery for the burial.

Low hopped into Razor's Lamborghini, and skirted out of the church's parking lot. Driving up N.E 2nd Avenue, he reached for the half-empty bottle of Barbancourt Haitian Rum, and pressed his foot down on the gas pedal. Images from the night at Silk's Lounge flashed vividly in his mind's eyes.

Even after seeing Razor's body lying in the casket, Low still couldn't believe Razor was suddenly gone. It felt surreal. Low cringed in regret wondering what he could have done differently that could've saved his cousin's life. Many questions were racing through his brain. What the hell were Lavisha, and her ex-boyfriend arguing about anyway? Was he just jealous? Why did he shoot Razor, and not say anything to him when Lavisha was clearly flirting with him at the bar? How did Lavisha's ex get into Silk's Lounge with a gun? Only Zoe Pound members were allowed inside strapped. So did Zoë Pound turn on Razor? Where were all the Zoes when the shooting went down?

Nothing was making sense, and this sent Low's mind into overdrive. None of the Zoes, not Sunny, Walter, Lavisha, Ghost or Gunner bothered showing up to Razor's funeral. They were all suspects and couldn't be trusted. Razor was his first cousin, and Low wanted revenge. Maybe Razor's death was an inside hit by a Zoe member wanting to erase Razor for money and status. If that was the case Mildred was definitely in danger.

Low took a sharp right turn, and gunned down N.E 79th Street. He popped open the car's glove compartment, and fished through various papers. In search of a car title or anything that could lead him to Razor's house, Low finally found an insurance statement with an address.

Zooming pass a red light on Biscayne Blvd, Low placed his gun on his lap. A murderous feeling came over his entire body. A look of death clouded his eyes as the luxurious Palm Beach community came in full view. Low gripped the steering wheel tightly and accelerated. Suddenly a vibration on his hip broke him out of his trance. A page was coming through one of Razor's beepers. Peering down, Low didn't recognize the area code number *1804-911* code on the end. Then the second beeper on his hip went off. It was the same number.

911 emphasized an urgent page. Low tossed the code over in his head for a few seconds. 1804 was the birth year of Haiti's independence from France. Suddenly the thought fell on him like a ton of bricks. Whoever was paging had to be a Zoe.

Easing his foot off the gas pedal, Low began to scan both sides of N.E 79th Street, trying to locate a phone booth. He found one up ahead on the opposite side of the street. Low made a sharp U-turn, and pulled into the front entrance of a Winn Dixie supermarket.

Tucking his Berretta back on his hip, Low hopped out the car, retrieved some loose change, and entered the phone booth. His heart was racing when he dialed the number from Razor's beeper. Then a voice picked up on the fifth ring.

"Is this Low?" The deep male voice on the other end asked.

"Um, yeah. Who this?"

"King Zoe is giving you twenty minutes to make it to Sunny's Shop. Don't be late. You've been sent for..."

The loud sound of the dial tone was jarring. Low swallowed hard, and hung up the receiver. Then he glanced at his watch. It was Sunday afternoon, the volume of traffic coming in and out of the TiMache shopping plaza was heavy. Food Giant was the only supermarket on the North side of Miami that catered to that side of the city's great population of Haitian, Spanish, and Jamaican foods. It was packed to capacity with bargain hunting mothers.

Pulling into the crowded plaza, Low's head was on a swivel. He was suspicious, and scanned the crowded parking lot, searching for any signs of an ambush. After circling the interior of the lot, Low reached Sunny's shop. He pulled into the parking space exclusively reserved for the electronics store.

All the lights inside the shop were off. Low stared at the entrance of Sunny's shop. *Closed,* the sign on the door read. However, Low was convinced that there were people inside. Low reached for the gun on his waist, and took a deep breath. He cocked the gun, feeding a round into the chamber. Then he took the selector off safe before sliding the gun back into his waistband.

There was a high possibility he would never walk out, but he wouldn't be able to live with himself if he didn't go in to see why the Zoes sent for him.

"Ambition and sacrifice..." Razor's voice echoed in his mind.

In order to avenge his cousin's death, Low was ready to sacrifice his own life. There was no turning back. If Zoe Pound turned on Razor, Low was certain they would kill him too. He left the engine running, and he pulled down the driver's side suicide door shut.

Walking up to the entrance of Sunny's Electronics, Low took a quick glance around to make sure no one was watching him as he reached for the shop's entrance door that swung open to the sound of jingling bells. Then he stepped through the entrance.

The main floor was vacant, but the door to the basement was wide open. Removing his Berretta from his waist, he gripped the gun, and placed it in his pocket. Low started walking forward to the open door. The steep wooden steps leading down to the basement of the shop creaked louder with every step. He gripped the handle of his gun. Stepping onto the smooth concrete surface of the basement floor, Low was ready for any surprises.

With anxiety running through his body like hot knife through butter, Low entered an empty, dimly lit hallway. It led toward two separate white wooden doors with a big surveillance camera above them. Low gripped his gun tighter as he cautiously approached. The sound of the metal door handle turning caused Low to immediately pull out, and take aim. The door to his right swung open. A tall man dressed in an all black business suit emerged.

"You're late. King Zoe doesn't like that. Come on in and put that gun away, you ain't gonna need it," Walter said.

He turned and walked back into the room leaving the door open for Low. He reluctantly followed behind Walter, and glanced at his watch. It was now 3:36.

The basement level of Sunny's shop resembled a social club. Thin wall-to-wall carpeting, four huge leather sofas covering each side of the room's black tiled walls. A casino styled card table, one professional-size pool table that sat in the middle of the room, two wall mounted thirty-inch television sets positioned on each side of a full-length bar. A set of magma colored strobe lights sat above the bar, installed into eight holes in the ceiling, illuminating the entire room a gloomy red.

Low entered behind Walter, the first thing that caught his eyes was the massive sized blue and red Haitian flag, adorning the wall behind the bar. Seated at the bar, on two of the five cushioned stools, Ghost and Gunner turned their attention to the doorway. Low locked eyes with them, and they nodded, acknowledging him.

"He's here, Zoe," Walter announced, making his way to where Sunny, and Caine were standing at attention.

Their hands were folded in front of them. They all seemed businesslike dressed in black suits as they stood on either side of the leather sofa. A man with long dreadlocks clad in a black business suit sat with his head down. He focused his attention on the newspaper in his lap.

Lifting his head without looking up from the article he was reading, he motioned with his finger for Low to come closer. Low got within a couple steps of him then he motioned for Low to stop.

"You don't have to hold onto that pistol in your pocket so tightly, son. We're not the enemy," the man said.

After finishing with the newspaper, he folded up the paper and put it away. When he looked up, Low's heart skipped a beat. It was Michelle's father. King Zoe hastily jumped up, and took a big step forward. This massive six-seven framed man towered over Low. The poisonous venom in his eyes could've killed Low instantly.

"So this is the man who tried to avenge brother Razor's death?"

"Yeah, that's him, King Zoe," Sunny said.

"Okay…" King Zoe nodded with a smile.

"Razor introduced him to us as his cousin," Sunny said.

"Oh his cousin?" King Zoe quipped with a raised eyebrow as he thoughtfully nodded.

He reached inside the breast pocket of his suit. Pulling out a fresh Cuban cigar, King Zoe made his way over to Sunny, who held out a light for him.

"Losing a family member is truly an agonizing ordeal," King Zoe said.

He took a few puffs on his Cuban then turned back toward Low, and continued. "Being a part of our family, Razor's death also hit us with great pain. Me especially, you see. Razor was like a son to me, and for you to be an actual blood relative of his, I must assume that his murder has brought you just as much pain as it brought us. But you know death, however distressful it may be when it hits close to home, is all just a part of our game, my man. It unfortunately comes with this life we lead, you know?"

Pausing, he puffed on the cigar. King Zoe allowed the thick smoke to linger in his mouth a bit. He gazed up, seemingly mulling something over in his mind. Exhaling the tobacco fumes into the air, a devilish grin crept across his face.

"But you know what also comes with the pain of losing a member of your family?" King Zoe asked, fixing his gaze on Low.

"The joy of getting revenge for their death. You see my man, I read this newspaper about the shooting, and it tells a half-ass story with many holes in it. It leaves the reader with so many unanswered questions. But me being the owner of the establishment where such a tragedy took place cannot be left with any questions. And since I'm not the most trusting kind, I tend to rely on visual proof that my employees are doing their jobs to my liking. It's the American way. In the event that something ever goes wrong, I made sure Silk's Lounge was equipped with the best surveillance technology money can by. Over three hundred cameras on that yacht, a person cannot sneeze without it being recorded," King Zoe said, and gazed at Ghost and Gunner. "Bring them in!" He ordered them.

Nodding their heads, Ghost and Gunner immediately pulled out their guns from under their suits jackets, and headed for the door. They disappeared into the hallway.

"Caine, bring me my machete," King Zoe instructed with a snap of his fingers.

Making his way behind the bar, Caine retrieved a large machete concealed in a customized brown leather casing. He promptly brought it to King Zoe. Ghost and Gunner reappeared at the doorway. They led three people at gunpoint into the room. King Zoe and Low were standing in front of them. Their hands were bound behind their backs with extension cords. Black pillowcases covered their heads. All three were forced to their knees. Ghost and Gunner stood off on either side of them holding semi automatic handguns aimed in the direction of all three.

King Zoe said, "After reviewing all the security tapes from that night all my unanswered questions were revealed. I noted several transgressions. I noted a major breach of security, an infiltration by a hated foe, and complete disloyalty by a once trusted family member."

Taking a step closer to Low, King Zoe continued. "But there was one positive moment that caught my eyes, and it was when I noticed a young man jump into action like a true soldier, and came to the aid of one of my fallen brothers. Even though the killer managed to slip out of sight through an emergency exit your bravery that night truly touched me my man… So we stand here in the presence of the three individuals responsible for Razor's death. I figured it just wouldn't be right if you weren't invited to take part in this retaliatory celebration with us."

After a short pause, King Zoe pulled the machete out of the leather casing. He handed the sharp sword to Low, glanced over at Caine, and said, "Unveil the infiltrators!"

Caine made his way behind the first captive, forcefully grabbed him from the back of his collared shirt, and snatched the pillowcase from his head. Lavisha's ex-boyfriend's eyes popped wide with horror. Frantically looking around the room, he tried to focus his sight in the illuminating red lights.

The room came into focus, and his eyes met Low's. Weighing the machete in his hands, Low saw the fear in his eye. Squirming in Caine's firm grasp, the man moaned loudly through his duct-taped mouth.

"This man is Bobby Sanchez. When Bobby stepped on my yacht he had one objective in mind. Carry out the mission given to him by his higher-ups, and slay the first Zoe he spotted in retaliation for the death of one of their members. Ironically, this man's blood brother."

While King Zoe spoke Bobby was groaning loudly, and becoming uncontrollable.

"Calm his ass down!" King Zoe snapped.

Gunner viciously struck Bobby above the right eye with the butt of his weapon. Bobby collapsed to the ground. Gunner kicked him in the ribs, causing Bobby to painfully groan, and squirm in agony on the floor. Blood oozed from a deep gash on Bobby's face.

"It seems Bobby is dying to say something," King Zoe said, pulling the duct tape from Bobby's mouth.

"Please don't kill me! I'll do anything!" Bobby cried.

Staring into the eyes of Razor's murderer, Low found himself in a trance-like state. All the anger and bitterness in Low's life began to quickly accumulate like fireball inside him. Images of his dead loved ones flashed through his mind. Everyone Low ever held close to heart, seemed to always get tragically taken away from him.

"Please, I don't wanna die. Please, I got a baby on the way!"

Tightening his grasp around the machete, Low took a deep breath, and said, "So did my cousin, muthafucka!"

Seething, Low lunged forward in a fit of rage, and drove the blade of the machete through Bobby's chest plate. The sword's sharp steel tore apart Bobby's sternum, ripping through his internal organs, and slicing his spine in two. The steel's sharp tip exited out his back.

"That's for Razor!" Low spat.

With a tug of the machete, Bobby collapsed face-first to the ground. Then King Zoe said, "Uncover the next one!"

Caine immediately grabbed the next captive by his collar, and snatched the pillowcase off his head. Silk locked eyes with Low, and the look in his teary eyes screamed his fear. Muffled sounds escaped his duct-taped mouth.

"Here is chief of my security unit. There was an obvious breach in security that night, and he's guilty for Razor's death," King Zoe said, motioning for the duct tape to be removed from Silk's mouth.

With a loud ripping sound, Caine tore off the adhesive tape. Silk instantly began speed talking. Pleading his case, he said, "Aye bruh, I'm sorry man. It wasn't my fault—"

One hard slash with the machete was all it took, and his plea was immediately cut short. The sharp blade brutally severed Silk's head from his body. The swing from Low decapitated him, sending blood squirting out of his neck, and his head tumbling to the floor with a thud. Silk's beheaded body slowly descended backwards. Lost in a trance, apathetically watching the blood leaked out of Silk's headless corpse, Low was completely numb of feeling.

"This one here hits a little closer to home," King Zoe said, moving to the third captive. "It actually pains me to do this," King Zoe sighed, taking a knee beside the captive then looked up at Low.

"Zoes are a unit, a team…but most importantly, a family. In this family there are rules that apply to each and every one of us. A minor infraction can always be overlooked when a family member does it… But to betray your family is to rock the very foundation on which we stand. If you cannot trust your own family then who can you trust?"

Taking a short pause, King Zoe stood, and looked down at the hooded captive. Then he shook his head, and sighed.

"But the consequence for the betrayal of a family member is punishable only by death. There's no way around that," King Zoe said, glancing over at Low before continuing. "So we lost two members of our family today, and another brother shall be born," King Zoe declared, staring at Low.

He removed the pillowcase, and Lavisha's sorrow-filled face instantly broke Low out of his murderous zone. Staring at her moistened light brown eyes, Low saw the tears flowing down her cheeks like a stream. He immediately glanced at King Zoe for an explanation.

"Our sister, Lavisha is guilty of betrayal. Knowing she would be allowed to get past security armed, Bobby set his deceptive plan in motion. He convinced her to carry his gun onto the yacht for him. She was fully aware of the growing tension between the Zoes and the Zombies, and against her better judgment, Lavisha agreed to her ex boyfriend's request. She was spotted on camera passing Bobby his gun as soon as they got through security. Had it not been for her negligence our brother, Razor would still be here with us. So in consequence of his death Lavisha must sacrifice her life."

Reaching down, King Zoe removed the tape from Lavisha's mouth so she could speak her peace. Lavisha instead took one last look at everyone around the room before she shut her eyes, bowed her head in shame, and accepted her fate.

Sweat ran down his face, his pulse raced at a rapid pace, and his eyes scanned the faces in the room. He looked at King Zoe, Ghost, Gunner, Caine, and eventually locking eyes with Sunny. A slight head nod from her uncle was all it took to seal Lavisha's fate.

Lifting the machete high in the air, Low came down with the sharp, steel blade slicing through the back of Lavisha's neck, beheading her with ease.

✦ ✦ ✦

WELCOME

"A Zoe is a leader. A leader must think through every move he plans to make ahead of executing it. A Zoe is a warrior. A warrior approaches every battle with fearlessness and fights until he defeats his enemy or his own life is taken in battle. A Zoe is strong for he is a part of a body of soldiers. There are no weak links in Zoe Pound. Zoe means bone in Creole. To be a Zoe is eternal...to survive in this game you gotta be bad to the bone, Zoe."

King Zoe lifted the bloody machete, and placed it on either side of Low's shoulder, knighting Low. Then he finalized Low's initiation by sliding each side of the machete's bloody blade on his outstretched palms, signifying with the blood on his hands that Low was now a Zoe for life.

"Welcome to the family, Zoe," King Zoe said.

Then he leaned forward, and whispered in Low's ear.

"But if you ever put your hands on my daughter again, next time I'll kill you," King Zoe said, taking a step back then smiled.

"Ghost, Gunner, clean this shit up," he ordered, motioning toward the three bodies. "Then come join us at the bar. Let's celebrate."

PART 3

THE
TAKEOVER

CHAPTER
19

KILLING SEASON

(Day 1- 3:00 pm)

News of Razor's death spread across the city like wildfire. The reputation, and livelihood of the Zoe Pound were in great jeopardy. Now the entire underworld of Miami was waiting to see how Zoe Pound would respond to the brutal hit on one of the top members. Razor's drug empire brought in the biggest percentage of Zoe Pound's income. Rival drug cartels were moving in on his vast drug turf, jockeying for position in hopes of expanding their own individual territories.

The amount of money to be made was substantial, and crack was bringing in astronomical profits. Zoe Pound couldn't afford to lose the stronghold that Razor had held down. Drug sales accounted for over sixty percent of Zoe Pound's income, the numbers racket was still profitable, their hands were all over Biscayne Boulevard's prostitution market, and Zoe Pound's legit businesses were thriving. However, Razor's drug empire was very much the focal point of their financial portfolio.

Low sat with the rest of the top Zoes at a round mahogany table. A blueprint layout of the entire city was in front of them. Low was appointed to fill Razor's shoes. He was in on the plan to kill two birds with one stone. Not only would Zoe Pound execute every single top Zombie responsible for Razor's death, and take their territories, but they would simultaneously move in on all other competing top adversaries within a fifty-mile radius of the operation.

It was a war of annihilation launched against the unsuspecting enemies of Zoe. Low's proposal to take over the entire north side and form a super cartel was met with great approval. Before long, every Zoe was down with his plan. Low was given top priority by leadership.

"One nation, one Pound…" Low said, closing his presentation.

He was greeted as a real Zoe, and even the King immediately liked the idea. Gunner and Ghost were assigned to him for security. Once every Zoe was made aware of who this new guy was, Low was given the green light to execute his plan.

✦ ✦ ✦

"Slow down a bit, Ghost. Let that car get in front of us," Low said from the backseat of the tinted minivan.

Checking to make sure the thirty-shot banana clip was filled, Low reloaded the magazine of the AK-47 assault rifle on his lap. Ghost eased up on the gas pedal, allowing the white Pontiac to get in front of the minivan. Gunner was seated next to Low in the backseat, gripping the handle of the matte black carbine machine gun clutched in his gloved hands.

"Where the fuck are these niggas headed now?" Gunner fumed.

The past hour seemed like forever. They were tailing an emerald green Mercedes-Benz that was making runs in and around the city. Waiting for the perfect time to strike caused Gunner some anxiety.

"Be easy, Zoe. Everything is coordinated. This has to be done right," Low said.

A few cars behind, another black minivan with Sunny, and Walter followed at a safe distance. They were awaiting the signal from Low to make a move. Ghost glanced through the van's rearview mirror, and saw the edginess under the ski-masked face of his twin brother.

"Looks like they heading for the pork and beans projects. We'll have a sure go at them there," Ghost said.

"Okay let's see..." Low said.

"Fuck this cat and mouse shit. We had them motherfuckers at the red light, and we fucking hesitated. Fuck that shit. They pull in...we move. That's it!" Gunner said.

"We'll do it at the right time. That's it," Low said, pulling back the AK's slide, chambering a round.

✦ ✦ ✦

He was sitting comfortably in the back seat of the four-door C280 Mercedes-Benz. Dante, the leader of the Zombies, and Rip, second in command, were in discussion over a Swisher Sweet. The driver, Shanikwa paid attention to the road while chauffeuring them around. They were making the daily runs to check the dozen trap houses, collecting money, and dropping off work.

It was another good week for the Zombies. Ever since the successful hit they had put out on the Zoes in retaliation for the death of a Zombie lieutenant, business was booming. Razor was out of the way, and now the Zombies were showing that they were no pushovers, but there were questions still unanswered.

"I don't know. It's just not like Bobby to go MIA like that. I think something's up," Dante said.

A week went by, and Bobby hadn't check in, but Rip didn't sound worried when he said, "Trust me, Dante you're just being paranoid. Bobby's good money." Rip kept on reading the newspaper article on the shooting at Silk's Lounge. After a few beats, Rip continued. "He more than likely just laying low. I wouldn't even give it too much thought cause it says right here that the Miami-Dade Police still have no leads or suspects, and haven't made any arrest."

He passed the Miami Herald to Dante. After browsing the news article, Dante said, "You're probably right."

Dante took a deep toke of the weed filled Swisher Sweet, and allowed the smoke fumes to linger in his lungs a bit while gazing out the window.

"I just got a weird feeling 'bout this. I told Bobby to get back to me as soon as the job was done. He ain't page me. You can't put nada past them Zoe niggas... they some sneaky-ass muthafuckas. When they find out that we put that hit on 'em it's gonna be on and poppin'. We gon' have to be ready to go to war."

"We'll be ready. I got plugged in with some new gun supplier—major firepower. I'm talking choppas on deck. I'm still feeling him out though, but we should be good in the next week."

"A'ight, keep working on that end..."

"The team's strong, all our goons have been briefed and on point. They ready for any surprise attacks. All our traps are secure. Shit, the money's flowing in like water. We just have to continue on our hustle. Fuck the Zoes! We up, not them."

"A'ight, a'ight, I hear you, Rip," Dante said, nodding in agreement.

Dante hated wars. Beefs made the streets hot and served only as a deterrent to the main goal of getting money. Dante knew a war with Zoë Pound wouldn't be an easy one. They were fucking unpredictable. But he had a plan for them. As soon as Rip's Jamaican gun supplier connected, he was sending a missile straight at King Zoe. Dante knew that if the Zombies had any chance of defeating Zoë Pound then he'd have to go straight for the head.

Another toke of the swisher, and Dante felt secure that they'd weather this storm. His mood lightened, as he passed the weed. Rip was probably right. Maybe he was just paranoid. There was one last stop to be made, and Dante shook off any bad vibes. This game was like chess. Zoë Pound opened up, he countered by making a game-changing decision, and now they held the advantage. The sunshine was brightest on his side.

Shanikwa made a right turn into the infamous pork and beans projects. Dante saw two of his dayshift workers coming out the trap house, and heading in his direction. One of them held a black duffle bag in his hands. They both approached the car. Shanikwa pulled the Benz over to the side of the curb. Two baby-faced workers were waiting with the cash-filled duffle bags.

Reaching under the passenger seat, Dante pulled out a Winn-Dixie paper shopping bag containing half pound of weed in nickel bags, two ounces of coke, bagged in twenties and forties. Four cookies of crack broken down in dimes.

"What it do…?" Dante greeted, and handed the twenty thousand dollars worth of supply to a worker.

"It do what it does…" the worker replied, and gave Dante a duffle bag filled with the day's earnings.

The loud screeching of tires distracted the worker. His attention shifted to the sight of two black minivans traveling at full speed toward them. This unexpected commotion caused him to panic. He lost grip of the duffle bag, and tried to get out the way.

Shanikwa saw that it was an ambush, and attempted to floor the gas pedal, but it was too late. The first mini-van completely blocked the Benz in. Suddenly the side-door slid open, and two-masked gunmen immediately hopped out, clutching fully automatic assault rifles.

Dante and Rip were caught wide-eyed in a surprised attack. Rip made a desperate attempt to reach for the gun on his waist. Low squeezed the trigger of the assault rifle, unloading a burst of slugs that exploded through the Benz windows. The bodies of all three occupants were riddled with bullets. Gunner followed the onslaught with a burst from his Carbine 15, sweeping the Benz front to back, chopping the car down with rounds as.330 bullets peppered everywhere.

"Come on!" Walter shouted.

He slipped opened the second minivan's side door, and waved his troops on. Low and Gunner bolted for the second minivan. Ghost hopped out the driver's seat of the first minivan with a slight limp, and hobbled his way over to the getaway van. He jumped in and Sunny floored the gas pedal making a smooth getaway.

It didn't take long before the rest of the Zombies found out that Dante and Rip were killed, and who did it. The gang members soon fell in line, and came under the command of King Zoe and Zoë Pound.

✦ ✦ ✦

Day 4 – 2:44 am

"Come on, youngster. I just need to take a quick shit," the fiend said, clutching his stomach in pain.

When the fiend didn't receive the response he wanted, he pressed on. "I spend all this money up in this muthafucka. It's the least you can do for me. Please man,

I'm 'bout to shit on myself!"

"I told your fat ass already. This ain't no fucking McDonalds!" Lanky Fred barked from behind the gated door of the trap house.

"A'ight, a'ight. I need four nicks," the fiend said, pulling a wrinkled up twenty dollar bill out of his dingy pants pocket.

"Okay…" Lanky Fred said.

"I got a deal for you. I really got the bubble-guts like a mutha. So I'll throw you an extra twenty, and I got this bud for ya," the fiend said, pulling out a balled up paper towel, and showing Lanky Fred the weed.

"It's about a half a zone. I only smoke this to help me sleep at night. It's some good shit too. I'll give you a few joints worth. Just let me in to take a shit, please!"

The fiend was doubled-over, and holding his stomach. Lanky Fred quickly debated his offer, but knowing the rules about unlocking the steel gate, he chose to stick to his guns.

"Fuck outta here. I'm straight," Lanky Fred frowned.

Just then Sicko, the trap's other midnight shift worker and Lanky Fred's best friend came to gate after overhearing the fiend's offer.

"Let me see that shit," Sicko said.

The fiend lifted fourteen grams of high-grade bud up to the gate, and unfolded the paper towel so Sicko could take a better look. The potent aroma of the weed instantly hit his nose. Peering down at the fiend's hand, he examined the bud. His eyes immediately lit up.

"Damn, looks like some fire!"

Fred was still reluctant to make any deals, but Sicko nudged him with an elbow to persuade him to open the gate. Then Sicko said, "If we let you take a shit we want all that bud."

"Damn, if I give you my whole stash I won't be able to get any sleep tonight," the fiend said.

"You wanna sleep or shit?" Sicko asked.

There were no other choice, and the fiend reluctantly agreed when he said, "A'ight, you got yourself a deal. But hurry up, and unlock this door cause I can't hold this any longer."

Shaking his head, he cut his eyes at Sicko. Then Lanky Fred reluctantly reached in his shorts for the keys. After a short moment of hesitation, Fred finally unlocked the gated door.

The fiend stepped inside the trap house, and Lanky Fred instantly realized he made a grave mistake. Grabbing a hold of his wrist, the fiend swiftly jerked his arm. It was Sunny, and he pulled Lanky Fred's lightweight frame toward him, and into a chokehold with his huge arms. Suddenly a black handgun appeared out of nowhere, and Sunny held it against Lanky Fred's skull.

Walter immediately rushed in behind Sunny, and Low busted into the trap house with an infrared equipped semiautomatic.40 caliber handgun leading the way. They both took aim at Sicko's head, instantly freezing his attempt to reach for the gun on his waist.

"Where Big Tuck live?" Walter scowled in a menacing tone.

Meanwhile Low was searching Sicko, and found the gun in his waistband. He quickly disarmed him.

"Boss? Man wha-what cha talking about?" Sicko stuttered.

This really made Walter angry and he delivered a wicked blow to Sicko's face. Walter viciously struck Sicko on his nose with the butt of his massive.40 caliber handgun. Sicko collapsed on the ground clutching his bloody nose. Taking a knee beside him, Walter angrily snatched him by the collar, and stuck the barrel of his gun at Sicko's head.

"Now I'm a ask you again. Where does Tuck live?"

"I swear. I dunno where da boss live."

Sunny had Fred in a chokehold. His gun was pressed against Fred's temple. Walter had enough of the bullshit. He glanced up, and spoke in Creole.

"Sunny, tiere mesior!"

Without missing a beat, Sunny pulled the trigger of his 10 mm exploding a round into Fred's temple, killing him instantly.

"No!" Sicko screamed.

"Now let's try this again. Where does the boss live?"

"Okay, okay man! I'll show you! I'll take you to his house. Just don't kill me, please."

"Now that's what I wanted to hear," Walter said.

✦ ✦ ✦

A worried look appeared on Big Tuck's sweaty face. The leader of model city B-Gang entire structure froze as his whole body shook under the restraints bounding his arms and legs. Big Tuck's three hundred and thirty pound, six feet, six and half inches frame abused the puny metal foldout chair he was confined to. His horrific loud moan escaped through the duct tape on his mouth. Big Tuck tried taking a series of rapid breaths in anticipation of the next shockwave. The pain was excruciating. Every jolting shock of electricity completely froze him, inducing a violent convulsion that caused every muscle in his body to spasm. Snot mixed with blood oozed out his nostrils. He grinded his teeth in agonizing pain, and his eyes bulged out of the sockets. Fifteen hundred volts of electricity were like sharp razors ripping through his veins. After several seconds, the torturous electrocution suddenly stopped.

Low rotated the knob on the portable tractor-trailer compatible battery charger, setting the voltage exactly fifty watts higher than before. Then he calmly flipped the switch on. An electric current instantly sent fifteen hundred and fifty watts of electricity through the two electromagnets precisely taped over the nipples of the bare-chested Big Tuck. He violently shook and moaned in complete agony, jerking, bouncing up and down.

The 8th round of Low's precisely timed electrocution came to an end. Once again, he flipped the switch off. Big Tuck's wife let out a dreadful yelp. She was sitting across from him while Sunny and Walter stood guard on either side with Russian imported choppers.

"Oh God! Tuck, please tell them or they're gonna kill you!" She pleaded with her husband.

Low watched the woman fell into another fit of uncontrollable sobbing. A menacing smile easily formed on his face when he said, "Damn, Big Tuck do you see what your wife is going through right now? She sounds pretty concerned for your wellbeing. I really hate the fact that I'm putting you through this...and in front of your wife at that...? It's really not my style honestly, but we've been here for a good hour now, and you still haven't told us what we want to fucking hear! Now it's simple. Tell us where your stash is, we'll kindly take it, and be on our way. No harm no foul."

Big Tuck stared into his wife's teary eyes, feeling sorry that she was witnessing him like this. However, Big Tuck was very stubborn, he was just squirming. Low glanced at him, smiled, and said, "It seems our friend here has something to say."

He reached for Big Tuck's mouth, and ripped off the duct tape. Then he angrily spat out the sock that was stuffed in his mouth. Big Tuck looked up, locked eyes with Low, and shot him a murderous glare.

"Kill me now, nigga! I ain't telling you shit, bitch!" Big Tuck angrily shouted.

Low laughed. Sunny and Walter were equally amused. Tuck was not. He was seething when he shouted, "Y'all don't know who y'all fucking with! I'm a muthafuckin' boss! When I get my hands on y'all mutha-fuckas, I'm a kill all a you!"

Low flipped the switch on, and a jolt of electric-ity went through Big Tuck's body. Grinding his teeth. Fifteen seconds passed, and Low didn't seem the least bit concerned about flipping the switch off.

Yolanda could no longer watch her husband being tortured. Finally, she shouted, "Stop the fucking char-ger!"

The angry woman attempted to rush toward Low, but Walter immediately delivered a blow to the side of her jaw with the butt of his weapon. Her fragile body col-lapsed on the floor at the feet of her husband. Reaching for the switch, Low flipped it off. Peering down at Tuck's wife, he shook his head.

"Tie her ass up too!" Low ordered.

Walter and Sunny picked up Yolanda, and pulled her up by her weave. She was violently tossed back onto the leather couch. Low pulled out a Glock handgun from his waist. He was about to step to Yolanda, but some-thing stopped him in his tracks. The sudden outburst of a baby's cry caught everyone off guard. Low glanced at Big Tuck, still recovering from thirty-five seconds of traumatic electrocution.

"Bring me that baby," Low ordered with a sly grin.

Low finished applying the last strip of duct tape across the infant's chest. Examining the charger, Low ensured that the single electromagnetic plate was prop-erly centered on the bare body of the baby boy. He clipped the blue negative clamp then the red positive clamp onto the two small hooks on the magnetic plate. Big Tuck was screaming threats, and obscenities. He twisted and turned in his seat, trying to break free from his restrains. All his efforts were in vain.

"You're really testing me, huh?" Low said, adjusting the voltage on the battery charger.

Rotating the knob all the way up to the right, Low set the charger on its highest capacity. Then he looked at Big Tuck and said, "I'm done playing games with you! Three thousand watts is enough electricity to start up a small yacht. Now even your fat ass won't be able to withstand this juice. I'm going to give your bitch-ass one last shot to tell us where the stash is."

Low ripped the duct tape from Tuck's mouth, and the captive spat out the saliva soaked sock. Big Tuck warily glanced over at his firstborn. The sight struck unnerved Tuck. A rush of anger and pain shot through his entire body. Locking eyes with his wife, Big Tuck sighed.

"Fuck y'all muthafuckas! You going to have to do what you gotta do cause I ain't telling you shit!" Big Tucked seethed.

"Bad move. Dumb motherfucker!" Low said, shaking his head.

He shrugged then immediately reached for the battery charger's switch. Suddenly Yolanda started hysterical screaming.

"STOP! I'll tell you! It's in the floor! The safe is in the fucking floor under that couch! The combination is four - seven - three - five - four – one - one! Take it all! Just please, let my baby go!"

She was sobbing uncontrollably. Low glanced at Big Tuck, and smiled. Then he said, "The love of a mother..."

"A mother's love..." Sunny, and Walter echoed.

✦ ✦ ✦

"Bingo!"

The safe opened with a loud click. Tugging the long steel handle on the huge safe, it took a little assistance from Sunny and Walter to get the heavy, fortified armored door to lift up. But as soon as the three got the safe's door fully opened, and peeked inside. It was crystal clear that they just struck gold.

"Okay then!" Walter exclaimed with glee.

"Muthafuckin' jackpot!" Low hollered.

Sunny clasped his hands, and rubbed them together in excitement. The Champion safe was as big as a mini storage closet. Inside, everything was lined up. On the left sat an arsenal of military assault weapons, two twelve-gauge shotguns, and a dozen handguns. The right side was divided into three metal shelves. Several dozen boxes of ammunition, containing various caliber-sized rounds were on the top shelf. The contents on the second, and third shelves made Low's eyes sparkle. On the second shelf, ten gold bars sat next to one hundred thousand dollars in cash, saran-wrapped in a square block. The third shelf was stocked with fifty kilos of cocaine packed on top of each other in five rows of ten. The Saran wrapped black duct taped bricks glowed like light bulbs.

"Okay, here we go boy!" Walter excitedly exclaimed.

He bent down, and picked up one of the bricks. Then he pulled out a small knife, and pierced the bag open. Placing the white substance in his mouth, he immediately felt the effects of the drug.

"Um hmm…dis dat Madonna!" Walter shouted.

Sunny made his way to the kitchen to get some garbage bags. After packing all the loot from the safe in three black garbage bags, Walter gave Low the signal. Then he and Sunny hit the front door, and headed toward a black van. Ghost was in the driver's seat.

Low remained in the house to clean up any evidence of the Zoes' presence. There was no longer a need for Big Tuck. Low had a murderous glare in his eyes. Immediately pulling out his Glock, Low pointed it at Big Tuck's head, and pumped two deafening shots into him.

Locking eyes with Low through his ski mask, Yolanda looked completely horrified. Low knew the rules—no witnesses should be left behind. He glanced down toward the glass coffee table, and saw the baby crying.

Low pointed his Glock at Yolanda. She was helpless, restrained in a metal chair with her mouth duct taped. He ripped the tape from her mouth then untied her hands, and feet. Yolanda rushed over to her son, picked him up, and began to sob loudly. Low walked out of the house, ran across the front yard, and hopped into the waiting minivan. They screeched off, leaving destruction in their wake. Big Tuck was dead, and the entire model city B-Gang eventually fell in line under the direction of Zoe Pound.

BRAINSTORMING

Day 120

7 p.m.

At this juncture, the entire north end of the city, from 163rd Street in north Miami down to Little Haiti, and across the entire Model City as far west as N.W. 62nd Avenue into Liberty City became Zoe Pound.

Their efforts to control it all were met with some resistance from a few stubborn loyalists of the deceased Zombie and B-Gang's leaders. Then word of Rip, Dante's, and Big Tuck's torturous deaths spread throughout the underworld, and there were no more resistance to the Zoes' takeover.

Slowly but surely, everyone started to get in tune with the Zoes' movement. With the entire northeast, and a large portion of the northwest on lock, Zoë Pound had instantly grown from a couple hundred members, to over four thousand strong, and growing by the month.

Low, Sunny, Walter, and the twins, took their roles as the top five, Caine took on more of a overseer's role and really didn't involve himself in too much dirt. He was out on bond, fighting a murder charge. King Zoe was getting more involved in politics, and stayed away from the criminal limelight. This left control of the movement solely in the hands of the new generation, and they led Zoë Pound headfirst into the booming Miami drug trade.

The top five also demanded a percentage from the profits made from other crews' illegal activities taking place on turf ran by Zoë Pound. No matter what other profits they received through any deals including, gambling, prostitution, and robberies, money from the drug game trumped all other rackets put together.

Cocaine money was the most lucrative. One hundred and sixty-three blocks were on lock, and open for business. Within two months, all fifty bricks that the top five had stretched to over eighty-five and a half bricks, taken from Big Tuck's stash were beginning to dry up. There was no connect to re-up, and Low was becoming agitated by the problem.

Finding a plug to connect with them so they could supply the amount of work they needed, became the issue. Connects were afraid of getting robbed by Zoë Pound, and would back out at the last minute of transaction. Even the plug Razor used when he was alive kept stringing them along on a date to re-up.

"He said give him another week... We need to have a little more patience," Sunny said, hanging up the phone with Razor's plug.

"Another week...? Man fuck patience we need work now!" Low fumed, pounding his fist on top of the wooden round table.

"I hear you, Zoë," Sunny said.

"What...? This muthafucka think our money ain't good?"

"Man, I think the muthafucka scared like every other fucka that refuses to fuck with us. Just hearing him speak on the phone, he sounded shook. I don't think he gon' connect. He used to be acting scared with Razor. And that was only for about ten to fifteen. Now Razor's out the picture, and we just went from needing ten to a hundred bricks. That nigga just giving us the runaround," Sunny said.

"Fuck!" Low fumed.

"Shit's going bad, huh?" Sunny asked.

"We down to our last few bricks, our customer flow is slowing down, and our soldiers in the streets are getting worried," Low said, glancing around at his cohorts sitting at the roundtable.

There was silence for a beat. Gunner, Ghost, Sunny, Caine didn't respond. Low looked at all the Zoes, and it became painfully obvious on everyone's face. They had reached an unexpected roadblock. Suddenly the sound of the basement's side-door opened, causing everyone to turn, and look in that direction.

A black Miami Dade police officer walked through the basement door, and Low immediately reached for his waist. Pulling out his gun, Low swiftly took aim.

"Whoa! Slow ya roll, cowboy!" Walter said, halting Low with a raised hand. Before continuing. "You haven't met Pierre yet, Low?"

The rest of the Zoes chuckled while Pierre walked around the table, saluting everyone with Zoë Pound greetings.

"Nah, I haven't," Low said.

"This here is Pierre. Don't let the uniform fool you. Pierre is Zoë to the bone. He just our guy on the inside," Walter said.

Pierre greeted Low, and took a seat at the roundtable. Low stole a quick glance at the single silver bars on each side of his police uniform. He was a lieutenant, Low noted.

"Any progress yet?" Walter asked, looking at Sunny.

"Not a damn thing. The connect still bullshitting," Sunny said.

"Kind a figured that... Pierre got some information that's useful," Walter said.

Everyone glanced at Pierre, giving him the floor. Clearing his throat, Pierre addressed the Zoë Pound hierarchy.

"I've been keeping my ear to the streets. And through a few sources, along with the info I've received through the wire, it's looking like your connect might not be bullshitting. There might really be no work to supply anyone."

"Really...?" Low echoed.

"Yes, one of the main suppliers' ship just got knocked off last week by the Florida coast guard and federal DEA. They were carrying a half a ton of coke. It happened just off the coast of Key Largo."

"That's not good for our business model. It cuts into our bottom line," Low said.

"And if you know anything about how these major suppliers operate—like a fraternity. One knock off is like basically sounding the hibernation alarm to every other supplier working in the Miami ports. Like a domino effect all the top suppliers find a hole, and don't come out 'til after the heat cools. This guarantees a shortage of supply for everyone. From kingpins on down."

"You just confirmed that there's a drought. How does that help us?" Low asked.

"Oftentimes what happens in these situations it could all just be a smokescreen. Usually when competition gets fierce between these major drug cartels, a supplier may intentionally cause a drought by sending a decoy ship out there just so it gets knocked off. Competitors will rather fall back for a month or two than risk getting any of their shipments jammed up. And while everyone's sleeping—boom! Another shipment with a much, much larger supply slips through uninterrupted by authorities or contested by competition. That cartel has a good two months to flood the streets exclusively with their product. By the time everyone else catches on, they done cleared millions, and now they are the ones ready to hibernate."

"That's a good history lesson on the drug trade and all, but it sounds kind of hypothetical," Caine said.

"This time I'm certain it's real. A half-ton—four hundred and forty-eight keys of coke—no smuggler is putting half-ton on the seas unless it's bait. I've been doing surveillance on one of my old informants. He's an employee working as a crewman for the Louise's Seafood Imports—a fishing company that's linked to the Peruvian drug cartel. After checking his work schedule, it happens that the same informant's scheduled to be on Louise's fishing boat when it docks at Jones boatyard tonight. I believe it's going down tonight."

"Tonight, huh…? How much work we talking here?" Sunny asked.

"From logging these cartel's patterns, if a half a ton was the bait, I'll say the real haul could be about three times that amount," Pierre said.

"So you mean there's gon' be a boat pulling into the Jones boatyard with three fucking tons of coke on it?" Gunner asked.

Pierre nodded his confirmation. A rush of adrenaline had been shot into everyone present. Members of the Pound could no longer sit. The air was buzzing with excitement.

"What time will that bitch be pulling in? And why the fuck we still sitting here?" Sunny impatiently asked.

"Hold on. Let's just say this is real. Y'all actually think seven muthafuckas can just walk on the boat and rob them without someone spotting? At nights, Jones Dock still has dozens of boats out there. We gotta think this all the way through," Low said.

"You're right. If y'all got spotted rushing onto a boat that could potentially raise suspicion, but not if the boat in question was raided for illegal activities, Pierre said.

"What'd ya mean?" Low asked.

"What I mean is if y'all go as officers then..." Pierre said with a nod.

✦ ✦ ✦

Miami River

August 21st, 1989

11:54 PM.

It was the last night of summer. A fishing boat named Louise 11 was slowly making its way up Miami River. During the mid-seventies, Miami River became a major port for drug smugglers importing large quantities of cocaine and marijuana into the United States from the Atlantic Ocean through the city of Miami.

The river was usually congested with boats and ships from all over the world. Everyday this port was the host to all types of boats from the big commercial cargo ships, independent fishing boats, cruise liners, and yachts to all kinds of small fishermen and leisurely boaters. The high volume of traffic made the Miami River a perfect place for the shipments of major drug cartels to easily slip through and unload completely undetected.

Louise 11 made its way approximately four miles up the river, and began pulling into the Jones boatyard. Transportation and dockworkers waited patiently for the Louise 11. It was forty-five minutes late. Gunner adjusted his elbows, and tightened his grip on his mounted M-110 Army issued sniper rifle. He had one trucker in his sights, and that was the driver who was picking up the load from Louise 11.

Zeroing in on the truck driver's face through M2 adjustable scope, he was completely locked one hundred yards away. Lying comfortably on top of a spread out blanket from the rooftop of a five-story Jet ski and boating equipment warehouse, Gunner waited for the right time.

From his location, Gunner couldn't hear a thing going on in the boatyard. He scanned the perimeter through his sniper rifle's night scope, and had a bird's eye view of the entire property. He kept his vision peeled on the truck driver's face. Then his focus shifted to Pierre in full police uniform, sitting behind the driver's seat of his Miami Dade police squad car discreetly parked in the lot of the boatyard. Next Gunner trained his night-vision scope on a black storage van parked on a side street approximately a half a block away.

In the van, Ghost sat behind the wheel gazing through a pair of night vision binoculars. Dressed in Miami Dade Swat team tactical gear, Sunny, Low, Walter, and Caine sat in the back. They were patiently waiting for the signal to move.

Glancing over to the boatyards watch Tower, Gunner noticed the night watchman on duty activate the bright red alert strobe light that sat on top of the tower, signaling that a boat had just successfully docked. Gunner zeroed in on the back of the watchman's head, preparing himself for the signal that was sure to come any second now.

"Let's ride!" Pierre said.

Gunner took a breath, and squeezed the trigger on his M-110 sniper rifle sending a bullet crashing into the back of the watchman's head, instantly killing him.

"All clear, move in!" Gunner said through the small microphone attached to his earpiece.

Pierre activated the squad car's dome lights. Sirens sounding off, Pierre floored the gas pedal of the black Crown Victoria. He came to a screeching halt between the docks leading to the Louise 11, blocking the path of the Steco's furniture moving truck.

Quickly jumping out, Pierre brandished his service weapon, and slowly crept toward the dock totally oblivious to someone's presence behind him.

A truck driver reached for his gun resting on the truck's passenger seat, but Gunner squeezed off another round. The truck driver was instantly killed. The commotion he made falling out the truck caught Pierre's attention. Glancing over his shoulder Pierre saw the headlights of the black van speeding his way.

Ghost came to a skidding stop in front of him. The two front doors of the van simultaneously swung open. A squad hopped out with their submachine guns ready. A smile came across Pierre's face.

"Let's do this," Pierre said.

The squad broke into a sprint, heading to the loading docks of the Louise 11 fishing boat.

"Miami police! Everybody on the floor! Get the fuck down!" Pierre shouted, leading the charge onto the boats main deck.

Two flash bombs instantaneously went off temporarily blinding all seven crewmen on board. They were in the boats main deck getting their belongings.

"Get down!" Pierre shouted.

Caine and Sunny rushed in two steps behind him clutching infrared equipped assault rifles.

"La policia! Todos corel!" A Spanish crewman shouted.

They all began to scatter and scramble for the rear exit. Low and Walter came busting through the two exit doors with the illuminating infrared laser beams on their Mac 11's pointed squarely at the crews.

"Get your fucking hands up cabrons!" Low barked.

The crew surrendered, and Low ordered them to their knees, and the rest of the Zoes immediately scoured through the boat.

Twenty minutes later, Sunny's exhausted face reentered the main deck, and said, "Nothing!"

"These crates ain't got nothing but fish and ice in them Zoe. This is fucking bullshit!" Walter shouted.

Caine continued prying open box after box of crates filled with fish. A few steps behind Sunny, Pierre made his way back onto the main deck.

"Fuck y'all mean? Did y'all search thoroughly?" Low asked, fuming, and shot Pierre an evil glare.

"Man, we searched this entire boat from top to bottom. Every fucking crevice, closet, and cooler, and didn't turn up a damn thing. Unless that shit's hidden really good, ain't nothing but a bunch of stank fish on this damn boat. And they're definitely ain't no fucking coke anywhere on here," Sunny said.

"Damn Zoe, you sent niggas on a blank mission?" Low asked Pierre.

"C'mon Zoe, don't even try me like that. Peze neg punyal avec chemise rouse la," Pierre said, giving an order in Creole.

"Press the Spanish guy in the red shirt."

Pierre communicated in Creole, secretly giving up his informant without any of the other crewmen's knowledge. Low strolled down the line of the crewmen facing a wall with their hands behind their heads. He grabbed the only one wearing a red shirt by the back, and aggressively pulled him down to the docks steel surface with one arm. Then he stuck the muzzle of his Mac.11 to the informant's cheekbone. A bright, red laser on top of the submachine gun instantly blinded the man's vision. Low asked, "Where the fuck is the cocaine!"

"Que dise? Yo no comprendre," the man said.

"You no speak English, muthafucka?" Low spat and immediately lifted the barrel of the weapon in the direction of the informant's fellow crewmen.

"No Ingles—"

Without hesitating Low pumped a silent burst of bullets into the back of the crewmen standing the furthest to the left.

"You got five seconds to tell me where the coke is before another body drops... Cinco... quatro...tres... dos...uno!"

"Por favor! Pada!" The informant shouted.

Low squeezed the trigger, and another close comrade from the ship's crew collapsed in a bloody mess.

"Por que!"

"Cinco... quatro...tres...dos..."

"Okay! Okay! I'll tell you! I'll tell you! The Coke is in the fish!" the informant said, pointing at all the fish filled crates lining every corner and crevice on the fishing boat's main deck.

"Good we understand each other," Low sneered.

"Yes, the yayo's stashed in the fuckin' fishes!"

With a wave of his Mac11, Low summoned Walter over, and spoke to him in Creole.

"Zoe, voye mwen ou pwason."

Reaching down Walter obliged, and threw one of the frozen fishes to Low. Catching the frozen fish, Low examined it for a few seconds. Then instinctively, he grabbed a hold of the head, and tightly squeezed both sides of the jaws, forcing its mouth opened. Stuffing his hand halfway down the fish's throat, he immediately felt something plastic-like between his fingertips. Low forced his entire hand inside, and pulled out the prize.

"Jack fucking pot!" Low exclaimed.

Gazing at the white substance rolled up in a Ziploc bag, Low marveled. It was tightly compressed, and the drug in it looked like a huge piece of chalk.

"This got to be an ounce, Zoe," Low finally said, tossing Sunny the package for confirmation.

"Yeah, this definitely about a zone… If not more," Sunny said, nodding.

Sunny took a small amount of coke in his nail, and tasted it. Then he said, "Damn this fire! Now I know why they call it fish-scale."

Low took a long look around the fishing boat's main deck. The crates of fish that lined damn near every corner and wall, it immediately became obvious to him, that he and his crew had indeed hit a huge prize.

"Subtract all witnesses. Everybody has to die!" Sunny said.

Turning around with his Mac 11 clutched tightly in his palms. Low locked eyes the informant who immediately begin to plead for his life.

"Thanks for the tip, papi," Low said.

Squeezing the trigger, he pumped a silent burst of bullets into the informant's head, taking him out. Without missing a beat he quickly followed up his murderous assault on the remaining four crewmembers.

The city is mine

In '89 Zoe Pound officially took over Miami. Taking advantage of the bloody '89 riots that took place across the city for two months straight. The brewing racial tensions between Blacks, Haitians, Hispanics, and Whites finally came to a head. Coupled with the fact that many immigrants were fed up with injustices aimed toward them by the police, they took to the streets, and began to rebel against the law.

Low and Zoe Pound took full advantage of the chaos. By investing a large percentage of their drug revenue to boost their criminal enterprise, Zoe Pound began a campaign of aggressive recruitment of soldiers, and purchasing a massive quantity of artillery. Zoe Pound simultaneously declared an all out war on every major drug cartel in the city for control of all the seaports of Miami.

With an Army of seventy-five hundred strong, Zoe Pound began laying the hammer down. On a daily, there were about twenty murders across the city attributed to Zoe Pound. Many of them public executions to show the entire underworld they were in charge. Between the full-fledged drug war, and an escalation of riots, the amount of blood and carnage on the streets of Miami was anarchic.

Unable to combat such an astronomical rapid increase of violence, the Miami Dade police force became overwhelmed. The resultant weakened strength, resources, and numbers, caused the bloodshed to continue. Many once dedicated officers began veering wildly off the line of duty. A great number of them began to succumb to the pressure of Low and Zoë Pound, and turned to corruption. The lure of fast cars, cash, and cocaine corrupted the best of them.

The amount of police officers on Zoë Pound's payroll increased tenfold. The relentless nonstop violence, and carnage against rival drug cartels helped Zoë Pound to take control over all Miami seaports. Competing cartels that were losing millions of dollars fighting back became sick of warring with Zoë Pound, and began to compromise.

Zoë Pound had seized control of illicit activities in Miami. Eventually every criminal faction in the city collectively agreed on a democratic solution guaranteeing Zoë Pound a percentage of everything coming in through the seaports. A unified peace agreement was ultimately signed, and the world confederation was formed between all the drug cartels.

Low was fast becoming a legend for his brashness, and elite street savvy, and was voted in by the head delegates of this newly formed union. He became the unofficial president of the drug trafficking capital of the United States.

CHAPTER
20

He's up

Low cruised down N.E. 2nd Ave in a new '91 midnight-blue Maserati sports car. The air conditioner was on chill, and a smooth melodic track from Sade flowed out of the vehicle's factory speakers. Michelle sat sound asleep in the passenger seat.

They were coming from a prenatal appointment at Beth Israel Hospital in Miami Springs, and on their way to the house of Michelle parents. Gazing at the soon-to-be mother of his first child, a million and one thoughts about his life were running through Low's mind.

For once in his life, none of his thoughts were negative in nature. Low was looking forward to becoming a father. He was having a baby with a woman he truly loved made the entire experience feel complete. Michelle was the perfect woman. She embodied the true definition of a ride or die partner.

During the nine-month pregnancy, Low hadn't been around much. He and the Zoes were on a mission. Michelle never complained, instead she was always encouraging. Low moved him and Michelle miles away from the madness of Little Haiti, and into a massive five-bedroom luxury penthouse in Boca Raton.

Low also hired a full-time live-in nanny to assist Michelle in their new home. The nanny helped with everything from cooking, cleaning, grocery shopping, laundry, and sometimes she was someone Michelle could talk with. On Saturdays Michelle was treated to a pampering session at the city's new local spa. She received a full body, prenatal massage, facial, manicure, pedicure, and Brazilian wax. Low gave her a couple thousand dollars spending money.

Sundays were spent with Michelle, and he treated her to dinner and movie. They would go see a local comedy show, or a leisurely stroll in their backyard that was right on the beach. At the end of those evenings, Low made sure he topped date night off by making love to Michelle. As he drove, Low reached over, and laid an affectionate hand on Michelle's protruding stomach. He was already busy making plans to marry Michelle. Everything seemed to be finally coming together.

Money was no longer an issue, and since his Zoes had conquered the game, Low was left pondering his next move. He began thinking about life, being on the streets, and hustling. Low had never gone into the game with the intent of making the streets a full-time career. The goal was always to get in, get lots of money, and get out before the alphabet boys came knocking.

Low was thinking of an exit strategy. Walter, Sunny and the rest of Zoë Pound were falling deeper and deeper into the game. Each member was using the control they held on the Miami seaports to tie themselves and the organization into more lucrative criminal ventures. They were expanding in numbers and influence across the state of Florida, and eventually the entire southern region.

Sunny and Walter's latest business discussions were with a Boston, Massachusetts based group of international figures. They were made up of military men active declarative officers and generals in the new Black Irish Republican Army. They were looking to broker an artillery purchase from Zoë Pound. A venture that the purchasers were willing to ditch out eight figures.

Expansion had always been extremely lucrative for Zoë Pound. Each new business deal that arose called for an increase in soldiers, and usually meant an uprising in bloodshed. In order to sustain Zoë Pound's empire, violence was a must. Being a boss was time consuming for Low. Profits skyrocketed, but it seemed as if he never had enough time to enjoy any of the money.

In his attempts to share his thoughts and views of getting out the game with his Zoes, Low soon realized that they were too blinded by the moment to look forward, and see the future. They were all too involved in the present, enjoying life, and living for the day. Low's comrades thought that they were already too deep in the game to even consider getting out.

Low loved his Zoes and enjoyed the comrade of Zoë Pound. They were his brothers, but he and Michelle were about to start a family, and he knew he would have to make a transition out the game now. Low didn't want it to swallow him whole, and he wouldn't be able to find a way out. Low saw giants like Tony fall hard. He dodged a bullet in that car theft case. After being questioned by the Feds, he was let go. Tony didn't snitch on him. Then he witnessed Razor's life snubbed out without even get the chance to see his firstborn. Low definitely had come to the conclusion that he was getting out with or without his beloved brothers' approval.

He had even mapped out an exit strategy, and immediately began to execute that plan. Moving to Boca Raton was the first step. Over the past few weeks, Low was in discussions with businessmen. He first met them at an exclusive jewelry store while purchasing an engagement ring for Michelle. The four young, black, wealthy men were in expensive Italian business suits, and had legal money in the bank. They were plotting legit business venture investments. After an impromptu meeting for a couple hours at a local coffee shop, the four men instantly took a liking to this small business owner that Low claimed to be. They also filled him in on their plans for their next business investment.

This investing plan was for budding stocks of the music industry with particular emphasis in the rap genre. After reviewing the revenues, and profit numbers from the last five years, and taking into account all possibilities for losses, they were looking at substantial increase in the national sales and revenue of rap music, as well as rising potential in international sales.

Their goal was to launch their own record distribution company, and compete for artists, record label contracts, and distribution sales. While at the same time, they would have inclusive ownership of the corporation's decision-making and stock shares. This move would ultimately allot them a hundred percent return on all capital gains earned.

Low made a verbal commitment to their cause, and officially became a fifth investor. Low advised his new partners that he would need time to get back to them with his two million dollar investment. Rainy days were unfortunately inevitable in the game. Low had a lot of his money stashed away.

After the boat heist, he purchased an old alligator farm that sat on two acres of land on the countryside of the Everglades. Then he began burying trash bags full of cash on the property every chance he got to make the two and a half hour drive down there from the city. No one, not even his Zoes knew about the property, or the amount of money he stored there.

The problem Low had was how to gracefully bow out of the game, and Zoë Pound. He knew leaving would cause his fellow Zoes to feel bitterness toward him. This could lead to them being envious, and caused them to seek retribution against him. Low knew he had taken an oath, and was bonded to Zoe Pound for life. So he wasn't trying to cut his ties with them completely. He had just begun to see life outside the game, and like King Zoe—now an American Ambassador to his native country, Haiti, Low wanted to explore other avenues that weren't criminally driven.

Over time, Low figured he would convince his brothers to make the same transition from thug to corporate. In order to accomplish such a feat, Low had to act now. His exit strategy from the game was officially in motion.

Low pulled into the driveway of Michelle's parents, and eased the gears on his Maserati into neutral, the sudden piercingly loud beeping coming from his sky pager completely broke his train of thought. It promptly awoke Michelle out of her peaceful nap as well.

"So sorry, babe," Low apologetically mumbled.

Fumbling with his seatbelt buckle, Low quickly read the number on his pager. He didn't know who was paging him, and stared befuddled by the unfamiliar number. Only his closest Zoes, and immediate family had access to this pager number. There were no codes following the number, and that threw Low off. Clipping the pager back on his belt, Low knew he had to get inside the house quick so he can use the phone.

"Rise and shine sleeping beauty," Low said, planting a tender kiss on Michelle's cheek.

Michelle gave Low that sarcastic a look, and said, "I just want this baby out of me!"

Low shook his head, and said, "He'll be out soon."

"You mean she, right?" Michelle quipped.

The couple continued their playful banter while Low escorted Michelle into the house. They had picked up food to go from Michelle's favorite Haitian eatery. He immediately picked up the house phone, and dialed the number from his pager.

"What?" Low exclaimed through the phone's receiver. He waited for an answer then continued. "So how much is the bail...? All right, say no more. I'll be right there!"

✦ ✦ ✦

Rob awoke to the booming sound of the hospital's loud-speaker outside his room. He heard an announcement paging a doctor. Opening his eyes, Rob tried to gather his thoughts. The conversation with his primary nurse earlier that morning left questions in his mind, and he couldn't fall back into a deep sleep. The slightest sound immediately awoke him out of his slumber.

Rest wasn't an issue. Rob had been doing that for the past ten months. After being in a coma for an entire year, he was immediately going to be discharged, and released to the custody of the Miami Dade police. It was forty-eight hours now since he was out of the coma. Then yesterday, he had a briefly evaluation by a nurse, and had not been seen by a doctor yet. Other than the nurse coming in to check up on him when it was time to feed him, and replace the surgical gauze covering his eye socket, no other post-surgical assessments were done.

Yesterday the nurse informed Rob that his case was high profile, and the hospital's administration wanted nothing to do with the media firestorm soon to hit. The negative publicity would be too much for the public relations department. The hospital wanted him immediately discharged.

Rob was being transferred to Miami Dade police, and held in the Dade county jail at the H.S.U. unit. While there, he would receive all necessary medical treatment, and await trial by the state on two counts of attempted murder, and one count of murder on the k-9 dog.

Rob was given a bond, and this afforded him the opportunity to fight his charges from the outside. The bond was set at one million dollars. Even at ten percent, Rob knew he would never be able to post a bail that high. Sighing he thought of Low, and wondered how his friend was living. Leaving Low by himself in the streets made him feel worse. Rob had put in all that work together, and didn't get a chance to spend any of their fifty-grand pay off. His pain suddenly became unbearable.

He was still alive, and survived a shootout. Being handcuffed to a hospital bed, and looking at three capital charges was depressing. Rob was certain the law was going to be playing for keeps when it came to the courtroom game. Gazing out the window, Rob saw the lively beam of Miami's afternoon sunshine. It was a complete contrast to the many gloomy days, he knew lie ahead. The thought of fighting the state of Florida for his freedom, and getting his life back looked dismal.

It was comforting to know that Low was still out there, and free. The nurse told him she would attempt to contact his aunt, Lucille, and his brother Milow. They were the only two people on his contact and visit list. She would do this before he was bonded over to the county jail, but Rob hadn't gotten any response since she told him this yesterday. He considered the idea to be another lost cause. Glancing over at the wall-mounted clock, it was one minute from three O'clock shift change. The afternoon shift officer for the day would be ready to transport Rob to the county jail any minute now.

His eyes followed the second hand on the clock until it struck twelve. It was time to face the music. He wasn't prepared, but he was ready. Suddenly a knock on his room door caught his attention.

"Mr. Matayer...?"

The nurse from yesterday stepped into the hospital room carrying a plastic bag containing folded clothes in her hands. An angelic smile was plastered across her pretty, mocha complexioned face. Her presence alone was very soothing to Rob, but a young, white Miami Dade County police officer entering the room behind her, and Rob's face turned into a frown. He impulsively sat up in the bed. The nurse walked over to Rob, and the cop slowly came forward.

"Are you Robinson Matayer?" the cop asked, opening a green folder.

Sucking his teeth, Rob rolled his eyes sarcastically, and gazed up at the young cop without a verbal response.

"I just have a few procedural questions for you, and I'll be on my way. Now all I need is for you to confirm your birthday, and social security number so I can remove the handcuffs and be on my way."

Rob gave the cop a skeptical look. His eyes darted at the nurse. Rob's clueless expression was evident. The nurse's smile was confusing to Rob. It wasn't the reception he was expecting when the time came for him to be transferred to the county jail.

"Um, what's this all about?" Rob asked, looking bewildered.

"Robinson, you've made bond!" The nurse delightfully said.

"What... What? You sure...?" Rob stuttered.

Then his eyes shot wide open, and he asked, "Bond...?"

"Yes, your brother's outside waiting for you!" The nurse said.

"Ah—" Rob said, but the nurse interrupted.

"I have some fresh clothes for you to change into,"

the nurse said, handing Rob the package she was carrying.

"If I can get you to just sign by this X I'll be on my way," the cop said.

Rob signed his discharge papers, bonds, and a summons paper for him to appear in court for his arraignment at the downtown courthouse in the morning. His right wrist throbbed from being handcuffed to the metal post on the hospital bed. Rob massaged the deep indentation in his wrists.

"Officer, I guess they can't keep a good man down, huh?" Rob said as the officer walked out of the room.

Rob was smiling when he walked out of the room, and gave the nurse a kiss on the cheek.

"Thanks for everything, nurse. I'm back baby!" Rob said, walking out.

The hospital's main entrance automatic, sliding doors separated, and Rob stepped out into the afternoon sunshine, Low's eyes brightened with excitement.

"My nigga!" Low exclaimed with a huge smile plastered across his face.

Rob squinted, adjusting his vision to the bright sunlight. Nodding, he laughed, and couldn't contain his excitement of seeing Low leaning up against a fresh looking sports car.

Low was dressed in white linen shorts, and looking like big money. The sight of Low brought an exhilarating feeling over Rob.

"If it ain't the man of steel in the flesh!" Low smiled.

Rob joyfully embraced Low with a heartfelt hug. Then Low said, "Damn, I'm so happy to see you right now, my nigga. You had me scared to death. I thought you wasn't going to make it."

Low's eyes were welling up with tears of joy as he held onto Rob, squeezing him tightly, and laughing.

"I'm good my nigga. Warriors don't die," Rob said with tears in his eyes.

The two broke their embrace and, Rob wiped his eyes dry. He glanced behind Low, and saw the new Bi-turbo Maserati with custom midnight blue paint job. Shaking his head, Rob smiled affectionately, and said, "Damn nigga, what's this...? I see you've been holding shit down while I was gone."

Rob was excited, and checked out the fifty thousand dollar sports car from bumper to bumper.

"It ain't hard to tell. Since you were gone I had to do my duty. Now we on..." Low smiled.

"Low, I'm loving the sound of that," Rob said, nodding his head approvingly.

"I knew you would."

"But damn, you just bonded me out. It's been ten months...but what the fuck you been up to?"

Low chuckled, and shook his head. Then he extended the key, unlocking all four doors, and said, "It's a long story. Hop in, Rob. I'll fill you in."

✦ ✦ ✦

163rd Street mall

Get Your Swagger Back

This was a department store located in the hundred and sixty-third Street mall in North Miami Beach where all the hustlers and jazzy ladies shopped. Bizzy-B was the store's owner, and a retired hustler, knew what was in, and what was not. He kept his store flooded with the most recent design and fashion trends. The latest styles, and fashionable gears were available before the competitors knew about them. Rob sat on the men's side of the store shoe section, waiting for a salesgirl to get back with the five pairs of sneakers he had requested in his size. It felt weird being out of the hospital.

Rob felt like he was lost in a fantasy world. During the drive from the hospital to the mall, Low brought him up to date on everything that went down while he was in the coma. Rob had to pinch himself to be convinced he really was out of his coma, and not lost in a dream.

Once they arrived at the mall, Low wasted no time splurging on his best friend. Their first stop was to BK's jewelry store, where Low dropped twenty five thousand dollars like it was nothing, buying Rob gold rope chain, three gold diamond flooded rings, a gold diamond nugget bracelet, and a ten thousand dollar-eighteen karat gold Givenchy watch.

Rob's jewelry game was now on point, and Low took Rob to every male clothing store in the mall. He bought Rob entire wardrobes, including a few dozen color coordinated designer track suits, about twenty different Kangol hats, fifty different pullover shirts, several designer silk pants, matching gator skin shoes, five expensive leather jackets, over fifty pairs of slacks, Dickey's pants and shorts, and countless LV and Gucci short sets. The last stop of the shopping spree was Swagger to get Rob's shoe game up to par.

"Sir... Sir..."

A slight tap on his shoulder broke Rob out of his daze. The salesgirl was trying to get his attention.

"Hmm...yes?" Rob said, putting his thoughts away.

"Sir, I got the rest of those sneakers you requested," the salesgirl said with a smile.

"My bad," Rob said, taking the sneaker boxes from her.

He placed them on the floor next to the other several boxes he already tried on. The salesgirl smiled, and said, "No problem. You're probably just fatigued from all the shopping," the salesgirl said. She saw all the shopping bags from different stores in the mall. Rob opened the first box, and pulled out a pair of white on white shell toes.

While putting on the sneakers, Rob heard the giggling, and noticed some girls several seats away chitchatting about their plans for the night. Rob gazed at honey complexioned girl, admiring her striking beauty. Her full lips, and captivating hazel brown eyes made her absolutely gorgeous.

She slipped her left foot into a pair of some fire red Prada pumps, glanced at Rob, and caught him staring at her. Her seductive wink, followed by a wave of her hand, and Rob knew he was on. He watched her mouthed something to her friend that cause the chocolate complexioned girl sitting beside her to glance at him.

It was on him to make a move. Thanks to Low, he was looking like new money, and had a pocketful, but all his self-confidence was no longer there. Low walked over to him, and said, "Damn Rob, you ain't see 'em fine-ass bitches waving?"

Taking a seat next to Rob, Low explained that he had been peeping the whole scene while talking to Biz.

"Yeah, I was just about to go holler at 'em," Rob said, lacing up the Adidas sneakers that fit perfectly on his feet.

Knowing his crony, Low shot Rob a strange look. He realized that Rob was conscious of the eye patch. Even though Rob was dressed freshly dip, and dripping with expensive jewelry, all his confidence was gone. Low immediately jumped into action.

"Okay, I get it big homie. You busy shopping, and want me to go get 'em, huh?"

Low saw that the two women were now checking him out. Coyly smiling, he walked over to where they were.

"Ladies, me and my man would like y'all to join us..."

Nonchalantly shrugging, the women glanced at each other. Then they smiled and nodded at Low. With an amused smirk, he signaled to Rob. They both took sat next to the women.

"I don't mean to be intrusive, but we were peeping y'all peeping us. I thought it was only appropriate that we cease staring, and just introduce ourselves," Low smiled.

"Oh, we were peeping y'all huh?" One of the women asked, sounding amused.

"Good one," the other smiled.

"I'm Chantella and this is my girl, Cynthiana."

"I'm Low, and that's the big homie, Rob," Low smiled.

"Nice to meet ya, Low," Chantella smiled, offering her manicured hand.

Low held onto her soft palm a bit longer than usual, and found himself totally captivated by her emerald green eyes.

"I'm sure you've heard this before, but I gotta say it anyway Damn, you're very beautiful," Low smiled.

He had never seen a woman so beautiful with dark skin, and green eyes. It was like icing on a tasty cake.

"What do y'all do?" Cynthiana asked with a raised eyebrow.

She spoke with a Spanish accent as thick as Chantella's, and just as sexy. The smell of her perfume made her desirable. A vibe was developing, and Low liked it.

"Hold on, y'all don't recognize his face…? Y'all must not be from around here then. Spanish?" Low asked.

"We're from Texas," Cynthiana said with a hint of embarrassment.

"Dominicans…" Chantella quipped.

"Okay, I understand then…"

"We're only here for the weekend," Cynthiana quickly added.

"Oh, then that explains it," Low smiled.

"That's Robertocito Matayer. He runs Matayer Entertainment, and that's one of Miami's largest fashion modeling companies," Low said.

"Wow…" both women chorused.

"I was just surprised that y'all didn't recognize him. I mean…you two look like y'all have definitely done some modeling."

"Yes, we have," Chantella said.

Both women begrudgingly glanced over at Rob, and smiled. Rob was doing his best to keep a straight face, nodded politely.

"It's really nice to meet ya, Mr. Matayer," Chantella said, extending her hand out to Rob.

Low could see the shape of the women's ass, and while licking his lips, he winked at Rob. Lust overtook Low's senses, and he immediately shifted gears with the conversation.

"So ladies, what are your plans for the day?" Low asked.

"We're just finished at the nail salon, and decided to stop by had to do a little shopping for shoes that'll match the new dresses we bought. Then we're headed back to our hotel, and rest up for later," Cynthiana said, glancing down at the Prada pumps on her feet that she was trying on.

"Okay…"

"But we might have to check out another shoe store. I totally love the shoes, but these prices are way out of our budget," Cynthiana sighed.

Low's pager suddenly went off. Glancing down at his hip, he peered at the pager screen, but didn't recognize the number.

"It's the Denise from makeup. I totally forgot all about her," Low lied, winking at Rob.

"I see…" Rob said.

Glancing at his Chopard, Low said, "She scheduled

an appointment with you for eight. It's twenty after six. We got to get going boss."

Low quickly stood, and prepared to exit. Then Rob said, "How could you let such an important business meeting slip your mind…? You know Denise is an important client."

"My bad, sir, Low said to Rob. Then turning to the women, he continued. "Ladies, I really hate to leave so abruptly, but we have to get going."

Rob bowed and smiled. Then both Low and him walked toward their shopping bags. Chantella and Cynthiana were left with dumbfounded expressions on their faces.

"Wait…maybe when you're all done with business, y'all can stop by the hotel?" Chantella said.

"Yeah, we're right at the Flamingo on South Beach. I'll just write down the room number for you."

Chantella began to scramble through her purse for a pen, and Low asked, "Did you say the Flamingo on South Beach?"

"Yes…" Cynthiana said, nodding.

"Wow… Isn't that a coincidence…? It just so happened that our business appointment is in the same hotel," Low said.

"No way," Chantella beamed.

"Yeah, the Flamingo on Collins Avenue right? That's crazy! What a small world…"

"Sure is," Chantella said.

"Well now we know you guys will definitely be stopping in later to hang out with us," Chantella said, handing Low a piece of paper with their room number, and her pager number on it.

"I'm really looking forward to it," Cynthiana announced, shooting Low a seductive wink.

"Well ladies, since we're all headed in the same direction. You guys might as well roll with us," Low smiled.

"We would love to, but we haven't finish our shopping," Cynthiana sighed.

Low looked at the half-dozen shoeboxes on the floor, and shot the women a questionable look. Then he quickly glanced at Rob, and summoned the salesgirl over.

"Um, sorry to bother you. It seems my two lady friends here are having a hard time choosing between these selection of heels," Low said.

"I could understand that. Our selection of shoes, especially women's, is very vast," the salesgirl said.

"Without question," Low said.

"Choosing the perfect pair can be quite a chore. Maybe I can help them through their selection process," the salesgirl said.

Rob looked on, wondering what Low was up to. Chantella and Cynthiana were in the same mind frame as Rob. Looking on, they were totally lost.

"Any other day, that definitely would've been very helpful," Low said, rubbing his chin thoughtful. Then he glanced at his watch, and continued. "Me and my boss are actually pressed for time. I personally think these Prada's are it."

"Alright…"

"But since we're running kind of late, I think it will be best for them to just make up their minds at home. So you can add all these to the ones my boss was trying earlier. And bring them all over to the cash register for us, please. Thank you."

"You're going to…um… For purchase?" the salesgirl asked.

"Yes," Low smiled, glancing at the startled faces of Chantella and Cynthiana. Then Low continued. "Ladies, y'all rolling back to the hotel with us right?"

This time there was no protest from either of the women. It took couple salesgirls four trips to get all the boxes of heels and sneakers to the cash register. By the time they were done, they were sweating up a storm. The commission from the sales was worth the labor.

Low, Rob, and their new Dominican girlfriends exited the store, all smiles. Their hands were filled with shopping bags. Today was definitely a good day.

✦ ✦ ✦

The Flamingo Hotel

"Aye papi! Si...si!" Chantella screamed in ecstasy.

Low plunged his dick deep inside of Chantella's gushy pussy, entering her from the rear. Hot water from whirlpool faucet of the shower rained down on their naked bodies.

"Aye papi! Duro! Duro!" Chantella wailed, begging him to go harder.

Rubbing her clit with her fingers, she pinched her breast. Then Chantella squeezed and massaged her erect nipple, enjoying the feeling of Low fucking himself into a sexual frenzy from behind.

His massive tool tore viciously through her womanhood. She braced herself to prevent the top of her forehead from slamming against the porcelain tiles. A loud clapping sound echoed on impact as his thighs collided against the softness of her plump ass cheeks.

"Duro! Duro!"

Squeezing her eyes shut in pleasurable pain, she moaned while Low aggressively plugged her moistened hole.

"Oh yeah! Si papi... No parez... Rapido! Rapido! Rapido!"

Low's swollen pipe snaked through her insides, activating her G spot, and igniting a fire within her womb.

Her body temperature climatically overheated, and she reached her zenith. The explosion caused her body to shudder in small orgasm spasms.

"Ooh-o-oh Pa-pa-pi!" Chantella delightfully cried.

Tightly squeezing her thigh muscles together, she tried to control the overflow of love juices streaming from her body. Reaching his highest sexual point, Low pumped and pushed himself as deep as he could. Then he froze, and exploded, filling the tip of the Lifestyle latex condom with the results of his pleasure.

Meanwhile in the bedroom, Cynthiana was licking the shaft of Rob's long, firm penis. She lassoed her tongue up the tip of his rock hardness, and circled the swollen head with her warm mouth. His pre-cum lathered her soft lips like lip-gloss. Gliding his dick against her cheeks, she smacked herself with his stiffness then engulfed him whole into her mouth, taking him in until she was deep-throat his dick.

The tip of Rob's cock completely blocked her air-waves. Cynthiana gagged, and slurped until Rob's body shuddered and jerked. When he let out a groan of satisfaction then Cynthiana knew it was her time. Picking up the pace, she switched it up, and went in for the kill.

Focusing solely on the head of his penis, Cynthiana bobbed her head up and down then around, sucking Rob's dick with serious precision. She popped his swollen cock in and out of her soft, wet lips with such intensity that Rob's toes curled. His orgasmic count down was over.

Rob was unable to hold back any longer, and with his eyes squeezed shut, he reached for her head. Grabbing a firm grip of her long, black, silky hair Rob guided her head up and down, fucking her lips. Cynthiana tightened her jaw muscles around his massive cock, and his entire body tensed and squirmed. His lower half lifted off the bed, and he squeezed his ass cheeks together, blasting off the most intense explosion of his life.

"Ah-ah-ah…ugh…" Rob shouted, ejaculating with a pleasure-filled grunt.

Cynthiana sucked on the spurting semen, swallowing every drop. Then she seductively watched Rob's body collapsed onto the hotel's bed while his head shook uncontrollably.

A knock at the door suddenly startled Rob. Taking a deep, Rob warily gazed over at the door then at Cynthiana. She knew that she had just sucked all of the energy out of him, and smiling she said, "Don't worry, papi. I'll get it."

Buck-naked, Cynthiana rose from her knees, and strutted across the presidential suite master bedroom's plush carpet. After unlocking the room's massive mahogany door, she threw him a robe, and nonchalantly walked into the bathroom.

"I'll be in the shower waiting on you," Cynthiana purred, and disappeared behind the bathroom doors.

Low strolled into the room, and shook his head while rubbing his crotch through his silk pants.

"Damn bruh, seems like you been having yourself some fun up in here," Low smiled.

Rob rose to a sitting position, and pulled up his boxers. He glanced at Low, smiled, and said, "I'm pretty sure it was just as much fun as you just had with her friend."

"I guess you're right," Low chuckled.

"Where she at?"

"Fast asleep in her room. For the past couple of hours I been straight fucking the shit out of her fat ass. Maybe later on, we can switch," Low suggested.

"Hmm…" Rob said, thinking of the possibility.

"Shit, we got this room for the rest of the weekend. We might as well make the best of it," Low said.

"Sounds like a plan," Rob said, nodding.

Low glanced at the time then said, "But for now

you need to be getting dressed boss. Cause we 'bout to hit the town."

"Oh yeah…? What'cha got planned?" Rob asked, letting out a tiresome yawn as he made his way to the closet.

"I figured for your first night back on the scene, we should hit club Desire. I just got off the phone with the promoter, and he going to have the entire VIP on standby for us. That bitch will be thick as fuck with stallions tonight. Plus, all the fellas gonna be in the house. So we finna hit that bitch up, and do it big for you big homie."

"Okay then…" Rob said, nodding approvingly.

"You down?"

"Hell yeah. Just give me about an hour to get ready. I'm about to hop in the shower."

Low shook his head, and smiled. Reaching into his pockets, Low pulled out a condom, and tossed it to Rob.

"I'll be downstairs in the lobby waiting," Low smiled, and walked out.

CHAPTER
21

He's up (Club Desire)

Club Desire was located in North Miami. Low pulled his Maserati up to the valet parking of the club. Glancing out from the passenger seat window, Rob took in the festivities going on outside the club. A wide variety of fine honeys were making their way from the club's parking lot. The sidewalk in front of the club was overflowing with scantily dressed woman. The line of revelers waiting to get inside stretched an entire three blocks. It seemed like everyone in the city was trying to party tonight.

When Low's Maserati came to a stop. A valet promptly made his way to the car, placed two bright orange hazard cones on each end of the car, and left a numbered ticket under the car's windshield. Then he moved along as a stretch limo pulled up.

Bobbing his head to a new fresh cut from the Gheto Boys, Rob enjoyed his turn on a tightly rolled Garcia Vega, and admired the mass of pretty ladies. Curious women were continuously breaking their necks staring at him as they passed the luxury sports car.

They were trying to get a glimpse of who was inside the confines of the smoked out luxury vehicle, but it was virtually impossible to make out their faces through the thick fog of weed smoke. Low and Rob were having a Bob Marley type smoking session before going inside the club.

"I see Sunny and 'em boys up in this bitch already!" Low said.

The car parked in front of his Maserati was Sunny's midnight blue Spyker Laviolette. Low could tell it was Sunny's car by the Florida license plate that read, '*Zoe 4 Life.*'

"This bitch thicker than a muthafucka!" Rob said, taking a deep drag off the cigar.

"Hell yeah! We might have to get another suite at the Flamingo. With all these bad broads flocking around this bitch, we might have to book that muthafucka for the whole week!" Low said with a wide grin.

"Yeah...? Well this time, I wanna be a successful R&B artist. They get all the bitches," Rob joked, and the two of them shared the laughter.

"Get used to it. This is what life's all about now. Stacking this money, on niggas in these luxury European toys, and fucking all these exotic looking broads. The city is ours," Low said.

Low's boast brought and endearing smile to Rob's face. Reflecting, Rob said, "Damn Low, you really held it down while I was gone. You really carried on the torch, put in crazy work, and made it happen!"

"Man, I didn't do anything you wouldn't have done if the tables were turned. I'm just happy you survived all that shit."

The two enjoyed the rest of their weed filled Garcia Vega in silence while the music played on.

Reaching over Low opened the glove compartment, pulled out a small plastic bag, and said, "We about to hit this club, and do it big for your first night back on the scene." Low gave the bag to Rob. Then he continued. "I just wanted you to have this before we go inside."

Shaking his head with a bashful smile, Rob reached inside the bag and pulled out a white square box. Lifting the top off the box, the first gift Rob pulled out caused his eyes get cloudy with tears. It was a black custom-made, rubies, and diamond flooded eye patch.

It was flooded with five-carat diamonds, and had a big capital R in the middle. The R was made of red rubies. Rob had to take a deep breath, and compose himself to keep from crying.

"Slick Rick ain't got nothing on you now," Low said.

Rob removed the hospital issued eye patch. Then he replaced it with his new custom-made patch. Rob didn't quite understand the second gift. He pulled out a single car key. Eyeing the key skeptically, he stared at the insignia that read Spyker in gold letters. He glanced at Low, who lifted his head, and motioned in the direction of a brand new 91 midnight blue Spyker Laviolette super sports car parked in front of them.

"I had Sunny drive it up here for you," Low said with a sly smirk.

"Damn Low, that bitch is hard as fuck!" Rob said, staring excitedly at the back of his new expensive gift. Then he asked, "But what's the plate all about? I ain't a Zoe—"

"Welcome to the family, Zoe," Low smiled, cutting Rob off as he held out an outstretched hand.

Rob was truly speechless, but his silence spoke volumes. Clasping Low's hand, he embraced Low, and said, "I'm grateful, Low."

"A'ight Zoe, let's hit this club, and party like there's no tomorrow!" Low exclaimed.

Turning off the Maserati's engine, Low reached in the backseat for his jacket.

"Damn, it's kind a cold out. I should've brought my jacket too," Rob said, feeling the chill of the brisk March Miami night.

"Here just take my jacket. I'm good," Low said, tossing Rob his calfskin Hermes jacket.

They hopped out the Maserati to the admiring eyes from all the fine honeys, and envious stares of all the haters stuck on the club's long line. The two dapper men casually strolled to the front entrance.

Slipping Low's Jacket on, Rob briefly gazed over to his left, checked out his new sports car, and smiled with an approving head nod. He slipped his hands in the pockets of the Hermes jacket and was about to catch up with Low. Then he felt a piece of paper in the jacket's right pocket that caused him to pause. Pulling the piece of paper out, he inspected it before tossing it.

At first glance, Rob thought it was just a regular shopping receipt and was about to ball it up. Then he noticed a note written on the back. Rob gazed at the note inquisitively. It didn't take much examining of the message with a telephone number followed by an address, and a time to meet up.

A woman had written the note, and he realized who signed it. This realization caused the smile on his face to instantly vanish. Rob recognized Lovely's signature, followed by short message that read, *And you better not be late this time mister. I'll be upset...* A smiley face followed.

"Yo Rob, hurry up, my nigga. This shit's packed to capacity, they 'bout to shut the doors," Low shouted, standing in front of the club next to the club promoter, waiting to escort them inside.

"I'm coming right now, Low," Rob said.

He folded up the receipt, placed it in his pants pocket, and forced a smile back onto his mug. On the other hand, he was seething so hard on the inside that his stomach was churning in knots.

"Hurry…"

Windows to wall, Club Desire was jam-packed. Bobby Brown's latest single, *My Prerogative* blasted with deafening bass from the club's mega speakers. The twenty five hundred partygoers reveled, enjoying themselves. Team of dancers moved enthusiastically, break-dancing, and battling each other. Sexy women moved to up-tempo tunes while the male onlookers chilled on the outer edges of the dance floor. Some were two stepping, and rooting for several small dance competitions that were on the way all over the club.

The top B-Boys were definitely in the house, busting their freshest dance moves. Onlookers were unable to contain their excitement screamed, and shouted enthusiastically. Making their way through the crowded dance floor, Low and Rob followed behind the club promoter, and two bulky security guards, escorting them to the clubs a private room with a full bar, separate deejay, and strippers dancing on stage.

They went past a couple of fulfill your desire rooms, catering to the crème de la crème of Desire's VIP's. Low and Rob had all eyes on them as they strolled through the main floor, looking like Hollywood movie stars, dressed in their color-coordinated silk suits, matching gator skin shoes. Low's was all Crip blue, and Rob's all Blood red.

Five shining gold chains swung from each of their necks. The dance floor's disco lights reflected off their four-fingered rings, and diamond flooded jewelry. Their apparel had all eyes mesmerized. Low and Rob were looking, feeling, and moving like money. They made brief eye contact with the honeys, and smiled gracefully at all the envious stares from the playa-haters.

"Okay, okay El Presidente has arrived!" Gunner said as Low and Rob stepped into the Desire room.

"Yeah nigga. The boss is on deck!" Low said, flashing a smile.

Gunner got up from the stool with a smile on his face clutching the bottle of Moët he was guzzling. He embraced Low.

"What it do G–Zoe!" Low greeted.

"Everything's everything, Low!" Gunner said, taking a swig of champagne. Then he continued. "Take a look around, Zoe. It's off the chain up in here. Nigga, I am going in!"

Holding out an outstretched fist, Gunner greeted Rob with Zoë Pound salute, and said, "How you living, Zoe? Welcome back."

"Thanks, everything's everything, Zoe. You already know," Rob said.

"So where my niggas at?" Low asked, glancing around the Desire room.

"Man, my bro somewhere around this bitch chasing some young, fine redbone with a fatty. I haven't seen Caine, and Pierre all day. I don't even know if they are here or not, but Walter and Sunny is at the stage making it rain for this Cherokee looking stallion that can beat box with her ass cheeks. You should go check that shit out, Zoe. I swear that shits a sight to see."

Bursting out laughing, Low bellied over at Gunner's animation. Then he said, "Nah, maybe in a few, but for now me and Rob bout to get our drinks on…"

Low and Rob took their seats next to Gunner at the bar, and a fine looking Cape Verde bartender came over to them.

"What can I get you, gentlemen," she asked in her soft, sexy Creole accents.

"Yes umm, can I get—"

Low started to speak, but his request was cut short when two soft hands covered his eyes from behind.

"Guess who?" the female voice whispered in his ear.

Before Low could guess, the hands uncovered his eyes. Lovely giggled and said, "What's up, baby boy?" Then planting a wet kiss on Low's cheeks, she continued. "Damn fool, I was paging you all day, and you never hit me back. Let me find out you hiding from me, Low?"

"Nah Lovely. Never that," Low smiled nervously.

"Oh… What then?"

"I been out and about with Rob all day, enjoying his first day back," Low said.

"Rob? Who's that?" Lovely asked.

"Oh wow! Robinson… How are you?" Lovely asked.

"I'm breathing so I can't complain," Rob said completely stoned-face.

His serious demeanor had no effect on Lovely. Smiling courteously at Rob, Lovely brushed him off, and turned her attention back to Low. The bartender made her way over, and placed three bottles of Moet on the bar in front of them.

"So what's up with you tonight, mister? Where you headed after this?" Lovely asked with a hand on her hip, looking sexy as hell.

"I told you, Love. We just doing it big with Rob tonight. So that call's on him," Low said, getting up.

Grabbing two of the bottles, Low handed one to Rob. Gunner cracked the third.

"Let's hit the stage," Low said, motioning for Rob and Gunner to follow him.

All three of them walked away, and Lovely was left standing alone with a confused expression on her face.

"If it ain't the untouchable one!" Sunny greeted Low.

Jumping from his cushioned seat, Sunny was making it rain one-dollar bills for the dancers on stage. Cherokee was making her ass vibrate like a washing machine. Another stripper poured champagne from two Moet bottles down her plump backside. The bubbly flowed into the mouth of a third stripper on her back fucking herself.

"Sun dawg and Dubs! What it is, pimps?" Low exclaimed, greeting Sunny and Walter.

Rob, Gunner, and Low joined them at the front of the stage.

"Shit, you see what I'm doing playa!" Sunny sang in a joyous chant.

"Nigga, I done threw about five stacks on these ho's so far. Next stop is the 'Fulfill Your Dream Room'!"

"That's straight up pimpin'," Low laughed.

Sunny passed him the weed-filled EZ-wider joint he was puffing on. Then he said, "Shit, why not? Ghost up in one of those bitches right now with some fine ass red bone."

"Oh snap! The one with the see-through skirt?" Gunner asked.

"Yup. And one of you niggas better give that fool some money for gas. That pussy ain't going for cheap."

Then he grabbed another hefty amount of bills from the large Prada knapsack lying on a small table besides him, and flung some more dollar bills skyward towards the stage. Music from the 2 Live Crew blasted keeping the Desire Room jumping. Suddenly the deejay's voice was heard.

"Shout outs to Low, Sunny, Walter, and all the Zoes up in the house tonight. I see ya playas! A special welcome home shout out going to Rob-Zoe. They can't keep a good man down. I see you boy! This ones for you."

After hearing the raucous urgings from the crowd, Rob hesitated but eventually gave in, and made his way to the stage. He sat between two naked, voluptuous strippers with nothing but designer pumps on their feet.

Low and Gunner both popped the corks on champagne bottles, and began to guzzle down the ice-chilled Moet. Roaring and cheering on as Rob enjoyed his personal freak show while two strippers gave him the business.

Removing a big wad of cash from his pockets, Low found himself caught in the moment. He threw the entire stack up in the air in the direction of the stage making it rain with hundred dollar bills.

"Money ain't a muthafuckin' thing!" Low yelled.

He was feeling the urge to hop on stage, but before he could, his pager began vibrating. Glancing at the pager's screen, Low didn't recognize the number.

"Oh shit!" Low exclaimed with excitement. Turning to face Gunner, he continued. "We gotta get the fuck outta here, Zoe!"

"What da fuck hap—"

"Michelle's water just broke."

✦ ✦ ✦

Jackson Memorial Hospital

"Push!" the nurse shouted encouragingly while Michelle held onto her hand, and squeezed with all the energy she had left inside of her. A screeching shrill accompanied her every breath as Michelle pushed with all her might.

"Here it comes! Push!" The doctor said.

He stuck both his hand a few inches further into Michelle's vagina, until he had a perfect grip around the baby's head.

"Push...!"

Low was stuck in awe. He watched closely as Michelle belted out one final ear-piercing cry, and pushed through the most excruciating pain she ever felt in her life. A rush of emotions washed over him when he saw the contortions her face went through. Completely stunned at the sight of the doctor pulling at the shoulders of his newborn baby, Low bit his lips. The rest of the baby's body slipped out of Michelle's vaginal canal, and into an awaiting bath towel, four seconds of uncertain silence was immediately broken with the baby's shrill of a cry, and the entire delivery room broke out in a rousing applause.

"It's a beautiful baby boy!" the nurse said.

The doctor handed the screaming baby to the nurse, and she gladly placed the newborn into Michelle's waiting arms. Low moved forward, and peered into Michelle's arms. He felt tears of joy as he stared at his newborn son. Looking up at him as joyous tears raced down her face, Michelle smiled, and said, "Come hold him. He's yours."

✦ ✦ ✦

Two Years Later

Two years went by since Low had his son. The infant bore his name, but was called 'Two-Five'. King Zoe gave him this nickname. The baby was his twenty-fifth grandchild, and life for Low and Zoe Pound remained harmonious.

New Millennium Records, a record company Low and his four business partners had invested in, and launched back in '99 was well on the way to solidifying itself as a music industry powerhouse. Over forty artists were under contract, and two already cracked Billboard's Top100 list with hit records. New Millennium ventured into genres far beyond just rap music. The roster included a number of R&B artists, pop acts, reggae artists, and several in-house producers. New Millennium also signed a male country and western singer to the label.

Tasting success not only gave Low an exhilarating thrill, it also gave him the chance to clean up a substantial amount of his dirty money. The record company was already generating figures in the multi-million dollar range. Low was now getting a chance to experience life outside the illegal grind, and at the same time building solid legitimate business relations. From Fortune 500 company owners, other entrepreneurs boasting financial portfolios in all types of businesses. Low was taking full advantage of doing deals with owners of restaurant franchises, car dealerships, casino developmental plans overseas including princes and kings of wealthy Arab nations, notable American politicians, and corporate lawyers.

Rubbing elbows with the world's elite, and being able to pick their brains was like gold to Low. He was like a sponge, busy soaking up all the advice and knowledge. Low's legit company of friends and business associates, were not only putting him onto countless investments opportunities available to him in the vast business world, they showed the czar of the drug game a way to execute his plan to transition himself, and his entire criminal family out of the illegal life to the corporate world. Low was making power moves in the music industry.

Sunny and Walter also were making moves in the game. Their two-year long business discussions between themselves and an international militant group known as The Black Irish Republican Army finally developed into a multi-million dollar business venture that was set to take place within the next coming weeks.

It took two long years of extensive background checks—conducted via Pierre's numerous law enforcement connections. Sunny and Walter were aware of the risks involved with this venture as oppose to major deals they had brokered in the past. This one was between foreigners they had never met in person. Even though they had done a substantial amount of homework, the potential risks were greater than they had ever experienced.

It could be the first time Zoë Pound would have to venture beyond the state of Florida to close a deal. That fact alone was enough to veto the entire thing. But with eight-figure deal on the table, and the potential to catapult Zoë Pound's financial reach to corporate levels, Sunny and Walter were finally ready to pull the trigger on this deal.

✦ ✦ ✦

"He's a fucking peon. Forget about it!" Timothy Danuzio said in a thick Italian drawl. "Peon I tell you."

Holding the glass door opened for Low, and his client, the three men stepped out of the Miami-Dade Superior Courthouse through a side exit, and walked toward the parking meter along the sidewalk where their cars were parked.

"I'm telling you, this is his third write up for excessive force. Internal Affairs is fed-up with his shit. This pig has a pool full of documented complaints against him—civilians and in-house. Trust me Robinson, all you have to do is continue how you've been doing—keep your nose clean, lay low, and steer clear of any unnecessary negative publicity. I guarantee you that I'll have this thing resolved within six months tops with a dismissal, or some light probation package."

Rob smiled, loving what heard. Then he said, "Shit, you ain't gotta worry bout me boss. I've been laying lower than a groundhog. Just get this case gone please... I need my life back."

"Don't worry about it, kid. This baby's good as done, wrapped, sealed, and just waiting to be addressed," Attorney Danuzio said in a boastful tone.

"Cool…"

"Just the way I like my checks," Danuzio joked, playfully nudging Low in the ribs.

The three men shared a laugh. Then Low said, "Oh fa sure T.D., I know what keeps the superman cape on. But you know we keep it straight cash around here my man. Paper trails only invite uninvited guests to the party. You taught me that."

Returning Low's smile, Danuzio nodded his head, and said, "You're absolutely right about that my friend. I gave that jewel for free. I must really like you."

The trunk of his Aston Martin popped open, and Low said, "Shit, with the amount you're making off this case the jewels should be added in as a bonus."

Low reached in his pocket, and pulled out his own keys to his car, parked in front of Danuzio's.

"I'll tell you what, Milow," Danuzio said, shutting the trunk of his car, and making his way to the driver's side door. "Tell your buddy Dimitri to give me a call."

He announced, referring to Caine who had skipped bond, fled to Haiti, and was now on the run for his murder case.

"Um—"

"I've been looking into his case. I'm pretty sure we can beat this thing, and at a reasonable fee. As far as the jewels go, I got one last one for you. The game is to be sold, not told, my friend. I'll see you guys next court date," Danuzio said, waving goodbye to Low and Rob.

He stepped into the cozy leather confines of his Aston Martin, started the super sports car's V-8 engine, and sped off. His Florida license plate read, *NOT GUILTY* was illuminated by the sun's bright afternoon beam.

"That motherfucker T.D. is the most Jewish-Italian I've ever seen. I swear!" Low said, shaking his head.

Timothy Danuzio was an unruly bastard when it came to his retainer fees, and picking his brain for knowledge, but being the best criminal lawyer one could buy gave him that right. He had thirty plus years of defending some of the most notorious gangsters on record. As long as it kept Rob free, the six-figure retainer fee Low was dishing out for his service was worth every penny.

"You driving, my nigga. I'm tired as fuck," Low said with a yawn.

He tossed Rob his car keys, and made his way to the passenger side of his '93 Artica white Lotus Turbo Espirit.

"Shit, as long as you rolling something up. This courtroom shit got a nigga straight stressed. I need to smoke one," Rob said.

"Oh, you already know. I got some fire on deck!"

✦ ✦ ✦

They were parked in front of Sunny's Electronics. Reclined way back in the Lotus' Saffron leather seats, Rob and Low passed the fourth crypie and hash filled Backwoods cigar between them. *2pacalypse Now* album played through the sports car's Alpine speakers. Low and Rob were discussing life, politics, and most importantly their next move.

"This record company is taking off just how we envisioned it. And have the potential to skyrocket us to the top. I'm telling you. We only one hit record away Rob," Low said.

"I hear you my nigga, shit, just keep ya focus, and you'll get it soon," Rob said.

"Exactly. That's what I know," Low said, glancing as his best friend. "I am gonna get it soon. Shit, our country act alone is already being nominated for all kinds of Country Music awards and shit. Collectively, New Millennium's knocking on the door of success, and sooner than later these corporate muthafuckas gonna be calling. And when that time comes, I gotta be ready. I can't have a foot in the game doing dirt. That's how niggas lose. I gotta be completely out. It's the only way to eventually get us out of this shit…"

2Pac's *Soldier's Story* serenaded in the background, and Rob puffed on the Backwood, inhaling the smoke deep into his lungs.

"So, what's your plan?" Rob asked, exhaling the fumes.

"Man, Sunny and Walter got some big deal that's been in the works for a while now. They're finally ready to put it into motion—double digit millions—if everything goes through smoothly. It's a make, or break shit. There's a lot of risk, but if this shit pops off as planned not only will the team be set for life, but it also guarantees me a smooth way out…"

"Okay that sounds real good…"

"Yeah, I'll always be a Zoe. That's for life. But in life change is constant. With King Zoe, Zoë Pound was more political. He stuck mostly to the traditional way of getting this money. I brought us to the forefront of a new wave, and conquered the game… And with you…"

Rob's heart sank when Low continued to speak.

"With you… You'll get to write your own chapter to this saga…"

"What you saying, Low?" Rob asked, staring at Low.

"I'm saying, we leave for Boston in three weeks. And while I'm gone, I'mma need you to hold it down out here in these street, keep an eye on my fiancé and my son for me. When I get back, I guarantee you the city will be yours, Zoe…"

Rob's silence was that of a man who had come full circle. The humble silence of a Triple A Prospect, finally called up to the big leagues. Glancing over at Low, Rob saw the true meaning of brotherhood. Low was his ace, his right-hand man, his crony, and fellow Zoe.

"Trust me, I got you, Zoe."

CHAPTER

22

Make or Break

To live is to suffer...
To survive is to find meaning to that suffering
—DMX

The year 1992 proved to be a difficult, and trying time for many Irishmen living in Ireland especially those of African descent, AKA the Black Irishmen. Blacks made up less than five percent of the entire population in Ireland, and this caused mistreatment, unfair civil rights, second-class citizenship, and racism, were tolerated.

Blacks living in Ireland were sick and tired of being strong-armed by the masses of majority Whites. The government pandered to the dominant White race. No matter what their class, or social status, would time gain their needs came before their black counterparts. Whether it was for employment, access to day-to-day economic essentials, or political positioning, Blacks living in Ireland were always on the back burner.

That year the Black race in Ireland was on the brink of obliteration. Hope came in the form of the son of a wealthy businessman, Thomas O'Malley. Nick O'Malley was the great-grandson of General Burns O'Malley, a general in the original Irish Republican Army of the early 1900's. The racist system had forced him to reach an unspeakable boiling point. He was ready to act.

In a land dominated by Whites, the son of a very rich, notable, and respected White man rebelled. His mother was a Black college professor from Belfast. Nick's mom taught history at a very prestigious university in Dublin. Nick had the light–tan complexion of his mother's family, and on a daily basis dealt with the problems of being Black in a White ruled country.

Nick found out at an early that even with all his rich inheritance being of mixed race wasn't easy. His tanned skin opened the floodgates of racism, subjecting him to the same brutal ridicule every other Black person in the country faced. His whites peers, fueled by a mutual hatred for the color of his skin treated him with the same contempt as every other Blacks they came across. Even though Nick came from a deep rooted and respected family The fact that he was half white caused everyone to totally disregard his social status, and family ties.

Growing up, Nick O'Malley had always been fascinated with war, especially war for a cause. As a youth, he grew to love watching old history documentaries of the original Irish Republican Army, and their well-documented struggle to overcome Britain's oppressive rule over them as they set out to gain their independence.

Being a direct descendant, and part of the bloodline of one of the actual contributors to such a vital, and historic movement, Nick felt somewhat of a personal connection to the IRA. He supported their ideological views pertaining to fighting the oppressor, AKA the British, for civil liberties, and regaining possession of their individual identities.

Nick grew from a young boy into a young teen, and began being ostracized by the same White family, friends, and heroic-type figures he once loved, and admired. It was very clear that the only reason was that he was slightly tanner than they were. Viewing chronological videos, and researching written data of his ancestry were once Nick's hobby. He eventually adopted all the IRA's philosophies. It was like a biblical guideline, and blueprint to Nick.

By the time Nick was twenty-one, and with his philosophical viewpoints leading his surge, Nick rallied up a small army of afflicted Ireland natives. Consisting of both Blacks, mixed race, and sympathetic Whites who were below class and considered social rejects by their elite Irish peers. Nick formed a brotherhood that mimicked the ideologies of the original IRA. Then he set out to start a resurgent revolution. Nick's plan was to wage an all out armed rebellion against the elite White masses of Ireland.

He recruited five thousand members and affiliates. The mission of Nick's organization, affectionately named the Black Irish Republican Army, was to engage in a guerrilla-styled rebellion against Ireland's government while simultaneously seizing control of the entire northern city of Belfast and Bangor. His plan was to seek, and demand complete ownership of these two cities, and order Ireland to declare them their own independent republic.

It had taken three years of strenuous underground campaigning to recruit all his soldiers. He used a lot of underground networking on a local and international level to raise the rest of the funds he couldn't get by conning his father. Nick had already secretly stolen millions from his father. It took Nick another two years just to break through to his American artillery connection, and struck a major purchasing deal.

Thirty million dollars was made available to purchase an arsenal of weapons for a battalion of soldiers. The enormous cache consisted of thirty thousand firearms. There were all types of shotguns including single barrels, pump action Remington shotguns, double barrel Mossberg shotguns, sniper rifles, assault rifles and machine guns. On the list were AK's, AR-15's, SK's, Tec, Macs, fifty Cal. street sweepers, and Thompson submachine guns. A requirement for explosives ordinance such as a variety of grenades, mounted missile launchers, along with anti-aircraft, and intercontinental ballistic missiles, thousands of bullet proof vest, and body armors. Nick lusted for hundreds of barrels filled with incendiary chemicals. This was just in case his chips were down, and it was time to go all out.

After brokering a multimillion-dollar agreement with Zoe Pound. He mapped out a clandestine war strategy to terrorize the Irish government that would only come to life if his demands were not met. The stage for the Black Irish Republican army's revolution was completely set. Now all Nick needed to do was pick up his guns.

✦ ✦ ✦

Everett, Massachusetts

"It's official. We're fucking lost!" Walter said, pounding his fist against the steering wheel of the Jeep Cherokee.

Low glanced at him. He realized that Walter was right, and said, "A'ight but how—"

"I know because I done seen the same fucking gas station 'bout three times. We just driving in fucking circles!" Walter seethed.

"See, I knew that dumb-ass blonde bird at that Burger King didn't know what the fuck she was talking 'bout, when she was giving us directions," Low said, shaking his head, and letting out a frustrated sigh.

"Shit, if Gunner wasn't distracting the simple-ass broad, trying to get her number. Maybe she would've been able to focus. She gave us some retarded-ass directions," Sunny said.

The comment brought the widest grin to Gunner's mug. Chuckling he said, "Okay, blame it all on Gunner. Y'all just mad I got the digits."

Gunner was smoking a Newport cigarette, and gazing out the Jeep's backseat window. He seemed to be the only person not fazed at the fact that they were lost. They were already half an hour late for their rendezvous, but Gunner's mind was elsewhere. He was looking forward to picking up the pretty, young white Burger King cashier from work later on that night. Gunner was thinking of Charlestown, and where it was. That was where she lived, and he would be getting cozy with her for a nightcap.

"I know one thing, we can't just keep driving around this damn town with what we got in the back. That's for sure. So you might as well pull up to that bodega right there, nephew," Sunny said to Walter.

"Okay…"

"Maybe somebody there will know how to get to this fucking motel. Plus I'm thirstier than a fat bitch, and I need to get me a box of Swisher Sweets. Y'all muthafuckas' stressing me the fuck out…"

✦ ✦ ✦

"Quatro Pepsi… Quatro Snickers, un Boston Herald papel, Y el dos cejaha's de Phillies. That'll be eleven-seventy-five," the old man said from behind the counter.

His eyes darted up to the store's wall-mounted television. A baseball game, Boston Red Sox versus the New

York Yankees was being aired.

Sunny handed Miguel a twenty-dollar bill. He glanced at Low and Walter, and they were also focused on the baseball game.

"Low, don't get anything, man. It's too expensive 'round here," Sunny said.

Low chuckled at Sunny. Then he and Walter got sodas, and chips before Miguel placed everything else in the plastic bag.

"We ain't in Florida. Prices are higher up north," Low said.

"Papi, you're sure this is how we get to the Townline Inn in Malden?" Walter asked.

Miguel double-checked the directions he had written down on the back of a cash three lottery receipt. Then he passed it back to Walter, and said, "Si... Si. Next city over, the Townline Inn will be on the right."

"Okay, gracias," Walter shouted over his shoulder.

Squeaking brakes coming from outside the motel's room, and bright headlights illuminated the motel's dark room. Nick jumped to his feet. Hustling to the front window, he pushed aside the thick curtain, and peeked out at the parking lot.

"Looks like they've finally arrived, mates," Nick said to his two comrades.

Sean Mulcany, and Liam Griffith were tin the room with him. Both men were his army's first and second lieutenants respectively.

"It's about darn time. I was on the verge of thinking these punks were jerking our fucking chains for a second there lads," Liam said, getting up from his seat on one of the motel's double beds.

"They're here?" Sean groggily asked.

"Get your Paddy ass up, and look alive mate. This is serious business," Nick barked.

Nick didn't approve of Sean's lack of motivation when it came to their organizations business dealings. They were about to broker a major multimillion-dollar deal with a group they've never met in-person before, or even really knew a great deal about. All they knew was that this group was made up of criminals, and were willing and able to supply what was on the arms shopping list.

This deal that was critical to the successful execution of their ultimate plan. Taking back control from an oppressive government, and finally gain a voice for their people. The revolution was on the way, and Sean, the first lieutenant was in bed. He was the only paddy completely hung over, and acting as if they were about to just have a dinner date over some milk and cookies, with the American Girl Scouts Committee.

Nick knew that working with Sean could be frustrating, but Liam and Sean were still the only two lads Nick truly trusted. He had known both since grade school. Like himself, Liam and Sean were of mixed race. They had dealt with the same struggles growing of being Black and wealthy. From a very early age, they had bonded like brothers.

Sean was second in line, and when it came to plotting, strategizing, and brainstorming ideas to further their organizations cause Sean was of great help. He found a connection to Zoë Pound and devise a plan to link with the American gangsters. Sean was gifted with intelligence, but his pal's lack of passion often left Nick baffled. Meanwhile on the outside, members of the Zoe Pound had arrived, and were getting organized.

"We here niggas," Walter said.

"It's about time," Sunny said, tossing the roach he been smoking.

"Damn Zoe, you really took that whole blunt to the head, and didn't even give me a hit," Walter said.

"I told you y'all were stressing me da fuck out. Catch a ride on the next one, nephew," Sunny grinned.

They could hear Gunner and Low's guns being loaded with clips. All four occupants in the Jeep were strapped, but Low and Gunner were packing fully automatic Mac.10 submachine-gun. Gunner eyed the noise-suppressor on the gun's muzzle then toyed with the equipped laser attachment on top of the Mac. Clicking it on and off couple times, he tested the infrared beam until he felt satisfied. Then he placed a nylon shoulder strap attached to it around his neck, and zipped his black leather Pelle Pelle jacket, fully concealing the weapon.

After lining up the seven.50 caliber hollow-tips perfectly in the metal cartridge, Low pushed the clip back into the chrome Desert Eagle, and cocked it. Low placed the massive handgun back in a holster above his right rib cage. Then he picked up another Desert Eagle, and went through the same preparatory routine before placing it in a holster above his left rib cage.

"You niggas ready?" Low asked.

It was time. Low and Gunner stepped out the back of the Jeep. Their eyes were intensely scanning the perimeter of the motel's parking lot for anything that seemed out of ordinary. There was the usual random order of empty cars and trucks parked in front of rooms, but nothing appeared out of place.

Walter and Sunny came out, and made their way to the rear of the Jeep. The back gate immediately popped open from the sensor on Walter's keychain. After taking one last cautionary glance around, both men retrieved two black Cole Haan duffle bags.

"Let's do this," Sunny said.

Walter, and Sunny carried the four duffle bags walking behind Gunner and Low. They were heading toward room 154.

"Here they come. Look alive lads," Nick said.

Low was caught off guard when the door to room 154 suddenly opened. He was about to knock, and was shocked by the greeting.

"Howdy mates, welcome," Nick said courteously at Low and Gunner.

They walked passed him, ignoring his outstretched hand. Both entered the motel room on guard, their eyes peeled, and scanning the entire room. Gunner quickly glanced underneath both beds. Then he checked the lone closet, and a tiny bathroom. He gave an approving nod to Low. Then Low spoke breaking the tense silence.

"All clear," Low said, relaying the code.

Sunny and Walter entered the room. With stone cold serious demeanors, they took a glimpse at Nick, and his two comrades. Always the toughest in the pack, and known as the one with the biggest balls, Nick appeared ill at ease.

"It's good to see that you guys made it here safe," Nick said, locking the door with the chain. Then he continued. "I am Nick, and these guys here are my two best lads. Sean, you guys have met several times already in person, and my lad here, Liam."

All three Irishman attempted to salute the Zoes with handshakes, but their courtesy was ignored. Low, and his crew nodded silently.

"Um... Okay... Well can I get you gentlemen something to drink...? Scotch...? A smoke or something?" Nick offered.

"Nah bruh. We ready to get straight down to business," Walter said.

"Alright then mate," Nick said, motioning for Sean and Liam to pull out some chairs for their guests. "If you lads will kindly take a seat. Then we can get right down to that."

Sean and Liam brought four metal fold out chairs, placing them with three other chairs already formed around a makeshift conference table. Nick and Sean sat next to each other. Then Sunny and Walter assembled the duffle bags in the pile. Then they sat across from the Irishmen.

Nick quickly realized that the two other stone-faced men had no desire to take part in small talk. He and Sean both sat at attention. Liam, the only armed Irishman, remained standing, observing the discussions, and stayed vigilant.

"Well lads, as we all are aware that we've been in discussions for the past two years. I take it you have done a significant amount of homework, and came to the conclusion that we are in fact whom we claim to be," Nick said, reaching for a pack of cigarettes on the table, removing one, and lighting it. Then he continued. "My organization, and movement is deeply rooted. The fellas and I stand for a just cause. We—"

"Honestly bruh," Sunny said, interrupting, reaching for Nick's pack of squares. After helping himself to one, he continued. "We did our research. If not, we wouldn't be here. We understand your cause and all, and after chopping it up with your boy, Sean on his many trips down bottom to talk with us. We actually support you guys' movement. But no offense…we didn't drive twenty-two hours to discuss politics, my man. We came to talk money, you dig?"

"Unh, huh… I understand?" Nick muttered then smiled, and nodding graciously, respectful of Sunny's wish, he said, "Let's talk money… Shall we?"

He smiled again and threw a glance in Sean's direction. Sean nodded at him and turned toward Sunny and Walter.

"Well, Jason and Mike since I'm the bloke you guys have been doing discussions with these past two years, it's only right that I handle all business related questions, or inquiries. But before we discuss numbers. I take it that those duffle bags you guys brought with you aren't change of clothing. So if it's possible...may we check out the inventory, mate?"

"Oh fa sure," Sunny said, grabbing the closest duffle bag.

Sunny lifted it onto the wooden table. Then he unzipped the bag, slid it across the table to Nick and Sean. He waited for them to take a peek then he continued. "These here are just some samples."

Sean took a look inside the duffle, and pulled out two of the thirty boxes that were stacked on top of each other. Placing them on the table, Nick and Sean inspected it.

"Wow mate, Beretta seven B nine-two FS handguns... Hmm, aren't these the side-arms the U.S. armed forces use?" Sean asked, admiring the non-glare bruniton finish.

Sean checked the gun's open slide design. He cocked the massive gun then un-cocked it, and toyed with the safety lever.

"Nick lifted the top of the second box, and picked up one of the weapon it contained. Smiling, he said, "HK–MK two-three SOCUM. Looks real good."

He continued admiring the rest of the weapons, scrutinizing magazines, and inspecting the cartridges capacity then finally nodded approvingly. Sean was doing the same, examining the artillery.

"All these handguns are brand-new, and never been used right?" Sean asked, putting a Beretta back into the box.

"We already went over all of that on your last visit with us," Sunny said, putting one of the duffle bags on the floor.

"You're right," Sean said.

Lifting up the second, and unzipping it, Sunny said,

"Now these babies here is just two samples of the choppers you requested, plus a sniper rifles."

Sunny slid the second duffle bag across the table. Then Nick removed an M1–110 U.S. Army sniper rifle from the bag. Admiring the new sniper rifle, Nick smiled at the possibilities.

"Now…in our last meeting, ah…we discussed the need for body armor," Sean said, lifting up a fully automatic Russian AK–47, assault rifle.

He ran his fingers along its matted black, wood trimming, and immediately taking off its banana clip while toying with its mechanical military features.

"Hold your horses there, mate," Sunny mockingly retorted, reaching down for another duffle bag, and placing it on top of the table.

His slight mimic of their Irish dialect got a deep chuckle out of Gunner and Low, but not Sean. He didn't find Sunny's mockery amusing at all, and shot a cold dagger stare in the direction of Gunner. It led to a tense stare-down between the two.

Inside the third duffle bag were fifteen police-issued bulletproof vest. Sunny removed a vest, and tossed it to Nick.

"These samples will give y'all a taste of the products that'll be coming in on the ship," Sunny said.

"What about explosives? Did you bring any samples?"

"Our supply channel will have them, and trust that they'll meet your satisfaction. I didn't want to drive with that in the car," Sunny said.

"Very well. That is quite understandable. I take it, the fourth bag contains ammunition samples then lad?" Sean asked.

"From twenty-twos on up to thirty–thirties," Sunny said, putting out the cigarette. Sitting back in his chair, he crossed his meaty arms, and continued. "So now that y'all had a chance to check out the samples. It's time to get back to money talk."

"So what time, and where is that ship going to dock?" Sean asked.

"All that info is irrelevant 'til we see some bread," Walter said, crossing his arms.

"Very well," Nick said.

Clearing his throat, Nick glanced at Sean then at Liam. After nodding to them, he got up from his seat. Sean headed for the front door, and walked out. Liam followed couple steps behind.

"No disrespect to any of you lads, but with the amount of money, and risk involved in all of this we took the precaution of putting the money in another room until we felt satisfied that your inventory samples would be sufficient to warrant a deal," Nick said, fishing for another cigarette out of his pack on the table.

He lit the cigarette, and inhaled deeply with a wide grin plastered across his face, and said, "I must say, mate. I am very much pleased."

Making their way back into the motel room, Sean, and Liam lugged a huge gray duffle bag. They lifted the heavy bag up, and placed it on top of the table. Sunny and Walter got up from their seats, and Nick followed suit.

"So as we agreed, lads. One million in US currency upfront... Take a look," Nick said, unzipping the large duffle, and revealing the contents.

"Okay then, baby! Now we talking!" Sunny said.

Walter peered inside the duffle bag. It was filled to the top with hundred dollar bills. Divided into rubber band bundles of ten thousand-stacks. The sight of the money caused Sunny to nod approvingly.

"Okay lads, now that you've seen some money I think it's time to tell us where the ship containing our products will be docking and what time," Sean said, reaching for the money filled duffle bag, and zipping it shut.

"Hold on, slow you roll partner!" Sunny retorted with a frown. He was clearly agitated by Sean's persistence, and said, "What we agreed on was fifteen million upfront. One million cash and fourteen wired. Then another fifteen million wired after y'all get y'all supply."

"All right—"

"Now this meal ticket is cool, and all. It shows you muthafuckas are good at following directions and shit," Sunny said.

Then he reached into his pocket, and pulled out a receipt that contained an eighteen-digit Swiss Bank account number written on it. Handing Sean the receipt, Sunny continued. "No more information on shipment 'til we get confirmation that the rest of our bread has been successfully transferred to that international account."

Nick briefly scanned the receipt in his hands. Sean angrily glanced over at his boss. He didn't trust these Yankees one bit, and most definitely not enough to transfer fourteen million dollars without knowing where their ship would even be docking.

Nick nodded to Sean, and said, "Do it."

From an exasperated expression on his face, it was clear that Sean didn't approve. He reluctantly turned and retreated to the back of the room. Gunner followed his every step then watched him like a hound when Sean took a seat on the edge of one of the motel's bed and picked up the phone's receiver.

Although Gunner hadn't intimately been involved with discussions over the two years, and wasn't even involved in any of the business discussions during Sean's many trips to Miami to meet with Sunny and Walter. Gunner was always around, and in earshot of all the talks that ever took place between the men.

Gunner sensed that something wasn't right. Sean had taken more than ten trips just to sit down in person with Sunny and Walter to discuss procedures, inventory, and prices. There should be no reason for Sean to really ask so many of the same redundant questions, and making so many qualms about where the ship would be showing up. Gunner found it odd that there were verbal issues about what amount should be paid upfront, and what Zoë Pound was supposed to have brought with them to Boston.

Over the two years of discussions between the two organizations, specifics where discussed so much even Gunner had the details of the entire transaction down. It seemed as if Sean was repeating the facts out loud for more than just to refresh his mind.

Staring at Sean from across the room, playing with the collar of his Northern Ireland Pirates long-sleeve rugby shirt, and speaking on the phone, Gunner's bad vibes toward Sean seemed to grow more intense.

"It's done," Sean said, hanging up the phone's receiver. He got up from the double bed, and made his way back over to the conference room.

"Splendid!" Nick said, sounding very pleased.

"Yeah, bloody splendid," Sean repeated sarcastically.

He reached over, and grabbed Nick's pack off the conference table. A motel issued pack of matches slipped out, and fell onto the carpeted floor.

"So I take it that the bank provided you with a confirmation number, right?" Nick asked, getting agitated by Sean's pussyfooting.

"Sure did," Sean said. He picked up the matches from the floor. Then he continued. "Here it goes, fourteen million US."

Sean tossed the receipt onto the conference table in front of Sunny and Walter. Then he asked, "Now don't you think it's about time you told us where our bloody ship will be docked?"

"Nah muthafucka!" Gunner interjected with a menacing scowl.

"Huh?"

Gripping the Mac tightly, Gunner said, "We ain't telling you a damn thing 'til you lift up that muthafuckin' shirt!"

He aimed the infrared laser attached to his submachine-gun so that the beam illuminated squarely on Sean's four head. Liam instinctually reached for the 9mm Ruger concealed on his waist, and pointed his weapon at Gunner. Low aimed and put Liam and Nick squarely in his firing line. Jumping up, Walter pulled a sixteen-shot Glock. 19 with the quickness.

"Hold on here, mates. What's the bloody confusing all about?" Nick shouted, looking perplexed.

Both his hands were raised in a compromising manner. Then all went quiet when Gunner said, "This bitch-ass muthafucka's wearing a wire!"

Gunner's voice was laced with venom, and his finger intimately caressed the Mac's trigger.

"A wire...? That's completely absurd!" Nick bellowed with a disgusted grimace on his face.

"That's nonsense. Our brother's solid, man," Liam said.

Liam and Gunner were staring down each other, their weapons aimed at each other, and fingers inching to the triggers.

"Man, I know what the fuck I just saw. Tell him to raise his shirt!" Gunner ordered.

"Say mate, just lift up your damn shirt, and show these gentlemen that you're not wearing a bloody wire, eh?" Nick said, wanting to prove to these disrespectful Yankees that they were dead wrong about his lad.

"Yeah mate, show them!" Liam said.

"I will not do such a thing! How dare these American fools question my integrity?" Sean seethed, his face going blood red with fury.

"Fuck all this bullshit! I know one thing! Now my dawg said he saw a wire, and that's a serious mutha-fuckin' accusation," Sunny said, rising from his seat with his chrome.44 in his hand. He aimed it in the direction of Nick, and continued. "Now I suggest you tell that fucka to lift his shirt, and prove my dawg wrong before we start squeezing off in this bitch."

Sean stood center stage in the midst of a standoff, seconds away from breaking out into a bloody carnage of catastrophic proportions. It was then he realized that he had made a grave mistake.

Nick and Liam had been nothing but good to him. At a very early age, Nick took a poor, White Sean into his home, and treated him like family. Nick sacrificed a lot of himself to assure Sean stayed in good standing.

Even on Sean's arrest in the U.S. during a trip to Miami to meet with the Pound. Sean was caught with a million dollars worth of American counterfeit bills and three currency engraving plates. Nick knew nothing about Sean's side-hustle, and felt put-off by the whole thing.

Instead of calling on a trusted brother for financial help and legal advice, too much pride prevented Sean seeking Nick's assistance. Sean's arrest tipped off the authorities, and they became aware of his ties to Nick, and his terrorist aspirations. A joint force was successfully launched after being able to get Sean talking about his crime without an attorney present. Sean talked himself into an incriminatory grave, and was forced to cooper-ate. The calm ended, and a wild storm was unleashed.

Screeching tires, police sirens, bright lights flashing, and Sean breathed a sigh of relief. Gunner pulled the trig-ger, letting off a sound suppressed burst of hollow tipped slugs, peppering Sean's face. Bullets ripped through Sean's dome left a piñata out of his exploding skull. It left a bloody mess.

Liam returned fire hitting Gunner below the shoulder, and causing his body to violently jerk in a one-eighty-degree angle. Gunner let out an agonized filled moan, and his gun fell from his arm. Liam attempted to let off another round, but was outmanned, and completely outgunned. Low, Sunny, and Walter joined in the firefight, hitting both Liam and Nick with a school of heated slugs that made Swiss cheese of both men's torsos.

"Zoë Pound, to the exit. We out!" Walter shouted.

A loud commotion of halting breaks, and sirens could be heard coming from outside. Walter and Sunny grabbed a handle on the money-filled duffle bag, and bolted for the front door. Low scurried over to Gunner, dragging him to his feet.

"You good, bruh?" Low asked.

"I'm straight, Zoe. That fuck nigga caught me good though," Gunner said, grimacing.

Low saw blood oozing from Gunner's two wounds, and said, "My nigga, we gotta get you to a hospital. Lets break!"

When Low and Gunner stepped out into the motel's parking lot. Three different law enforcement agency's task force units were assembled outside. A sea of bright lights instantly flooded the parking lot. It was all over. The alphabet boys had the entire place surrounded.

"FREEZE! DROP YOUR WEAPONS!"

His heart speeding at a million beats per minute, Low quickly scanned the sea of agents with their guns drawn. They were from the F.B.I. Anti Terrorism Division, A.T.F. and the United States Secret Service. The agents effectively covered every avenue of escape, including the rooftop of other buildings, and helicopters hovered above.

Reaching the fork in the road, Low was faced with two choices. He glanced at Walter and Sunny sprawled out on their stomachs with their hands interlaced behind their heads, and decided it was best for him to follow suit.

Unfortunately Gunner would never make it to the hospital. He wasn't surrendering. Instead he squeezed the trigger of his submachine gun, hitting an agent. Immediately all the agents fired a hail of bullets hammering Gunner to the ground.

"Don't move! Stay down! Stay down!"

The orders came from everywhere. Armed agents moved in closer. One of them kicked both guns out of Low's reach. Then he said, "Secure! Don't fucking move motherfucker!"

Pressing the bottom of his steel toe boot into Low's neck, pining his face to the rough edged concrete, he said, "Give me a fucking reason. I swear I'll blow your brains out."

✦ ✦ ✦

Plymouth County Booking

"Drop your boxers, shake 'em out. Then hand them to me," an officer impatiently ordered, waiting for Low to oblige to his command.

"Now lift your hands high in the air. Wiggle them. Lift up your nut sack…Turn around. Let me see the bottom of your feet. Wiggle your toes, now bend over and spread 'em. Now squat and cough… Again… Good. Now get dressed."

The correction officer tossed Low's silk boxers onto a pile of the rest of his clothes, piled up on the dirty tile floor of the search cell. The officer walked out, and the cell door immediately slid shut behind him. Low took in a deep breath, and let it out real slowly. The mean mug plastered on his face indicated the displeasure he felt being stripped naked, and examined like an animal.

Slipping his boxers, socks, and tank top back on, Low sat on the cold bench. He thoughtfully put his red and gold three-thousand-dollar Gucci sweat suit on. Low had gone through arrest before. He knew what being in jail was all about.

"Milow Pierre! Booking-station four!" A female voice announced.

With a loud clicking sound, the search cell door slid open. Low was about to go through the booking process.

"Can I make my intake phone call now? Low asked the white, gray-haired booking officer.

"There's a payphone in the tank," the old man icily said.

Entering the huge spacious cell known as the tank, Low saw hundreds of booked inmates. He quickly scanned the large, packed room, trying to locate the payphone. There was one in a far corner of the tank, and someone was just hanging up.

Low ignored the eyes on him. His face was all over the news that replayed on the wall-mounted television in the tank. The local news kept rebroadcasting details of the gun trafficking, and quadruple homicide case. Low reached the phone, dialed his house number, and waited for his collect call to be accepted.

"Thank you for using Evercom..." the automated voice said after a short pause.

"Hello...?" Low muttered through the phone receiver.

"No-o-o!" Michelle screamed when she heard Low's voice.

She broke down into a fit of uncontrollable sobbing. Low could feel her pain through the phone connection. Hearing his fiancé bawling her eyes out shook the core of his heart.

"It's gonna be alright, 'Chelle," Low said, trying to soothe Michelle's heartache.

"No, it's not. I saw the news, Milow. This is bad!"

Michelle broke down crying. Her loud sobs came though the phone's receiver, and Low just shook his head despairingly and sighed deeply. There was nothing he could say to her that would ease her anguish or make his current predicament less grave than it obviously was.

Michelle saw the news, and probably was fully aware of exactly what he was up against. There was no need for sugarcoating.

"Look, Chelle. You already know I'm a get a real good lawyer. Even though this shit looks bad I can still make bail, and fight it from the outside," Low said, taking a deep breath as he tried to keep himself composed.

"I'm a need you to make a few calls for me, Chelle. Call Danuzio first thing Monday morning. Tell him where I'm at and he'll take it from there. And as soon as we get off the phone, call Rob—"

"He's downstairs sleeping on the couch," Michelle sobbed.

"Rob's there?" Low asked, feeling a little elation jolt to his dim spirits.

"Ye-yes. He's been here ever since he found out you got arrested," she said, whimpering.

Low heard her sniffling, and said, "Put my nigga on the phone."

Michelle arose from her bed, Low heard his newborn crying, and it caused him to shake his head.

"Yo, my nigga?" Rob groggily said.

"Yeah bruh…" Low said.

It felt good to hear Rob's voice on the phone, but it pained Low to know what kind of trouble this could bring.

"Man, you should know by now what's going down," Low said, breaking the ice.

"Yeah man sorry. How you?"

"This is my first call, so I didn't get to contact anybody. But I'm a need you to call—"

"Don't worry 'bout nothing, Low. I already called that nigga, Danuzio, and got plans to meet up with him on Monday to hit him up with some bread, and retain him for your case. He said he 'bout to clear up the rest of his week. He wants to fly out there, and come see you. So y'all can chop it up about the details and shit. He's setting up a bail hearing for you…most likely get a date for that hearing in a week or two. He's gonna need to know everything about your case before y'all get up in that courthouse. I'm sending a five-thousand-dollar money order so you'll have bread on your books by Tuesday the latest. Everything out here good, and you already know, I'm a keep a close eye on Michelle, and make sure her and your son need nothing. Just keep your head above water in there, bruh. I'm a hold it down for ya out here, ya dig?"

"My nigga!" Low said.

"I appreciate you, Rob. Thank you."

"Man, it ain't nothing you didn't do when the tables were turned, Low," Rob said.

"Hey yo, you been on that fucking phone for mad long, son!" A deep, angry voice came from behind Low's back.

Slowly turning around, Low found himself staring in the eyes of a tall, Black muscle-bound man. A mean scowl was plastered on the man's mug. He was ice-grilling Low.

"Phone check, nigga!" The man barked.

"You straight, Low?" Rob said, hearing some of the commotion through the phone's receiver.

"Yeah, I'm good," Low said, brushing off the man's presence.

Low's total disregard for his order to get off the phone didn't sit well with the muscle- bound man.

"My nigga, didn't you hear me?" The man growled, stepping closer to the side of Low's face.

Putting his hand aggressively on Low's shoulders was the wrong action to take. With a vicious swing of the phone's heavy receiver, Low made contact with the man's face, striking him dead center on the bridge of his nose.

The hard plastic of the phone crashed against caused a split through the man's flesh. Blood began squirting out of his nostril like a ketchup packet that had been squeezed. Adding to his malicious assault, Low immediately followed up with a brutal kick to the man's nuts, causing him to belly over as he let out a pain filled moan.

Lining him up for an uppercut, Low was about to finish him off, but was beaten to punch by Sunny, appearing from nowhere. With a brutal kick to the jaw, Walter joined in on the fun, as all three men started stomping Chuck's face into the concrete.

"Break it up! Get the fuck down on ya knee, or I'm gonna let the dog loose!" A corrections sergeant shouted.

While several corrections officers dressed in riot gears began spraying pepper spray in the faces of Low, Sunny and Walter. The fight was quickly broken up, followed by a brief struggle. Then the three Zoes were handcuffed.

Segregation AKA The Hole

"Ah nigga! We beat the shit out of that big muthafucka!" Sunny shouted through his cell door.

Low was sharing a healthy laugh with Sunny, and said, "Man, y'all niggas popped out of nowhere."

"You know, Zoe...?"

"Once 'em alphabet boys cuffed us up, and threw us all in separate cruisers, I thought y'all muthafuckas was sent to different jails," Low said.

"Shit me and Walter thinking the same thing 'bout you. We were in the tank, and you wasn't nowhere in sight. Then we saw you walking in later. We was gon' holla, but I saw you racing for the phone. Me and nephew just kept an eye on you."

"Yeah, that was good. Cause that was one big-ass muthafucka!"

"Ha, ha, boy you ain't never lie…! That cocksucker was huge! But you know how we roll. We Zoë Pound."

"No doubt… Where Walter at?"

"Walter probably sleeping," Sunny yawned.

"You probably right. I'm a get some shut eye my damn self. I'll holla at you," Sunny said.

"A'ight…" Low said.

The whole operation went down badly. Everything that could have gone wrong—went wrong. Gunner was dead, and three important members of Zoë Pound were locked up. Walter sat on the bunk, thinking this was his fault. Low tried to warn him about this expansion move, but Walter disregarded Low's advice. Low made an offer to join him in the music world.

"Damn, why didn't' I listen?" Walter muttered to himself, dropping to his knees, he started to pray.

✦ ✦ ✦

"Code nine! Segregation! Code nine!"

The echoing sound of screams, cell doors being kicked by rowdy inmates, loud vibration of boots running up the segregation unit's steel steps broke Low from his slumber. He jumped up, and rushed to his cell's door, peering to see what all the commotion was about. Out on the tier, he saw about twenty officers. The two women dressed in all white coats had to be the jail's doctors. They were milling around a hospital gurney two cells down.

Then four of them hoisted Walter's lifeless body on the gurney. The officers held each metal corner, and carefully made their way down the steps. Low stared at the bed sheet still tightly knotted around Walter's neck. It quickly dawned on him. Walter decided to be his own judge, jury, at his own trial.

"R.I.P WALTER..." Low shouted in an emotionally charged rage.

One Week Later

"Pierre!" The young, pimpled-faced C.O. shouted. He gave Low's cell door a loud kick. Then he continued. "Let's go, Pierre. You have an attorney visit!"

Attorney Danuzio was dressed sharp as usual in a tailor-made blue Italian suit. His hair slicked back, a gold Presidential Rolex, and two diamond flooded pinky rings gleamed under the moderate lightning of the attorney conference room.

"Hey Milow, what the fuck, eh?" Danuzio said with a playful grimace on his face. Low silently entered the small cubicle conference room, and Danuzio continued. "We gotta get you out of that jumpsuit, kid. Orange doesn't suit you too well."

Low embraced Danuzio with a firm handshake, and said, "Tell me about it, boss..." The two men sat across from each other, and Low continued. "I appreciate you clearing your week, and flying up to see me."

"Ah, no sweat, pal," Danuzio said with a wave of his hand. Then placing his briefcase on top of the small conference table, he clicked it open, and continued. "I was born here in Massachusetts...went to Law school at

Harvard... Plus my mother still owns a house here in a small town called Cambridge. So every chance I get to visit, I do. Boston is a beautiful city. When I get you out, maybe you can treat me to a Celtics game or something, eh?"

"Shit, that's nothing... Just get me out. I'll even take you to a Red Sox game, and I'm a Yankee fan," Low said.

He saw the wide grin on Danuzio's face. The nattily dressed attorney pulled out a large manila folder from his briefcase, and placed it in front of him.

"Well coming from a die-hard Red Sox fan, that would be quite a treat," Danuzio quipped.

"A'ight..."

"But first things first, Milow. This case you got here is pretty messy, kid—If I must say so myself. We're talking gun trafficking, conspiracy, money laundering, four counts of felony murder, and one count of murdering a federal agent. And that's just what I can remember off the top of my head."

"Damn!" Low sighed, scratching the back of his baldhead.

"Damn, is right," Danuzio said.

"What can you do?"

"Fortunately for you sir, I can tell you that you're definitely being overcharged, and most likely none of these murders will be able to stick come indictment time. It's still early in the game, but from reviewing what I was able to get so far, since you willfully surrendered, it's obvious you played no physical part in killing the federal agent. And for them to attempt to pin the shooter's death on you as well is just plain absurd."

"Okay..."

"Now as far as the three Irish men, quite frankly they were criminals under international investigation for attempted acts of terror. The feds were supposed to have video, and audio surveillance setup in the motel room.

But from what I'm hearing through my federal sources on the inside, the audio is barely audible, and the surveillance footage is so sketchy it's unlikely to be admissible in court.

"Cool…" Low said, nodding approvingly.

"Now I haven't gotten a hold of your discovery to confirm what my sources are telling me, but even when I get to confirm what my sources are telling me, and get these bodies off your back then that still leaves these other three charges that won't be easy to get rid off. And the conspiracy count alone carries a minimum twenty years. So to keep it blunt with you, Milow, we have an uphill battle on our hands."

Taking a deep breath, Low shook his head. There was really one thing Danuzio hadn't mentioned.

"So, what's up with getting me bail?" Low asked.

"Well since you have no adult priors, it gives me a lot of leverage to fight for at least a dollar amount. And if it's too high, we can schedule another date down the line to get whatever dollar amount set, reduced. But since your crime took place thousands of miles from the state in which you reside, I know the US Attorney office will be vigorously pushing for a no-bail judgment on the grounds that you may potentially become a flight risk."

"Damn…"

"A deep sigh escaped Danuzio. Shutting his legal briefcase, he said, "Your bail hearing is set for two weeks from today. And don't get in anymore fights," he winked. Then stood, extended his hand to shake Low's hand, and said, "I'm going to throw my superman cape on, and see if I can work my magic for you."

Bail Hearing

"With all that said, your Honor, though five hundred thousand dollars maybe a bit much for my client to attain.

But I think it's a reasonable amount that will assure my client's appearance at any, and all future hearings, Thank you..."

Attorney Danuzio casually made his way back to the defense table, and took his seat. Low glanced quickly behind him where Michele sat holding his sleeping son in her lap. For a very brief moment, the two locked eyes, and Low smiled. Dressed in a suit, Rob was sitting next to her. Low took a deep breath, and gave his best friend a reassuring head nod before turning around to look at the judge.

Danuzio proved why he was viewed as one of the best in the nation. The way he presented his case before the federal magistrate left Low confident that bail would be set. He wanted desperately to be with his fiancé, and newborn son. Low was ready to go all in on his music career as an executive for his own label. Then he could always await his due process in the court, and clear his name of the erroneous charges against him. He was a legit businessman, and didn't want to waste away in jail while waiting for his day in court.

"Does the state's attorney have anything to say?" the federal magistrate asked, making notes on a legal pad.

"Yes your honor. We do," Attorney Spanner said in a feisty tone.

She rose from her seat, walked to the center of the courtroom, and continued. "Your honor, not only is this man a coldhearted killer, who is under investigation in the State of Florida for more than fifteen murders, but your honor, I would like you to take a very good look at this man sitting before us in this courtroom today because your honor, I must say you, I, and everyone in here are very privileged to be in the presence of Milow Pierre. The undisputed successor to the throne of Miami, Florida's most ruthless criminal organization, The infamous Zoë Pound..."

The rest of the proceedings went by in a blur. Spanner had a field day dragging Low's name, and reputation through the dirt.

"If Milow Pierre is ever released on the streets again, the United States of America will surely regret it," Spanner said.

In less than five minutes the magistrate said, "Your request for bail, Mr. Pierre, has been denied."

Chain and shackled, Low boarded the federal Marshall's cruiser en route to the county jail. His head down, Low looked at the shackles on his ankles, and wrists then let out a deep sigh. Reality hit him like a bombshell. He was in for a long ride.

C-3

Low was sent to unit C-3, after completing his thirty days in the hole for his role in the fight. Sunny was sent to another unit within the jail. Sunny and Low saw each other around the jail's hallways, going to the gym, and the medical department. Sometimes they bumped heads during attorney visits, but most of the time they kept in touch through kites.

In his unit, Low experienced no static from fellow inmates because around the jail, everyone heard of the brutal assault him and his Zoes had put on Boston Chuck. He was given respect or violators faced the consequences that came with their disrespect.

Eighteen months into Low's arrest, and no further misconduct, he was eventually given a job as a unit worker. The one dollar and fifteen cents he made daily to sweep and mop the entire unit at night was downright disrespectful, but inmate workers were allowed a lot more free time out of their cells than non-workers.

Low spent the extra time lifting weights, and watching sports and news on television. It also afforded him more phone-time, and Low took full advantage of the opportunities. He was able to keep up with his record company, and Zoë Pound through Rob.

After discussing business with Rob, Low would usually spend the rest of his phone time with Michelle, the highlight of his days and nights. She was his mental balance. Hearing her voice daily kept Low grounded as he waited for his day in court. Lately Low found that his conversations with Michelle weren't as pleasant as before. All they had been doing for the past month was a lot of arguing and bickering.

Low knew that the friction between the two was due to the fact that he was away and wasn't with her. All the fighting they were doing on a regular basis was causing Low a lot of stress. His time was getting much more harder to get through. Eventually Low knew something had to be done. So in a conversation he explained this to her.

"I love you Chelle, a'ight? I'll talk to you tomorrow. Please put Rob back on the phone," Low muttered dismally.

"No, you don't muthafucka! Cause if you did, you wouldn't have put yourself in jail!"

Michelle's icy response left Low in cold sweat with his fist balled up around the receiver. He heard Rob's voice.

"Man, don't even sweat that shit, Zoe. She's having a bad day. The baby's been stressing her out," Rob said.

"Yeah? How is he?" Low asked.

"Shit, he's a bad ass. Looking and acting just like his dad," Rob said.

When Low heard that, it brought the biggest smile to his face. Low said, "Damn, that's what it is!"

News of his son's antics always brought a bright smile to Low's face no matter what mood he was in.

"You got that money order I sent you?" Rob asked.

"Yeah, I got it. Back dat up," Low said in gratitude.

"Cool…"

"But I've been meaning to tell you something," Low said, shifting the conversation.

"Speak to me?"

"Man, I'm 'bout to fall back from these calls for a while. I got a little ways to go before the wheels on a trial get rolling. And arguing with my shorty on the phone everyday is only making a nigga time harder than it needs to be, ya dig?"

"Man, I can dig it hood. What you want me to do?"

"Shit, Danuzio is all paid for and my account is good. So I'm straight. I just need you to continue to hold shit down out here for us. Ya dig? Continue to take care of my lil' man and keeping an eye on Chelle. As far as everything else, you got the keys to the car drive safely."

"You already know, Low. I told you before you went in. I'm a hold shit down," Rob said, assuring Low.

One Year Later

When someone new entered a unit for the first time, an inmate's first reaction was to stop whatever he was doing, and turn his focus on the booth of the correction officers. This brief encounter between the new inmate and the officer on duty was critical. It was the only advantage an inmate already on the unit would have to determine if the new man was friend or foe.

This alertness was essential for an inmate, in order to have a slight heads up on any potential enemies. Lack of this vigilance could prove fatal if an adversary slipped through the unit's front doors without being noticed, made it to his cell to unpack, and potentially spotted his enemy first.

Low was from out of town, and didn't know anyone from Massachusetts. He had no issues with anyone, and usually never paid this new Jack routine any mind. When some new face hit the unit Low would quickly glance over to make sure it wasn't the big dude from the tank. Then he'd usually got back to whatever he was doing. On this particular night, the front steel door to unit C-3 slid open with a hissing sound then a loud click. Low was in the middle of a high stakes poker game with several other New England kingpins, he took a glance toward the front of the unit, and had to make a double take when he noticed a familiar face.

"Low, bets on you. Mel raised Luca five hundred more," Black Jack said, staring at Low, and awaiting a response.

"Um, I fold," Low said, without looking at his hand. Getting up, he continued. "Aye Jonas, deal me out next hand."

Dominican Jonas was from west Cambridge. Low left the game behind, and made his way to the front of the unit. He was now close enough to the booth to confirm his suspicion. Low hadn't seen Sicko in a while. After Low spared his life for revealing where Big Tuck's house was, Sicko eventually fell under Gunner's command.

Low, Sicko, and Gunner had got together to execute some missions on some non descript cliques that were constantly caught trying to shortstop on Zoë Pound's turf. It was during these few missions that Low gained admiration for Sicko. He got the chance to witness the young street warrior in action, and saw Sicko as a rider.

"Aye Sicko, what it is, homie?" Low greeted.

Low approached Sicko, who squinted his eyes at Low. Sicko had bad eyesight and was really supposed to wear thick-rimmed prescription glasses, but never wore them. Sicko was temporarily oblivious to who called his name, and was more paranoid about someone actually knowing him all the way in Massachusetts.

His paranoia quickly vanished once the figure approaching came into full view. Sicko saw who it was, and his face immediately lit up like a Christmas tree.

"Oh shit Zoe! What it do, nigga?" Sick beamed with joy at the sight of the boss.

The two men embraced using Zoë Pound salute, and Low couldn't help the wide grin plastered across his face. Low felt good to see someone from the home team, and the sight of Sicko amazed Low. Sicko looked like he put on a hundred pounds of muscle.

"Shit I'm cooling, Zoe. You already know," Low smiled, nonchalantly.

Low caught Officer Spencer, a stupid bigheaded, young officer gazing at them, and listening to their conversation.

"What cell they got you in?" Low asked.

"Um, two-nineteen," Sicko said, gazing at his bed assignment sheet that the officer just handed to him.

"Oh, that's on the second tier next to my cell. And the dude they got in that cell with you went to court today. I think he was supposed to be taking a plea, and going up the way. So you lucked up and got yourself a single cell and bottom bunk," Low said.

"Shit, that's what it is," Sicko said.

"I'll take you up there, and help you unpack," Low said, grabbing up Sicko's property bag then he continued. "Follow me."

"Yeah Zoe, I heard about how y'all boys got pinched. This nigga told me y'all caught shit in New York," Sicko said, making his bunk then he leaned up against the wall.

"Nah man. We got jammed up right here in good ol' Massasippi," Low said, shaking his head, and sighing at the thought.

"But shit, fuck you doing all the way up in Maine, hustling?" Low asked, a sipping from a cup of hot coffee he had just whipped up from Sicko's box of canteen.

"Shit Zoe, I was everywhere getting it," Sicko said.

I had met this gangsta bitch from Connecticut at this club one night, and started kicking it with her for a few months. Her brother's a get-money-hustla too. So once me and him linked up, we was hitting everywhere. Connecticut, Rhode Island, Ohio, Jersey, Philly, New York, nigga you name it. If a nigga was in the city getting money, and in need of an order, me and him was there with the delivery. We was getting it major too. You'd be amazed at the prices these up north niggas paying for birds, Zoe. The numbers unreal."

"Shit, I already know. I've been kicking it with quite a few of these niggas. The numbers they screaming was damn near extortion," Low said.

"Ain't it though," Sicko said.

"I used to tell Gunner all the time..."

Gunner's name caused both Zoes to pause, and remained silent for a few seconds. Then Low switched gears, and asked, "So your Connecticut bitch still holding you down and shit?"

"Yeah, she riding one hundred with the kid. Me and her brother co-defendants on this trafficking case," Sicko said.

"How's that looking?" Low asked.

"A nigga looking straight so far. I got a real good lawyer from out here in Mass named Tim Flaherty. He taxing a nigga some serious bread, but he screaming since I ain't got no priors on my record, he could most likely get me a five-piece in the Feds for this shit. But shorty's brother, his lawyer screaming his pleas will most likely start at ten, cause he got a few priors. But it ain't nothing either way we both staying solid that's all that matters, you know? We can do the time."

"Yeah, I can dig it."

"How about you? Who you still talking to out there?" Sicko asked.

"Shit, only to the family. Michelle, and Rob, Low said.

Low saw the way Sicko grimaced when he mentioned Rob's name. Sicko's facial expression, and wrinkled eyebrows didn't sit well with Low.

"What you know about Rob?" Low asked.

"Nah…" Sick muttered passively.

"What Sicko? Spit it out," Low said.

"Nah, it's just… I… Before I got locked up I was down in Miami…"

"What da fuck Sicko…?" Low snapped.

"I'm saying… You…you haven't spoken to Rob in a while, right? How long of a while you talking?" Sicko asked.

"Man… Shit, 'bout a year, give or take some weeks," Low said.

"It's none of my business, but I heard that Rob's the man now. Lately niggas been seeing him with Michelle, and your son a lot…"

"You think I don't know this?" Low asked with an amused smirk.

"You do…?"

"Who you think gave Rob the green light…? Me nigga. Of course niggas gonna see Michelle with him from time to time. That's my right hand man. He's also my son's godfather. That's his duty."

Sicko shook his head, glanced at Low, and said, "I'm a just say this bluntly. I realize that you don't have a clue to what's really been going on in the past year. Rob is the man, but not because of you. He's the man cause King Zoe held a powwow between the top Zoes. He officially sanctioned Rob your successor, and the new official leader of Zoë Pound. He's prince now. And when it comes to Michelle, she's not only his main bitch, but the both of them muthafuckas got your son thinking Rob's his father—"

Low was on Sicko like a wild predator. Instantly grabbing Sicko by his throat, Low began choking the living daylights out of him. The two collapsed onto the metal desk in the cell, knocking over all of Sicko's freshly organized hygiene products, and legal paperwork. Sicko managed to free his throat from Low's prying claws. He pushed Low off him then quickly squared up, preparing to defend himself.

Low was about to attack again, but the chatter coming from an officer's walkie-talkie, and the clinking of keys caused both Low and Sicko to quickly calm down. The officer gave them an inquiring glance as he went by the cell then kept on walking.

"Look Zoe. Don't kill the messenger," Sicko said.

"My nigga, honestly I thought you knew. That's why I looked at you all crazy at first when you referred to Rob as your right-hand man."

Staring at Sicko, Low's eyes were glazed over with a mixture of intense rage, malice, and fury. Low's heavy breathing was curtly interrupted as he took an anger-filled swing at the cell's walls. Letting out a loud roar, he gave the wall a few more knuckle breaking punches, before he turned, and glared back at Sicko.

"You know what Sicko? If you're lying, I can find out right fucking now," Low fumed then furiously stormed out of Sicko's cell, and went to used the phone.

"That number is restricted…." a female automated voice said.

Low slammed down the phone's receiver then immediately picked it back up. The automated voice promptly advised him to dial his pin then the area code, and number he wished. Low dialed his home number again. An uneasy feeling came over him. His sweaty palms tightly gripped the phone's handle causing his heart to race a million beats per minute. This feeling was truly torturous. Taking another deep breath, Low pressed the receiver to his ear and waited.

"That number is restricted," the automated voice said.

Letting go of the phone's receiver, Low said, "Fuck! This can't be happening right now," Low said aloud.

His mind was doing back flips, and he picked the phone's receiver back up. Low had contacted Rob on his phone only a handful of times since he was always at the house when Low would call Michelle anyway. There was really no reason to waste the prepaid minutes. The two only spoke on Rob's phone when they needed to discuss a topic they didn't want Michelle listening in on. Low was certain Rob's cell phone was clear for him to call. Rob had setup an exclusive prepaid account, just so Low could get through when he needed to contact him personally. Picking up the phone's receiver, Low quickly dialed his pin, and Rob's cell number, and waited.

"That number is restricted," announced the automated voice for the third time. Low felt like his entire world was crashing down around him. Glancing up at Sicko as he stood posted up on the top tier in front of his cell door. Low locked eyes with him then dropped his head and hung up the phone's receiver.

Furiously grabbing his canteen box off the top of the cell's wall-mounted, Low violently hurled the large, heavy metal locker toward the front of the cell. The chest crashed against the cell's fortified steel door with an amplifying bang. Drilling the cell's cemented wall with two fury-filled punches. Low groaned loudly, as the impact against the unaffected wall broke his right knuckles, and vibrated his bones with numbing pain.

Low had no control over anything going on the streets, and he was now aware of this. Taking in a deep breath a single pain-filled tear raced down the young boss's face. He emptied his lungs real slowly and attempted to clear his mind. The streets, and everyone in them would have to be forgotten for now. Low had bigger issues on his plate to get prepared for. The trial was starting in two weeks.

✦ ✦ ✦

"Damn Sunny, you just gonna bow out and cop-out to eighteen years for this shit, Zoe?" Low said, shaking his head as he spoke with Sunny through the cage-like screen that separated the two in the back of the County transport van. Both of them along with eight other inmates were being driven to court.

"Shit, I gave this shit some deep thought, my nigga. And I figured I might as well go on ahead and take it. I mean we had a good run out there. Life was real good while it lasted, but I refuse to die in one of these mutha-fuckin' places, feel me? If I cop to this plea I'll be home in fifteen. Fuck it. I ain't fit'n a play with these crackers. At least I'll have a date to look forward to," Sunny said.

Shaking his head, Low sighed. He didn't agree with Sunny's decision, but understood it. Low said, "Shit, I feel ya. But I Just can't do it. I ain't taking no damn deal. I'm going all the way to the hoop with mine. These crackers gonna have to run it. Free me or kill me."

THE VERDICT

"Has the jury reached a verdict?" The Judge asked, addressing the foreman.

"Yes, your honor. We have," the foreman said.

Getting up, she handed a small, folded paper to the waiting bailiff. He casually strolled away toward federal Justice Roger Mathieu Sr. The Judge took a brief look at the verdict, and nodded slightly to his bailiff then handed the paper back.

"The jury is ready. Can every one please rise to their feet for the reading of the verdict," the judge said in a deep baritone.

Standing along with his attorney, Low had a stare down with the judge. Then Low's eyes veered in the direction of the twelve members of the jury. He zeroed in on the blonde-haired female foreman as she unfolded the paper and began reading the verdict.

"In the case of docket number FD0075193. The United States Versus Milow Francois Pierre The Second, we the jury find the defendant guilty…"

The rest was a blur to Low. The next thing he knew was sitting between two beefy U.S. Marshals while the federal helicopter airlifted him from the top of downtown Boston's Federal Courthouse, transporting Low to MDCC, New York. Low was to be federally booked, and held awaiting his classification process. Low took one last glance at the streets. While be briefly admired Boston's beautiful downtown skyline before his eyes darted straight ahead.

Six hundred and eighty months, followed by two consecutive sixty-month terms was a long time. Shaking his head at the thought, Low inhaled deeply, and exhaled loudly. This was the flip side of the game. Low was in for a very long ride.

7 Years Later

Lewisburg Federal Penitentiary—Lewisburg,

Pennsylvania

Carefully clipping his shit sheet up on a makeshift hook hanging from the air vent in his cell, Low made his way to the other hook that hung across on the opposite side underneath a wall-mounted shelf with all his hygiene products. Low looked at the other end of his sheet. Once his makeshift curtain was up, Low reached for his institution-regulated jar of Vaseline sitting on his hygiene shelf. Low made his way to the toilet, where the metal seat, already carefully rounded with a few layers of toilet paper, and two shower slippers for added comfort awaited him.

Along with the recently mailed issue of the latest Big Butt Magazine, featuring porn star, Ebony Dash on the cover. There was an eight-page photo spread, and interview on the inside. Low briefly skimmed thru when he received the magazine at mail call. At that time, his cellmate, Reeseboy was all over him, trying to take a look at all the fine ass women in the magazine. Low let him peep it first. Low really didn't mind. Reeseboy was on his half hour break from his job as law clerk at the prison's law library. Low knew that when the four pm count cleared, Reeseboy would be off to work until at least seven. It was enough time for Low to be alone and fantasize about fucking his bitches.

Making his way over to his bunk, Low lifted up his mattress and grabbed his 'nut rag', freshly washed yesterday on laundry day. Low made his way to the toilet, pulled down his boxers, and copped a comfortable squat. Then he immediately began flipping through Big Butt magazine until he reached the page where Ebony Dash was looking like a sweet delicacy as she posed on the railing of a building's roof top, scantily dressed the nude photo showcased Ebony's massively plump, heart-shaped ass with a clear view of the slit leading to the opening of her edible pussy lips.

Low applied some Vaseline to the tip of his swollen penis, and evenly spread the light grease down is manhood. Then Low slowly stroke his dick while staring at Ebony's misty eyes as she made love to the camera. Low was envisioning himself inside of Ebony's tight pussy, slowly stroking it from the back. Low was about to explode, and bit down on his bottom lip.

"Hey convict, take this fucking sheet down before I rip it down!" A female corrections officer barked.

The unwelcome interruption totally broke Low's concentration. He jumped, losing his grip on the magazine, and it fell to the floor.

"What?" Low scoffed.

Both inmates, and officers knew that when the shit-sheet was up in a cell it meant to give that cell fifty feet while the occupant handled his B.I. Usually if pressing issues arose, such as a visit or medical appointment then a friend would shout the inmate's name letting him know what was up, and keep on strolling. An officer never dared violate an inmate's privacy, especially not at Lewisburg Penitentiary.

"I suggest you keep it moving if you know what's best for you," Low warned.

His other hand slid down, and gripped the handle of his eight-inch shank placed between his tube socks on his ankles.

"Muthafucka is that a threat?" the female officer asked.

Then she boldly entered Low's cell, and angrily snatched down his shit- sheet. The officer's brazen disregard of Low's warning caught him completely off guard. He sprung to his feet, pulled his boxers up, and turned to see Lovely staring back at him with the widest, amused grin plastered across her face.

"Did I interrupt something here, Mr. Pierre?"

Her light hazel brown eyes briefly skimmed over the magazine, Vaseline jar, and rag scattered on the cell's floor. Lovely bellied over in laughter. Low was so shocked that Lovely was standing in his cell. He was totally speechless.

"What happened boo...? Cat got your tongue?" Lovely smiled, moving closer to Low.

Lovely's intoxicating perfume made Low's mouth water in lust. Finally, he gathered himself, and asked, "What the fuck?"

Low looked Lovely up and down. She was wearing a United States federal corrections officer's uniform.

"Um, are you trying to figure out how the hell I managed to get up this prison all dressed up like an officer, Low?" Lovely asked in a sarcastic tone.

"Ah...uh," Low mumbled.

"Well first, let me tell you that this uniform and badge are the real deal boo," Lovely said.

"How did you pull that off?" Low asked.

"Easy. Two years ago, I applied for a correction officer position at the Broward County Conte facility. I took the required written and physical exams, and after passing both, I was immediately assigned a position with thirteen officers. Then I did my research on you, and your location. It took me a while, but after staying on top of some old law enforcement buddies that I used to rub shoulders with back in graduate school. I finally was put on to a vacant Captain's position up here at Lewisburg. At first, the staff in Broward County jail's administrative department tried stalling my transfer request. I was trying to make a leap from county jail to a maximum federal prison in a short time, but after packing all my things, and moving into a condo here. There was just no way they could deny my transfer."

"Wow... And you got two bars...? How the hell did you go from rookie to sergeant then captain in two years?"

"You'll be amazed by what a Master's Degree in Criminal Justice can do when it comes to getting your way in the prison system," Lovely smiled. Reaching out, she gently rubbed the side of his face with her soft hands.

"I missed you."

Then she planted a gentle, wet kiss on his lips. The sweet flowery aroma of Lovely's scent mixed with the combination of her sensual touch sent all the blood in Low's body rushing in one direction.

"Um, someone's happy to see me," Lovely smiled.

Low's bulge through his prison-issued boxers caught her eyes. Lovely licked her lips and undressed her curvaceous body from the tight-fitting uniform. Low made his way back to the cell door, and picked up his shit-sheet lying on the floor, and quickly threw it back on the hooks.

Dropping her uniform pants down to her ankles, Lovely bent over, and gripped the edge of the cell's metal sink. With his stiffened cock gripped in his hands, Low traced the outer moist pussy lips of Lovely's fat twat. Then in one hard thrust, he shoved his dick deep inside. The stiffened impact caused Lovely to bite her bottom lip.

Grabbing a hold of her silky, jet-black hair, Low roughly pulled back Lovely's mane with one hand, while giving her round, soft ass a smack with the other. Digging his fingers into her fleshy rump, he tugged on her long hair, and viciously plunged himself deeper inside of her wetness with hard, aggressive strokes. Her suppressed pain-filled moans brought joy to his psych.

The harder Low pumped, the more Lovely's excruciating pleasure intensified. He was giving her some intense jail dick, and she loved it. She found herself euphorically climbing the cloud numbers, and Low eased his thumb closer to her forbidden hole, probing, and pressing his thumb in her ass, sending her overboard. Lovely's legs shivered and shook, Low's neck-muscles instantly ceased function, as his head cocked simultaneously freezing his entire body. Nine-and-half years worth of backed up stress was released inside her.

✦ ✦ ✦

It wasn't uncommon on a hot and sunny summer afternoon for the prison yard, as big as a professional football field, to be overflowing with more than two thousand inmates. Twenty officers always stood guard at different posts scattered around, watching inmates enjoy recreational activities. Several full court basketball games were in full swing, a couple of handball tournaments were underway, the weight cages were packed with cons getting in shape, and a few inmates were on the half-mile long track encircling the entire yard.

Under a large tent-like pavilion hundreds of card and board games were going down. Chess, checkers, and scrabble, hundreds of thousands of dollars were being waged on spades, and no-limit poker tables.

In a far-off corner of the pavilion, next to a large group of men enthusiastically cheering on two contestants involved in an intense, energy-filled free-style battle, Captain Shabazz stood guard. Dark Ray Ban sunglasses covered her eyes, and her arms were crossed in front of her body, she watched a prison-league softball game, and spoke with inmate, Pierre.

"If she's not the best criminal defense lawyer in the nation, this woman's one of the best. Her clientele is made up of America's elite, top politicians, and rich entertainers. She's almost guaranteed to be on a short list of super attorneys," Lovely Shabazz said.

"Okay, so what's the problem?" Low asked, taking a drag of the Newport cigarette.

The place erupted in loud applause as a softball player at the plate hit a towering line drive back toward center field.

"There are two very substantial issues that we have right now. One being that she's expensive as hell. Issue number two is that the demand for the woman is so great.

Even if the money is right, that still won't guarantee her availability."

She remained silent for a while. Low stared at the softball game, soaking in everything Lovely told him.

"Milow, you've been in prison for a while now. I don't know how your funds are looking, but I've been saving very well since like my last year of high school, and I know I can convince Mom to part ways with a few thousand. Honestly, that won't be enough to retain this attorney for your appeal."

He continued smoking the cigarette, exhaling fumes skyward. Then Low asked, "Why me?"

"What?"

"What makes me so special, Lovely? That you'd risk your career, freedom, and be willing to invest your life savings to help me get out of this bitch?"

With a sly smirk, Lovely said, "No one has ever fucked me as good as you do."

Low burst out laughing. Then he said, "You're crazy."

"Its true. I love you, Milow. Even though you used to treat me like one of your groupies when you were out there. There were times when you treated me like a real queen. And I really appreciated, and miss that."

Taking a deep breath, Lovely removed her sunglasses, and glanced at Low. He was nodding approvingly when he heard her continue.

"Plus, I hate how Rob did you dirty like that. He just left you for dead in here. You were a boss. I saw how good you were to Rob. I know you went above and beyond for your wife, and for it to end like this for you that just wouldn't be right. So I'm your angel, here to get you home…"

"What's really happening on the outside?" Low asked.

"You really want to know?" Lovely asked.

Her eyebrows were raised, and Low smiled then nodded.

SOMEWHERE IN FLORIDA

"Look me in the eyes," Michelle moaned ecstatically as she reached up and grabbed each side of Rob's sweaty face.

"Oh baby, I'm cumming!" Rob groaned.

Reaching a climatic peak, his whole body froze, and he exploded while staring into his wife's eyes. His love juice flowed inside her.

"I love you, Rob," Michelle whispered giving his lips a soft, wet kiss.

"I love you too, Michelle."

Low jumped out of his dreams, and sat up, staring at his cell's door through the pitch darkness. There was murder in his eyes. His breath came in spasms, and his heart burned with pain. There was only one thought weighing down his mind. It was going to be a daunting undertaking, but he needed to get home.

A tough decision kept looping through Low's mind. He had eight-and half million dollars buried on his private alligator farm in the Everglades, and that was his life savings. For the past seven years, the annual income he received from his investment in New Millennium Record kept Low afloat. He had to relinquish his CO-CEO position when the verdict went against him, but Low was able to retain a small percentage of ownership stocks. However, that wouldn't be nearly enough to retain the attorney Lovely referred.

His appeal was of utmost importance, but Low didn't trust a soul. In order to aggressively seek, and successfully retain the caliber lawyer Lovely had referred, he knew it would take a substantial amount of funds. He knew he would have to trust Lovely to give her access to maintain the money during the few years it would likely take for the appeal to go through.

The question Low was wrestling with was whether or not he could trust Lovely, and was her motives to help him truly genuine? If Low told Lovely where his stash was buried, and got fucked it would officially be over for Low. Two of his appeals were already exhausted. Low had one last shot to get this time off his back, and was one denial away from the being stuck in the federal prison for the next four decades.

His back was against the wall, and his chips were getting low. A final shot at the jackpot of freedom was a chance he had to take.

Two-and-a-half years later

His new lawyer was fully paid, his appeal was filed, and Low was awaiting the decision from the United States Supreme Court. This could take up to five years or more. Lovely was on board, she followed his lead. Although Low was still in prison, and had minimum freedom, he was living like a king in jail.

Lovely used her rank to work magic for Low. He was awarded a job working as an orderly in the prison's administration building. This position gave him full access to her office Mondays through Fridays. Once his detail that included, dusting, sweeping, mopping the entire building, and taking out every officer's trash were completed, Low would stop by Lovely's office. A couple times a week, he fucked Lovely's brains out on top of her office desk.

Once a week, Lovely brought him some good weed to relieve his stress. She got him a CD player, she kept locked away in her office at night. Low utilized it while working. He enjoyed bumping 2pac's collection she brought him. Pac had become Low's new favorite rapper.

Low was really hopeful about his appeal. In the meantime while he waited, Low got through his bid spending as much time as he possible could with Lovely. Lovely was able to help him diversify his investments his money into various business ventures, and the monthly revenues became substantial. Finally everything was looking up for Low again. Then as soon as he was getting used to living good, suddenly everything started coming apart.

8:00 AM

"Pierre!" The officer shouted, and gave Low's cell door two hard kicks with his steel-toe boots.

Low and his cellmate, Reeseboy were abruptly awoke from their sleep. Rubbing his eyes, Low heard the annoying officer's booming voice.

"Pack it up. You're being transferred."

Low's heart straight dropped. He quickly rushed to his feet, and made his way to the cell's door.

"Transferred…? Where…?"

"I'm not supposed to divulge that info. I heard you're going to Coleman Minimum in Florida. You should be happy. Your custody got lowered," the baby faced officer said.

"Man, I wanna see Captain Shabazz about this bull-shit! I didn't request any transfer, and I don't want no fucking transfer!" Low shouted through his cell door.

"Captain Shabazz is out sick today, inmate. You got twenty minutes to pack it up so I can take you down to intake," the officer said, walking down the tier to knock on another cell.

Coleman Minimum 3 years later

Jumping out of his dream, Low was sweating profusely, and panting. He glanced at his watch. It was three in the morning, August 21, 2007. Fifteen years went by, and reality finally hit Low like a ton of bricks. Lovely got him transferred, and it was three years since his transfer to Coleman. Within that time, Low hadn't heard from Lovely. Not a letter, no visits, nothing.

Low did a casual inquiry through a prison case manager he was friendly with, and she revealed that Captain Shabazz not only quit her Captain's position at Lewisburg, but she no longer worked for the corrections department. Low couldn't believe his luck. When he heard the news, all he could do was shake his head. He walked out of her office, his mind clouded in shame. Lovely still had twelve million dollars of his at her disposal.

His head was back on his pillow, and Low sighed in despair. Staring up at the desolate darkness of his cell, he listened to the sound of his cellmate snoring.

9:35 am

"Inmate Pierre! Inmate Pierre!" An officer shouted, giving Low's cell door a hard kick with the tip of his black, steel-toe boots. Then the officer called his name again.

"Inmate Pierre!"

"What!" Low angrily shouted, pulling his blanket down from over his face, and staring at the officer.

"Pack it up!" the officer barked.

Low sprung off his bunk, and rushed to his cell door. Then he asked, "Pack it up for what, man…? Where the fuck y'all transferring me to now?"

Looking back at Low with a crazy expression on his face, the officer shook his head then said, "Who the hell said anything about a transfer? Pack your shit, inmate. You just made bail," the officer said.

Shaking his, the officer whispered something vulgar under breath as he walked away. Low turned back toward his bunk, and locked eyes with his cellmate old man Haggerty, who was also awakened by the ruckus.

"You heard that…? I'm going home!" Low excitedly exclaimed.

Picture Me Rolling

The barb-wired gate slid open with loud squeaking noise. Low stepped through to the sight of the most beautiful woman in the world. He locked eyes with Lovely, and his entire face instantly lit up.

"Hey daddy," Lovely beamed with the brightest smile plastered across her face.

She was dressed in a pearl white Cavalli sundress with a printed silk scarf covering her head. She was wearing a vintage Gucci frames over her eyes, and a bomb pair of Christian Louboutin red-bottom peep-toe heels on her feet. Lovely was leaning against a magma red luxury sports car. She was looking better than every beautiful woman he had ever masturbated to, and she was in the flesh.

Stopping dead in his tracks, Low smiled, and said, "Look at you!"

He paused just admiring her stunning body, causing Lovely to blush. The huge smile on her angelic face grew even wider.

"Come here, girl!"

The two embraced in a blissfully long hug, and Lovely planted a soft, wet kiss on Low's smiling lips.

"Welcome home, daddy. Did you miss me?"

"Hell yeah! It's only been three years. What the hell took you so long, girl?"

"I had to let you sweat it out a bit, boo," Lovely smiled.

Shaking his head, Low couldn't do anything but smile then said, "Let's get outta here."

The two broke their embrace, and hugged each other all the way to where she parked her car. Low whistled out in total astonishment, and said, "Damn Lovely, a 2008 Bugatti Veyron EB one-six. I see you doing big fucking things!"

Low rubbed his eyes to make sure his vision wasn't deceiving him. The sight of the fastest road car in the world clearly impressed him.

"Girl this car cost a million dollars," Low exclaimed, giving Lovely a crazy look.

"One point six," Lovely smiled, correcting him.

"Okay…"

"But who's counting?" Lovely shrugged, and tossed Low the car keys. When he caught the keys. Lovely smiled and continued. "The boss gotta ride in style, right?"

"So where's this GPS taking us?" Low asked, easing into the fast lane.

Pressing his foot on the gas pedal, and bringing the Bugatti to an enjoyable eighty-five miles per hour.

"I also bought a two-bedroom condo down in Vero Beach," Lovely said, applying the final licks on the vanilla Dutch Master cigar. Then she continued. "It's nothing major, mind you. But it's in a beautiful little neighborhood, that's pretty cozy and very quiet."

Lovely lit the Dutch, took a pull, and said, "I figured it would be the perfect place for you to lay low while your appeal process goes through the courts."

"Yeah, I can dig it. It sounds perfect," Low said, nodding in agreement.

Lovely passed him the weed filled Dutch. Taking two pulls. Low inhaled the exotic tasting bud deep into his lungs. Then he exhaled, and said, "Just perfect."

Glancing down at the car's entertainment console, Low scrolled through the music titles in the iPod playlist. Low located 2Pac's, *All Eyes On Me* album and scrolled to track seven.

Picture Me Rolling instantly blasted out of the cars custom fifteen-inch Bose surround sound speakers with deafening bass. Low took one last deep toke of the potent bud into his lungs before passing the cigar to Lovely. Taking a firm grip of the sports cars corn silk covered steering wheel. He made himself comfy within the confines of the plush leather, and began to rap along with the lyrics enthusiastically singing along. Life was good. The song had him in a fantasy-filled daze then Low noticed the cherry lights closing in fast behind.

"FUCK! Love, put that shit out," Low said while hastily putting his seatbelt on.

"We getting pulled over..."

"Whose car is this?" A blonde haired female state trooper asked.

The Buggatti's tinted driver's side window rolled completely down, and the cop saw a Black man behind the wheel.

"Excuse me?" Low said, looking up at the trooper with a perplexed expression.

"Did I stutter? I said who's fucking car is this, boy?" she barked, staring down at Low.

It took everything within him to bite his tongue, and not flip on this bitch. Taking a deep, calming breath, Low knew he had to remain humble.

"Um, it's my car, but the title is under my girl-friend's name."

"Hmm, typical. This is a very expensive car. What are you a rapper?"

Low's blood was at its boiling point, and he said, "Excuse me?"

"You know what...? I don't like your attitude. Step out the car, sir."

"Why did you stop me?" Low asked, but was immediately cut off.

"I'm not gonna ask you again," the trooper warned.

Low shook his head in disbelief, and he stepped out the car. He hadn't even been out for two hours, and was already getting ready to be handcuffed. The trooper stared back at him through her rearview mirror, and typed away on her patrol car's police database laptop. Low sat in the backseat, sweating profusely. The a/c wasn't on all four car windows were shut, and it was ninety degrees outside. Low felt like saying something, but figured if he kept his mouth shut then the faster this harassment would be over. He was clean as a whistle.

"Says here that you just got out, huh? I figured you were an ex-con. All of you guys are. But damn, I didn't think you just left your second home a couple hours ago."

Low badly wanted to give this cop a piece of his mind, but something inside of him just kept telling him to remain humble. The sweat coming down his forehead had increased to the point where it was now dripping into his eyes. The cop finally started feeling the scorching heat. Low noticed her unbuttoning and removing her uniform shirt.

"Sure is a mighty hot day, huh Mr. Pierre?"

The trooper tossed her uniform shirt in the passenger seat. Instead of answering her stupid remark, Low continued to remain humble, and rolled his eyes.

"Uh huh, heard it might hit a hundred degrees."

She continued typing on her laptop then said, "Damn, I'm so hot, my pussy's sweating."

Low looked baffled. His eyes opened wider with surprise when she said, "Damn, I gotta take these hot-ass pants off."

The trooper took off her utility belt, and began sliding out off her uniform pants. Low's eyes and mouth sprung open in shock.

"Damn, I might as well take the rest of this shit off too."

She proceeded to relieve herself of her T-shirt, bra, and panties. Low couldn't believe his eyes. Before he could utter a word, the butt-naked trooper made her way into the back seat with him and immediately began to undo his belt.

Whipping his meat out with the quickness, she took a hold of Low's cock, and with a swift straddle hop. Stuffed all of his stiff manhood inside her gushing wetness. With his hands still cuffed behind his back, the trooper placed her arms around Low's shoulders, and began to ride him like a horse. Gyrating her hips, she began a sexual romp, moving up, and down then around. Bouncing on his big dick with hungry intensity, she fucked herself into in a sexual frenzy.

"Oh fuck yes!" She moaned, while her D-cups swayed in Low's face.

About five minutes into the trooper's intense sex game, Low's eyes were lost in the back of his head. He reached a climatic point, and erupted. Low's entire body froze, and the trooper reached her zenith. She buried her face in his shoulders, while their bodies shook and spasm in small convulsions.

"Oh God. I needed that," the trooper said, letting out a deep satisfied sigh.

Making her way back to the front seat of the squad car. She immediately began to put her underwear, and work uniform back on. After getting dressed, she stepped out of the vehicle, and made her way to the back. She opened the door for Low, removed the handcuffs, and shot Low a wink.

Then without saying another word, she hopped back in her cruiser, and sped off. Low was left standing on the side of the highway with a dumbfounded expression. Making his way back to his car, Low hopped in the driver's seat of the Bugatti, and couldn't look in Lovely's direction. His mind was still trying to register what had just happened, but it didn't take long before he realized that he had been had. Looking at Lovely, she smiled then revealed the culprit.

"That was Amy," Lovely said, letting out an amused girlish giggle at the sight of Low's stunned facial expression. "She'll be over later on tonight." Lovely shot Low a seductive wink, smiled, and continued. "Welcome home, daddy."

"You're crazy, girl," Low said, shaking his head, and laughing.

Shifting the Buggatti's gears, Low peeled off as the dash-mounted GPS immediately continued its course towards his new home. Once again, life was good.

✦ ✦ ✦

The blob of spit dropped easily between the crack of her ass. Low lubricated the entrance of Amy's rose pink anus with the tip of his swollen penis. He stuck the head in a few inches, and her body tensed, but she didn't resist. With one hard thrust, Low pushed the rest of his massive manhood inside of her. Amy screamed on impact then instantly her moans turned into sounds of pleasure. Low began to stroke her forbidden hole.

Low was fucking the shit out of Amy's ass, and Lovely was moaning uncontrollably while Amy's tongue sent her into a whirlwind orgasmic convulsions.

"Oh fuck! Yes!" Lovely screamed, exploding over, and over again.

Lovely shook and squirmed while Amy sucked harder on her clit, and Amy's two fingers inside of Lovely's moist pussy stimulated her G-spot, elevating Lovely's pleasure to heavenly heights.

Low was reaching his peak. Tilting his head back in total ecstasy, he pulled out of Amy's asshole, and spurted his nut all over her spine.

✦ ✦ ✦

Low sat on the edge of the master bedroom's king-sized bed. The only light illuminating the dark room came from a wall-mounted fifty-inch Sony flat screen TV. Earlier, Low had been watching *Never Die Alone,* but now the television showed a blank, blue screen. Staring at a beige wall, Low's face was stone cold. There was murder in his eyes, and on his mind. He glanced at the Mont Blanc on his wrist, took a drag off the Newport then put it out in a crystal ashtray sitting on the nightstand beside the bed. It was then that he decided that it was time.

Taking a look at the two women he had just fucked to sleep, Low made sure they were still knocked out before he rose to his feet, and walked out of the room. He entered the dark hallway, and made his way into the second bedroom. Low sat looking at the custom built steel-closet door. Placing his thumbs on the door's fingerprint recognition scanner. It took nine seconds for the small security light atop the scanner to turn green, granting him access.

The closet's steel door slid open, Low stepped into his fifteen square foot walk in closet, and briefly took a look around, admiring the way Lovely had everything arranged. One side had a row of brand new wardrobe for him. Business suits, and street clothes all hanging perfectly from a clothing rack. An entire arrangement of designer shoes and sneakers lined the thin-carpeted floor underneath in small square cubicles.

On the other side were three huge steel shelves custom built into the wall. There was an array of weaponry. Several nine millimeters, Rugers, a couple dozen Glocks, Remington 38s, Colt 45's, Desert Eagle handguns, and plenty boxes upon boxes of ammunition.

On the second shelf, four chrome Mossberg shotguns were laying next to three Matte-black fully automatic Carbine-15 machine guns. Hanging from individual hooks, on top of the third shelves were five Russian AK-A7s hung neatly in a row from their nylon shoulder straps.

Grabbing a bulletproof vest off the third shelf, Low slid it onto his bare chest, and tightly secured all four Velcro straps around his ribs. After getting dressed in an all black Champion sweat suit, Low picked up a P89 Ruger handgun off the first shelf and tucked it in the small of his back. Reaching down on the third shelf, Low snatched up a pair of military issued night vision binoculars, and threw the nylon-attached strap around his neck. Taking one of the chrome Mossberg pumps into his palms, Low checked to assure it was loaded. Filling his lungs up with a shot of fresh air, he exhaled slowly then turned and exited the room.

✦ ✦ ✦

"Your destination is on your right."

The Garmin GPS sounded off. Low slowly strolled by the basement's parking garage entrance of the massive twelve-story, luxury building. After all these years, Low still remember the five-digit pass code that would grant him access. He could never forget his son's birth date.

Low wasn't trying to park. Coming to a stop sign, he made a left turn, and proceeded up a steep, ascending road. After driving seven blocks, Low came to another stop sign. He made another left, arriving at a big white church named, 'The church on top of the hill'. Low pulled into the property's driveway, and proceeded to the back of the building. Coming to a stop at a short metal fence, he placed the Buggatti's gear in neutral, and stepped out the car with his shotgun in hand.

Almost instantly, the thick black cloud up above gave way. It began to rain down hard on the city of Boca Raton. Raising his night vision binoculars to eye level, Low glanced around until he located the Palm's luxury condominiums building. Scaling the floors. He made his way up the top of the floor and zoomed in.

There she was, sitting in a chair in the dinning room. Fifteen years had been good to Michelle. Her face was still as beautiful as the day when Low had first met her back in high school. Glancing a bit to his right, Low noticed a young teenaged boy sitting on the living room's sofa, enjoying a slice of pizza while playing with a remote clutched in his hand. Damn, Two-Five had grown so big. He looked like a grown man, Low thought. Then he glanced back toward Michelle. Rob appeared from the kitchen area with a pitcher of red juice, and Low felt the intense burning in his heart.

Making his way into the dining room, Rob placed the pitcher of juice on the dining room table then got on a knee between Michelle's legs. Rob rubbed Michelle's stomach, Low zoomed in closer.

Low lost his grip on his binoculars, a thundering boom exploded, and a bolt of lighting illuminated the entire sky a gloomy bright gray. Fifteen years, Low had dreamed about this day for fifteen long years.

Cocking his Mossberg pump back with a deadly click-clack, Low turned and sprinted with murder in his eyes toward his car. Fifteen years, the boss was gone, and left to rot. His status, statue, and family were stripped away from him. Now it was time to take it all back. It was now time for Low's revenge.

The End

The author:

Jeffrey Appolon, AKA Pain, was born in Boston, Massachusetts and raised in Miami, Florida. Early in life, he discovered his passion for writing, and his desire to turn thoughts into stories was born.

During the summer of 2005, after reading stories from countless classic storytellers such as Eric Jerome Dickey, Kwan, Carl Weber, Teri Woods, Vickie Stringer, Shannon Holmes, Nikki Turner, Wahida Clark, and Sista Souljah, Jeffrey set out on a quest to write his first novel. It took many years of dealing with obstacles, and setbacks for him to finally complete his debut project.

In **STREET KARMA, t**he author known as **Pain** takes it back to the essence. Bringing compelling, realistically vivid drama. The outcome will be shocking.

CPSIA information can be obtained
at www.ICGtesting.com
Printed in the USA
JSHW040258180321
12658JS00004B/5